SWORD AND SCION

INTO THE DARK MOUNTAINS
BOOK 1

JACKSON E. GRAHAM

YOUNG**OAK**PUBLISHING

Young Oak Publishing LLC
Hayden, Idaho

This book is a work of fiction. The characters, incidents, and dialogue are drawn from the author's imagination and are not to be construed as real. Any resemblance to actual events or persons, living or dead, is entirely coincidental.

SWORD AND SCION: INTO THE DARK MOUNTAINS

Young Oak Publishing LLC
P.O. Box 682
Hayden, ID 83835

Cover design by CraftArc
Logo design by KJ Designs
Author photograph by Rachel Stewart Photography

Quotations from (NIV) New International Version of the Holy Bible used by permission of Bible Gateway.
New International Version **(NIV)**
Holy Bible, New International Version®, NIV® Copyright ©1973, 1978, 1984, 2011 by Biblica, Inc. ® Used by permission.
All rights reserved worldwide.
Text set in Times New Roman

http://jacksonegraham.wixsite.com/jackson-e-graham

Library of Congress Control Number: 2017918018

ISBN: 978-0-9996059-05 (sc)

PRINTED IN THE UNITED STATES OF AMERICA

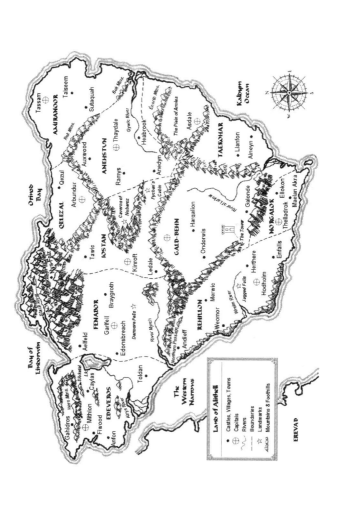

PRONOUNCIATION GUIDE

Places

Anehstun (pronounced: **Ah**-ne-stoon)
Gald-Behn (pronounced: **Gahld-Ben**)
Iostan (pronounced: **Eye**-oh-stann)
Nys-Felz (pronounced: Niss-**fellz**)
Qelezal (pronounced: **Kell**-eh-zall)
Rehillon (pronounced: **Rey**-hill-on)
Taekohar (pronounced: **Tay**-ko-harr)
Zwaoi (pronounced: **Z-why**)

Characters

Ardul (pronounced: **Arr**-dool)
Av400nyn (pronounced: Ah-**vah**-nin)
Dányth (pronounced: **Dan**-ith)
Dárig (pronounced: **Dah**-rigg)
Élorn (pronounced: **Eh**-lorn)
Etherul (pronounced: **Eth**-eh-rool)
Eyoés (pronounced: **Aay**-oh-ess)
Fódral (pronounced: **Foh**-dral)
Fychan (pronounced: **Fy**-kan)
Gwyndel (pronounced: **Gwin**-dell)
King Fohidras (pronounced: Fo-**high**-dras)
Ladur (pronounced: **Lah**-durr)
Llumiael (pronounced: **Loom**-ee-ell)
Makulazai (pronounced: Mah-**koo**-lazai)
Skreon (pronounced: **Skrey**-on)

Creatures

Kélak (pronounced: **Keh**-lak)
Norzaid (pronounced: Norr-**zayd**)

Months for the World of Alithell

Iaudyn
Nósor
Dichán
Biarron
Iaulan
Merchen
Yílor
Thurdál
Aevoran
Rotanos
Rynéth
Bivyn

To the one true God,
who helped me write this book.

It is coming.
The heartbeat of drums,
echoing through the wood,
Hailing the arrival of blood and sorrow.
What can men do against such tidings,
But do their duty to their King?
Yet, even as the sun rises,
Hope—seems far from me.

Song of Arógym, son of Eryndál,
commander of the armies of Men
during the War of Adrógar, the First Era

"It is mine to avenge; I will repay.
In due time their foot will slip;
their day of disaster is near
and their doom rushes upon them."
(Deuteronomy 32:35, NIV)

PROLOGUE

Hate. The fortress of Nys-Felz breathed it. *Thrived* on it.

Carved into a deep gash in the dark mountainside, the fortress contemplated the pitch black conifers that swarmed over the mountains. It seemed to devise a cunning strategy—observing the land before it as merely a step to greater horizons further inland. An outcrop clung to the front of the mountain, crowned by a sinister terrace. Upon the fortress walls were remnants of various geometrical reliefs, relics from another time. Torches fastened to the walls provided light into the dark recesses of the fortress exterior. Dark, hideous forms went about their duties on the stone ledge. In several places, regiments of these minions drilled, their hoarse, guttural war cries echoing with every thrust of their weapons, every stroke. Two massive double doors, studded with spikes of iron, towered above them all. Inside the fortress of Nys-Felz, soaring hallways branched off a single, empty antechamber, reaching into the depths of the mountain. Writhing shadows hid from the eerie, orange glow upon the walls. Like a blanket, the thick doors smothered the outside noise.

Far into the depths of one fateful corridor, a single door patiently anticipated victims. It guarded a massive chamber with an immense window overlooking the mountains. Unlike the rest of the fortress, this room was well furnished. Elegant, savage weapons hung on the walls opposite the door, bloodstains streaking the gleaming blades. A prodigious bed occupied a corner of the room, hidden by dark red drapes. To the left of the large window, a neat desk and chair betrayed the calculating nature of its dark lord. A hulking man sat with chin in hand, pensive. At least, he seemed to be a man—*at first glance.*

Long locks of straight white hair draped over his shoulders. His pale skin glistened in the overcast light streaming in from the window, giving him the appearance of a corpse brought back to life. Lavish, ebony armor accentuated his strength. A large, fearsome helm sat absentmindedly at his feet. From the albino face, dark, red eyes stared at the desk, seeing nothing. His thoughts consumed him. He would not be aroused until he so desired.

The din of his drilling troops carried through the window, their gruff cries—pleasing. Soon, the time for his rising would come. His eyebrows darkened in anger, a grave frown creasing the corners of his mouth. If he had not been alone, the withering expression would have inspired terror—now, it only served to vent his fury.

Llumiael was inadequate to bring King Fohidras to his knees. Now, it's my turn.

He cringed, wishing he had not let such thoughts into his mind. There was no assurance his master wasn't listening. If he had heard the slanderous comment…

He resumed his thoughts, eyes darting to the shadowy corners of his chamber. A loathing rose within his throat, and with it, an eagerness to summon his forces to action—now. Gruffly, he shook his head.

Patience. The Hobgoblins need time.

The albino stood, wandering toward the window with hands clasped behind his back. Gazing out toward his domain, Skreon considered his next move.

1

4th of Merchen, 2192 SE

Eyoés parted the stack of books, causing dust to spring up in protest. Searching longingly among the collections, his dark blue eyes considered the spines of each volume. Baffled, the young man took a step back, mumbling to himself. He examined the shelves, his straight black hair dangling to his shoulders.

"It must be here," he muttered to himself. Sighing with frustration, Eyoés stepped toward the bookshelf, hands groping among the covers. His eyes caught sight of a previously unseen book near the end of the shelf. He gave a cry of triumph. Grasping its spine, he pulled backwards. The book didn't budge. Eyebrows furrowed, he seized the book's spine and gave it a strong jerk. It almost sprang from his hand and loosed a second book, which tumbled to the ground. Grinning, Eyoés tucked it under his arm and stooped to re-shelve the fallen book.

I must hurry, or Master Aeryn will set me to work sharpening the awls and shears!

He suddenly stopped, curious, and stooped to examine the second book. Its old, tanned cover lay oddly askew, revealing another cover underneath. Eyoés tried to recall if he had seen this book before. Cocking his head, he set aside the thing he had so earnestly searched for. As he reached toward the fallen book, he hesitated. What gave it such an allure? Questions preyed at his mind as he lifted it from the floor. The tan cover slipped free of the book altogether and fell to the floor with a thud. The volume itself was nothing beautiful. Bound in old, tattered leather, it seemed that touching it would cause it to break apart. Instead of crumbling, however, the book remained intact, stronger than expected.

Respectfully—even reverently—Eyoés turned to the first page, holding his breath in expectancy.

His jaw dropped.

Numerous notes and curious diagrams littered every page—yet were surprisingly well-organized. Enraptured, Eyoés fell into the nearest chair, leaving the sought-after book—and his leatherworking apprenticeship—forgotten. An asymmetrical drawing caught his eye—a diamond within a circle, segmented by opposing lines. He frowned, creases forming at the corners of his mouth. What could this enigma mean? Intrigued, he turned to another page, greeted by a trove of mysterious illustrations. Moving the hair aside that blocked his view, Eyoés turned to the last page. His heart skipped a beat. His hands shook. There, in the middle of the page, was his father's name, written in elegant script.

Élorn, son of Aelar, Protector of Taekohar

5

Eyoés burst into Baron Dányth's office, nearly throwing the door from its hinges. Alarmed by this abrupt intrusion, the Baron leapt from his seat and seized the hilt of his sword. An armed guard darted into the Baron's office in hot pursuit with short sword drawn. Tripping over a nearby chair, the boy grasped the desk to steady himself. His frame heaved with each ragged breath. Dányth released his sword handle as he recognized Eyoés. Failing to see the Baron's lack of concern, the guard seized Eyoés by the arm, dragging him backwards with sword poised over his captive's neck.

Dányth raised a hand in objection. "I know the boy," he declared, his voice commanding. "Release him and let us speak privately." The soldier complied, exiting the room after giving a brief salute. Only when the door had closed did the two venture to speak. "What's wrong, lad?" Dányth inquired.

Catching his breath, Eyoés set a leather book upon the table. "I found this on the bookshelf at home," he answered in a measured tone. "It was hidden inside a false cover. If it hadn't fallen from the shelf, I wouldn't have noticed it."

The Baron raised an eyebrow, examining the book intensely. Pulling up a chair for Eyoés, Baron Dányth gestured for his companion to sit. After giving a nod of thanks, the young man sat down. He exhaled slowly, calming himself, but peace of mind remained far from him. Trying to recover from his show of disrespect, Eyoés reached for the book. He opened to a random page, exposing the mysterious diagrams to the light streaming from the window. The Baron shook his head ever so slightly.

Abruptly, Baron Dányth stood, pushed his chair from the desk, and strode toward the window. A sigh escaped his watch as he overlooked the castle grounds. A grassy plateau raised the keep above the surrounding buildings. Below, the civilians worked at their individual trades, while others spoke with their companions. The steady clang of a blacksmith's hammer rang like the heartbeat of the town. Directly across from the window, the main gate stood guard over them all, locked shut by iron latches. Parapets of stone were lined sequentially at different intervals upon the ramparts encircling the castle. Dányth couldn't hold back a grin at the sight of the children playing in the grass, untroubled by the duties of adulthood.

I remember when Eyoés played among them.

His smile faded at the thought. No longer did the youth have such childish innocence—at least, he wouldn't for much longer. Leaning on the window frame, he tilted his head against his arm. A gesture of defeat.

Disturbed by this sudden move, Eyoés stood, taking several steps forward. He had never seen the Baron so upset—the man was usually confident and reserved.

"Sir, my mother told me that my father was your scribe," he remarked, stabbing the book with his index finger. "This book tells a different story." A heavy silence hung in the air, almost choking the two of them with its strength. Dányth turned, regarding the young man that stood before him. He opened his mouth to speak. Eyoés interrupted before the Baron could answer. "Who was my father?" he asked.

Silent, the Baron remained still, thoughts distracting him from the current situation. He clenched his teeth in frustration.

It was Aványn's duty to tell the boy. I should have pressed her.

Motioning toward the desk, he indicated they should sit. Obediently, Eyoés returned to his seat, followed by the Baron. The older man pulled his chair alongside. Clearing his throat, he folded his hands upon his lap. "There are two things you must know," he began. "The first is that Aványn—" He paused, unsure whether to continue, but it was too late to abandon the disclosure. "Aványn—is not your mother." Dányth sighed.

Eyoés' head began to swim as the words fell from the Baron's tongue. His face contorting in confusion, the young man leaned closer. Seeing the boy's pain and bewilderment, the Baron laid a comforting hand upon his shoulder. After a lengthy silence, Eyoés spoke. "And the other?" he muttered.

Nodding, the Baron slid from his seat, crouching before the suffering boy. "Your father was never—a scribe. He was a warrior, and the most noble man I ever knew," he declared, his voice choked with emotion. Stricken, Eyoés looked into Baron Dányth's eyes. "You found his notes on combat," the Baron paused, letting the new declaration sink in. Eyoés let his head hang.

He didn't move, grief heavy upon his shoulders. "She told me that he died of sickness. How *did* he die?" he quavered. Silence met his question. Anger welled up in Eyoés' chest, and he lifted his head, indignant. "*HOW DID HE DIE?*" he shouted. The Baron opened his mouth to speak, then shut it as he swallowed a knot in his throat.

He steeled himself to deliver the truth. "Your father, Élorn, Protector of Taekohar—was lured into a trap and assassinated by a band of radicals the year you were born," he said.

Unable to control the strong emotions that churned within, Eyoés sprang from his chair, screaming a cry of rage. "Aványn has told me nothing but *LIES!*" he roared, the choked cry reverberating through the small chamber.

Dányth stood, his hands darting out and seizing Eyoés by the shoulders. Overpowered by the man's strength, Eyoés remained still. The older man looked deep into the young man's eyes. "She lied to protect you from your father's fate. To keep you *alive*," he announced, his voice stern, yet loving. The man relinquished his hold on the boy's shoulders. Eyes red, Eyoés staggered toward the door.

"Eyoés!"

The devastated boy stopped in his tracks, turning back toward the man who had been forced to tell him what he should have already known. Downcast, the Baron stood in the middle of his quarters. Raising an irritated eyebrow, the young man waited for what the man had to say. Their eyes locked.

9

"I miss him too," Dányth whispered, his voice robbed of its former strength. A single tear rolled down his cheek.

2nd of Thurdál, 2197 SE

"AAAH!" Eyoés roared, the cry of his hot fury resounding into the open sky. With a low, menacing hum, his blade sliced through the air, shimmering brightly in the sunlight. Biting fiercely into the oaken pell, the steel cut neatly, the nut-brown wood curling outwards like a book's folding pages. In retaliation, the hard wood brought the blade to a sudden halt, the jarring reverberation shooting up Eyoés' arm. He brought his other arm to his forehead, wiping the sweat away. With a vicious heave, he wrenched his weapon free.

He recalled his clumsy techniques at the start of training. Now the weapon was an extension of his arm, obeying orders. Chest heaving, the young man stood, appraising his target.

It is astonishing how the embers of anger are so quickly kindled into flame. Five years have passed, and I still have not found my way to forgiveness.

Retrieving the sheath from the tall grass, he thrust the sword into its scabbard.

If I had known that book would change my life forever...

Attaching his sword to his belt, Eyoés stepped back

to further examine his handiwork. The oaken pell now leaned to the left, its surface deeply scarred. Shaking his head, he gazed up into the deep blue sky.

It has been wounded—like me.

Eyoés turned toward the weathered cabin he called home. His hand dropped to the braided-leather hilt of his sword, fingering the intricate designs etched into the crossbar. For years, his father had wielded this sword in many a battle. In noble hands, the weapon had avenged many a wrong and protected the innocents of Taekohar. Now, the weapon was *his*. As memories began to surface, the youth's face fell, laden with grief.

The journal and the sword at his side remained the only links to his father. Too exhausted from training to hold back his emotions, Eyoés let a tear trail down his cheek. He was not even aware of his steps toward the cabin.

The melancholy of the moment suddenly broke when the clop of old shoes on wooden steps arrested his attention. Looking upwards, his eyes locked with the old woman who emerged from the back door. The young man scowled, yet his yearning eyes remained focused on her. Bound in a braid behind her head, silvery white locks were streaked with faded red. The top of her left ear was missing, the old scar *still* poignant. Her appearance was youthful for her age. Gleaming with elvish wisdom, her brown eyes peered questioningly at the young man.

She licked her lips and looked away. "Again, Eyoés?" she inquired, her voice laden with emotion.

Staring stubbornly at his aunt, Eyoés gripped his

father's sword. "Yes, Aványn," he replied through his teeth. "Do not keep me from fulfilling my duty." She took several heavy steps forward in the tall grass. Trembling, her hands began to reach out. Aványn paused, and after a moment of consideration, laid a comforting hand on his shoulder. His dedication to his imagined duty had cost him his leatherworking apprenticeship and barred him from the guild entirely. Without work, he would never be able to care for himself—and she could not bear to watch him descend into madness.

"Backwards are the feet of those whose hearts are hardened against all but their own counsel. They will set out on a long, dark path, only for their counsel to come to nothing," she protested, quoting the ancient proverb. Her despondent eyes flickered with hope.

Surely he will heed the King's own words.

Forcefully exhaling, Eyoés flicked his gaze upward in irritation. The light left Aványn's eyes. This was not the first time she had recited one of the Proverbs to change his mind. Over time, he had learned how to rebuff her.

"A liar has no place among kings," he retorted, pointing an accusing finger. "Yet an honest man shall receive the highest honor." As he expected, Aványn visibly drew back, wincing with a pang of guilt. Her past lies continued to haunt her.

I should never have lied to him. I could not see past my own selfish love.

Recovering her composure, she leaned closer to his face. "I am your mother! I want the best for you," she begged.

With a scowl, Eyoés shook his head. "My *real* mother was killed by wolves," he snapped, stinging her heart with a hornet's fire. Persisting, she glanced to the sword by his side.

"Just because your father was the Protector of Taekohar doesn't mean you have to follow suit," she commented, a quick smile passing over her face.

Eyoés glared at his adopted mother, rubbing the back of his neck. "My father died in disgrace," he snapped. "I *believe* that I can become the man my father was. I must only train and study what remains of his legacy."

Aványn's chin trembled. She loved him as her own true son—the thought of him venturing into the dangerous world sent chills up her spine. She could not let his mother's sacrifice be in vain. Gently, she reached toward the sword. "The world is more savage than you know. It robbed Taekohar of both your parents," she pleaded, "I can't let it destroy you as well."

Eyoés swatted her gentle hand away, leaning close to his aunt's face. "I can right the wrongs in our world," he replied, his voice strong. He gestured toward the stone walls that encircled the castle grounds, his face shining with anticipation, "I've never stepped outside of these walls! It is time for me to venture out and fulfill my calling."

Eyoés' eagerness faded as tears filled Aványn's eyes. The sight made his heart twinge with regret. When he could have been left for dead, she brought him up, adopting him as her own son. In his heart, she was still his mother.

"Forgive me," he apologized, his eyes downcast. Feigning a brief smile, Aványn stepped back, looking away. She fingered a small locket that dangled about her neck. The boy had come of age. She was thankful he hadn't already departed. A stray lock of hair dangled from her forehead. She pulled it backwards behind her ear.

A ghost pain shocked the side of her head as her hand brushed against her old wound. She hesitated. After his mother had entrusted the child to her, they fled, pursued by a reckless young wolf. Her agility and knife were an equal match for the beast's quickness and teeth. They had barely escaped with their lives. She had shed blood for him, and now he would soon leave her. Aványn wiped away a bitter tear. She turned to where Eyoés stood shaking his head while absentmindedly rubbing his bottom lip.

"If the King has given you a calling, I will not stop you," she declared, her voice wavering.

Without another word, she returned to the cabin, leaving the young man at the mercy of his thoughts. Eyoés watched her return to the comfort of the cabin.

A divine King. Had it not come from her mouth, I might believe it.

2

A heavy sensation of foreboding hung in the air like a blinding mist. Bent in a pensive posture, Eyoés gazed into the dark shroud of midnight from the porch of his home. As he adjusted his seat, the creak of the wooden chair rang in the empty silence. He suppressed a shiver as the frigid breeze sliced through his clothes. Wrapping his thick, black cloak around himself, he lifted his eyes to the frosty moon, noting the small patches of darkness covering its surface. The eerie glow it cast upon the landscape only heightened the tension permeating the cold night. Standing from his chair, Eyoés crossed the weathered planks and gazed down the grassy thoroughfare. Light was absent in the neighboring windows, except the white gleam of reflected moonlight.

Am I the only one awake and unsettled?

Memories of the previous day's argument had roused him from sleep—as if to prod him to an apology. Still, even as he dismissed the thoughts, a sense of an impending disaster refused to leave him alone. Something was not right, whether it be moral or circumstantial.

Eyoés retrieved his weapon from the cabin and descended the steps, boots brushing through the grass.

Scrutinizing the surrounding streets, he fastened the rough leather belt around his waist. He loosened the blade in its scabbard, then hesitated.

For what? Could I be imagining all this?

Narrowing his eyes, Eyoés began to unfasten his belt—unsure of his own senses.

At first, the sound was obscured by distance. Then it intensified—the steady beat of wings, carried on the night wind. The sound was ancient, emerging from a page of the legends of old. His stomach tightened. From the numerous descriptions in his books, the persistent thump was instantly recognizable. Hastily re-buckling his weapon, Eyoés crept along the path, searching the night sky. The sound died away. He glimpsed a dark shape glide swiftly across the sky, blocking the light of several stars. Riveted to the spot, he searched for the shadow again, to no avail.

I have to warn Baron Dányth.

His home exploded into flames with a thunderous percussion. Reeling, Eyoés fell onto his back, the heat making his eyes water. With an ear-splitting roar, a massive creature raced through the blaze, the flames parting in its wake. Its dark green scales sparkled in the light of the fiery surroundings, and serrated teeth crowded the beast's jaws. Two spear-like horns protruded from the back of its skull, while a single, leathery frill descended down its neck. It disappeared into the streets of Asdale.

Dragons were among them. The air teemed with the creatures—their screeches combining with the screams of terrified and dying civilians. The hellish cavalry raced through the streets and the sky above, unleashing fangs, talon and fire with bestial zeal. Amid the chaos, Eyoés stood, clothes covered in ash. Watching the death around him with a wild eye, he struggled to move from the spot. The legacy of his father fell upon his neck like a millstone.

I must protect these people with my life.

A tremor shook his body as one of the dragons ripped the roof off a nearby building to get to the inhabitants. The cold wind of terror clutched him as the odor of sulfuric smoke constricted his breathing. Seeing a trail of wreckage between several houses, Eyoés dashed forward to the path of escape. Dodging falling timbers as he fled, Eyoés shielded his eyes from the bright light. Flames slipped under house walls like serpents. Fence posts were transformed into pillars of fire. One of the houses behind him exploded with a spray of sparks as he burst from the alley. Disoriented, Eyoés dashed into the next street.

A gust from a dragon's wings blasted him off his feet, hurling him against the side of a nearby structure. Gasping for breath, Eyoés struggled to fill his empty lungs.

Hidden by shadow, he stared with horror as the creature paused, nostrils flaring. His blood ran cold. The eyes of the beast seemed to glow with fire, and the moonlight reflected off its pale hide. The icy blue underlid surrounding its eyes eerily reminded Eyoés of a pale corpse. Upon its back was an armored figure he couldn't quite make out in the darkness. He froze as the creature's red gaze moved in his direction.

A scream from a nearby house drew the dragon's attention. With a single beat of its wings, the ghoulish monster took off toward the sound, maw opened in a grisly array of fangs.

Finally recovering his breath, Eyoés looked down the road, catching sight of the main gate dangling loosely from one of its hinges. He cringed as the heat singed his face and clothes. His next move could be his last.

If he did not take the chance, the flames would claim him—if one of the bloodthirsty monsters did not find him first. He broke into a sprint, his gaze fixed on the wreckage of the gateway and the shelter of the forest beyond.

His feet did not seem fast enough.

Heartbeat pounding in his head, Eyoés struggled to breathe through the thick smoke. Sweat ran down his forehead, and his legs wavered. Fighting his way through time to cover the distance, safety seemed beyond his grasp. Eyoés strained forward as he passed through the gate, fearing he would die inches from freedom. The air cleared.

Relief flooded over him as he dove into the dark forest. Tripping over a rock, Eyoés hit the ground, branches and thorns cutting his face. Blind to the pain, he stood, turning back toward the destruction. He covered his ears as the towering keep exploded in fire and smoke, raining blocks of rubble over the town. Letting his arms fall to his sides, he watched the remains of the stronghold fall to the ground, quaking the earth upon impact.

Tears stung his eyes. Painfully, his left forearm hung limp, crooked and broken in his near escape from the dragon's jaws. Shaking violently, Eyoés fell to his knees. His father died protecting this place—these people.

I left it to burn.

Everything he had known—destroyed. All his friends, even those who knew his parents, lie dead— and his father's precious journal burnt to ashes.

I left them to die.

Still, Eyoés could not imagine *how* he would have been able to stop the destruction. His death in battle would have made his father proud—had he tried to make a stand.

Instead, he *ran*. His own cowardice shocked him. Innocents lost their lives, while he lost his head.

Aványn.

His mouth hung agape. The last things he had said to her were thoughtless.

I am inadequate to fill Father's shoes.

The pungent stench of death compelled him to retch with violence, nose and eyes running. Rising from his knees, he leaned against a nearby tree for strength. Watching one fire rise, another burned in his soul, demanding vengeance.

He clenched his fists, pain shooting up his bent forearm. Tears carved trails in the ash on his face. Silent, he trekked deeper into the forest, more alone than ever before.

Whoever destroyed Castle Asdale would live to regret it.

3

The light of day woke Eyoés from his slumber. Morning dew clung to the tips of the grass, reflecting thin streams of sunlight. Traces of distant birdsong accompanied the rustling of the wind in the trees. The sight of this unfamiliar landscape bewildered him momentarily. Memories of the previous night's carnage returned to haunt him. As he attempted to stand, searing pain bolted up the length of his left forearm, forcing him back to the ground. Rolling onto his side, Eyoés tucked his left hand into his belt, grimacing at the pain. The inability to move it unsettled him.

Flames. Screams. Rubble falling from the sky.

He shook his head in a vain attempt to end the revolting memories. Tears pooled in the corner of his eyes. Above him, the deep blue sky stretched endlessly upward, and the bright sun caused him to squint.

I'm the only one left.

The thought struck like a hammer. Gritting his teeth, he was unaware of the tears running down his cheeks. A wave of nausea increased his misery. Wrenched from the depths of his soul, an anguished cry escaped his lips, scattering the birds from their perches. The sudden exclamation released just enough pressure to keep him from breaking. Still, prodding thoughts assaulted his mind. With a heave, Eyoés rolled to his right side, his sore muscles crying out as he propped himself on his elbow. He stood shakily, staring vacantly into the forest.

Is there any way to redeem myself?

The memory of horrible dragon roars caused his hair to stand on end.

Slithering tails weaving between the burning ruins. The choking stench of death.

He woke from his stupor, self-pity transforming into a wild stare. Instinctively, his right hand fell to the sword that remained buckled to his waist. His misery was not entirely his fault.

Attacks by dragons are rare, and never by more than one. Who could have led such an organized massacre?

As he rose to his feet, Eyoés set his eyes to the sunrise, teeth bared in an bestial sneer. His breaths grew loud and ragged with each staggering step toward the edge of the small clearing. He rambled to himself, consumed with fury. A low growl rose within his throat.

Eyes wild with anger, he seized his sword, yanking it from its scabbard. "My vow to avenge *will* stand. I WILL DIE BEFORE I FORSAKE IT!" he shrieked, face turned to the sky as if it could testify to his pledge. As the echoes of his oath rang through the trees, Eyoés ventured into the unknown.

Eyoés stumbled into the brush, legs weary. Mind clouded with fatigue and hunger, he dug through the bushes nearby with his one good arm, searching for anything edible. Making out the blue color of berries in the darkening light, he picked several, pricking his fingers on the thorny brambles. The growling in his stomach urged him.

I must survive! My vow must not fall void.

Recognizing the berries as Bralossary, he filled himself, juice running out the corners of his mouth. He picked the bush clean, but his body demanded more. The light trickling of a creek met his ears, coursing quietly behind the bushes. Rushing past the bush, he knelt, cupping his hand and repeatedly bringing the cool water to his mouth. Eyoés tried to warm his numb hand, eyes darting from place to place.

The inability to fight off attackers and his vulnerability to the elements implored him to hide, away from the threatening creatures stalking the night. Trying to ignore the sharp pain in his broken forearm, Eyoés moved on, searching for a place to sleep. Not far from the small creek, a tall evergreen towered above the forest. Its boughs stretched to the forest floor, creating a formidable guard against predators. Wary, Eyoés crawled below a shorter bough. The needles coating the ground pricked his knees, but the cavity underneath provided suitable sleeping space. Grateful to be sheltered from the coming cold, Eyoés lay upon a bare patch of earth, falling into a tired sleep. He wandered day after day without his bearings, finding shelter wherever he could. Caught in the tedious cycle of foraging and sleep, he pondered his next move without resolution. With every passing day, his strength waned from the lack of meat and infrequent water.

Three days later...

She waited. Rumors had come, telling of a trespasser on Baron Dányth's personal hunting grounds. Perched in the limb of an oak, her emerald green eyes scrutinized the forest. To her right, she caught sight of a squirrel darting among the bushes. Eyes set for bigger prey, she paid no heed to the small creature and resumed her search. Braided and tied atop her head, her curly copper-red hair was smeared with mud in an effort to conceal her position. Dark green clothing melted into a multitude of leaves, sheltering her from prying eyes. An old, L-shaped scar on her cheekbone glistened in the sunlight. She glowed with the light of youth and vitality. Fingering her bow, the young elf tuned her ears to any sound, alert to all that stirred below her.

Suddenly, she paused, eyes riveted to a section of nearby brush. A large stick broke under the weight of an unseen intruder. Muscles tensed to pounce, she stared intently at the place of reference, waiting for the source of the sound to emerge. For several seconds, nothing appeared.

A man stumbled out of the brush, sword clenched

in hand. The young elf leapt from the oak, landing in front of the intruder. Pulling an arrow from her quiver with astonishing speed, she drew the bowstring to her cheek—aimed directly at his heart. Shocked, the man swung his blade toward her, clumsily missing his target. Carried by the momentum of his blow, he spun on his heels, falling into the underbrush on his sword arm. Unflinching at this awkward strike, the elf stared at her fallen quarry. His long, black hair lay disheveled over his features, and coarse stubble covered his chin. The man stared back toward his captor, his gaze wild and tormented. He could not be more than seventeen years of age.

"These are the Baron's private hunting grounds. State your name and business here," she commanded, her voice steady.

At the mention of the Baron, the man's face lightened—for only a moment. "Flames—blood," he muttered under his breath, loud enough for the young elf to hear. Before she could answer, the young man laid his head back, unconscious.

She dropped to his side, replacing her arrow and slinging her bow onto her back. Laying her hand on his shoulder, she shook him in an attempt to wake him, without success. The glint of the sun on the man's sword drew her eye. The weapon seemed—familiar. Pensively, she pulled the sword from his hand, bringing it up to the sunlight. As she took in the fine craftsmanship, a gleam of recognition dawned in her eyes. Her hand flew to her mouth, vision blurring with lightheadedness.

How did this weapon get into this man's possession? Who is he?

The young elf returned the blade to its scabbard. She retrieved several fallen limbs and brought them to where the man lay. Setting them on the ground, she constructed a travois, lashing the limbs together with vines from a nearby bush. Satisfied with her work, the elf set the structure parallel to the victim and kneeled. Splayed in an uncomfortable position, the man's left arm was loosely tucked into his belt, bruised and deformed.

A broken forearm.

Carefully, she laid the arm upon the young man's chest, slipping a straight piece of wood underneath the broken limb. Setting a similar piece atop the man's arm, she fastened the splint with the cords that bound her hair. Once she had finished, she rolled him onto his good side, sliding the travois underneath him. Jolted by the move, the man incoherently muttered to himself. Setting the man down, she adjusted his dangling limbs, crossing his legs and setting his right arm on his chest to keep him from slipping off. Gently, she hoisted the small end of the travois onto her shoulders and looked west. Through the trees, a gaping cave could be seen on the mountainside.

It will suffice.

With a deep breath, she trudged toward the cave, hoping for answers.

Sparks leapt toward the tinder, setting it alight as she struck her flint and steel. The young elf had set a temporary camp well within the exposed mouth of the cave. Close to the warmth of the fire, the stranger lay, still unconscious as to his whereabouts. A cloth containing bread—her afternoon rations—lay opened by his side. Set alongside these rations was a roughly whittled ladle, filled with the water from the bubbling stream inside the cavern. Doubtfully regarding the still form of the wounded man, she tried to discount the uneasiness she felt. Over the course of his sleep, she had reasoned two theories as to his identity. One option —the man was a young thief. She had seen the type first-hand. Prone to stealth, they appeared during times of absence, taking everything of value while the owner was unaware. Her reason for thinking so was simple— the last time she had seen that weapon, it had not been in *his* hands.

Yet, as she pondered, the second option loomed from the innermost reaches of her memory. She pensively eyed the forest. If not a criminal…

It could not be. After all these years.

The young elf woke from her musings as the young man stirred. Immediately, she moved to his side, propping his upper body on her leg. Tearing some bread into small chunks, she coaxed his mouth open. Despite the man's fatigue, he swallowed the bits she fed him, taking water in between.

As soon as she stopped, he began to mutter to himself. "Lost, everything," he ranted. "Can't stop— now."

26

The elf continued to kneel by the stricken figure, setting aside the food. "What do you mean?" she asked.

For a moment, the young man mumbled incoherently. "I have failed them," he croaked. He was fading from consciousness—fast. Shaking his head to keep him awake, the elf tried several times to glean something informative from him, yet was met with no answer. Then, with a cry, the young man stretched out his hands in an imploring gesture.

"Father, why did I fail you?" he wailed, falling back into unconscious sleep, ravaged by the effects of hunger and thirst. Tentatively, she withdrew from the limp form beside the fire. Leaning against the wall of the cave, she waited for him to wake once again, but soon slipped into the depths of her thoughts.

When Eyoés regained consciousness, he started, unsure of his whereabouts. A warm fire burned next to him, and he gazed up at the soaring cavern walls. The light of afternoon lit the space, giving it a pleasant atmosphere. Glancing at his broken arm, he realized it had been splinted. His stomach growled as he noticed the bread and water sitting at his feet. Grunting as he shook off the fatigue, he sat up, reaching for the rations. As soon as his hands laid hold of the bread, he bit off several chunks with zeal. With a greedy eye, he swallowed, opening his mouth to bite off more.

"Do not eat so much," instructed a voice behind him. "Your body has not adjusted well enough to begin eating full portions." Eyoés froze as someone reached over his shoulder and snatched the bread from his hand. He turned to identify the source of the voice. Standing behind him with an armful of wood, a young elf regarded him with a chiding eye, her long, copper-red hair covered in traces of dried mud. Her green eyes scrutinized him with an expectant, yet strong gaze. Keeping her eyes locked on the young man, she set the wood by the fire. Her similarity to Aványn unsettled him.

Eyoés eyed her with suspicion as he sipped from the ladle of water at his feet. Slowly, he began to rise. The young elf darted to his side, putting her shoulder under his arm to help him up. Once Eyoés had come to his feet, he swatted her arm away, wary.

"Who are you, and why am I here?" he inquired, his voice raw from his parched throat.

Stepping away from him, the elf crouched by the fire, setting the newly gathered kindling into the burning pile. "You stumbled out of the woods and fell unconscious," she replied, eyes kept on her task. "I brought you to this cave to recover." Although she had answered his second question, Eyoés narrowed his eyes in annoyance at her refusal to identify herself. He began to protest, when she stood to speak.

"I found you trespassing on Baron Dányth's hunting grounds—and with this sword in your possession," she declared, tapping the sword which now hung at her side. Eyes widening at the sight of his sword at her hip, he impulsively grabbed at it. The elf dodged his hand and kept the weapon out of reach. "What is your name, and how did you get this weapon?" she inquired, trying to remain passive.

Regaining his balance, Eyoés assumed a noble posture. He blinked back the tears that began to well in the corners of his eyes. "I am Eyoés, heir of Élorn—the Protector of Taekohar," he proclaimed, his voice confident, yet wavering.

The young elf's quiet gasp gave him a start. His name was not a common one outside of Castle Asdale's walls, due to his sheltered upbringing. He searched his memory for some symbol of recognition, bewildered by the woman's strange behavior. A vague recollection of his father's journal entered his thoughts. Early on in his training, he had discovered a note left by his father—yet the stress of his predicament and the chaos of the past two weeks clouded his memory. Moved by the thought of his father, he furiously tried to recall the message. He brought his hand to his head, trying to recollect.

Nothing. Growling in frustration, he fixed his eyes on the young elf, his elusive memory hinting that the sign he sought for was obvious.

Mouth hanging agape, the woman backed up a step. The change of light and shadows on her face revealed an L-shaped scar on her cheekbone. Memories of the mysterious journal entry rushed upon Eyoés.

They slashed their symbol on her—marked her as an outcast! How dare they mark your beautiful face with their vulgar emblem. Where are you? I wish desperately that I could hold you again. I cannot bear to think of being without you, Gwyndel.

Eyoés' hand fell to his side. "What is your name?" he quavered, unsure if he wanted to know the answer. Their eyes locked, and the young elf wandered several steps toward him.

"Gwyndel. Daughter of Élorn," she replied, her voice soft.

4

"You need food and water. Come, I'll take you to my home, where you can rest," Gwyndel urged, moving further into the forest. As she vanished into a thicket, Eyoés followed, the underbrush cracking with each step. Lush ferns swept against his legs as he walked. Gently, the breeze scattered the decomposed remnants of the last season's leaves across the ground. The rattle of a woodpecker's knock wafted through the breeze. Squirrels darted up the trunks of trees, disappearing into the leaves. Despite this beautiful sight, Eyoés gave it no heed, instead dwelling on the vow he had made. The hatred he bore in his soul set everything before its scrutiny, causing him to see only through the eyes of his anger. The thoughts ruling his consciousness distracted him from the passage of time, and the arrival at their destination surprised him.

The forest opened into a small clearing, where a single conifer towered above the others. Built in this tree, a small cabin was suspended at the height of two and a half average men. Several supports braced the cabin to the tree to provide extra stability. The tree itself pierced one of the cabin's corners as an axis upon which the building had been constructed. A small deck extended several feet from the cabin, sheltered by the boughs above. A sturdy railing surrounded the balcony.

Impressed by the sturdy construction, Eyoés stepped up his pace, taking in the simple, yet charming craftsmanship.

Gwyndel pulled out a long stick, previously camouflaged in a nearby rotting trunk. With the angular crook on one end, she hooked a small pin from the bottom of the balcony and pulled it free. A simple rope ladder tumbled down with a rattle, swaying erratically as it reached its full length. Gwyndel scrambled up the ladder and disappeared over the edge of the balcony. Still taking in the sights, Eyoés grabbed hold of the ladder with his free hand and set his foot upon the lowest rung. As soon as his weight shifted, the ladder sent him swinging. Clenching his good fist, Eyoés moved to steady the rope ladder and try again.

"Wait," Gwyndel said, grabbing a bundle of thick rope. Retrieving a pulley from a nearby limb, she looped the rope through and fastened one end around the center of a wooden plank. Eyoés raised an eyebrow as she heaved the makeshift swing over the balcony. The seat hung close to the ground, bouncing against the taut rope. Eying the improvised bench with reluctance, Eyoés straddled the knot and sat, grasping the bristly rope with his free hand. Gwyndel heaved against her end of the rope. The bench rose with every pull.

As Eyoés came over the lip of the balcony, he rolled onto the deck. He took Gwyndel's extended hand and rose with difficulty. Gesturing for him to enter, Gwyndel held the door. With a polite nod, Eyoés stepped over the threshold. Although small, the one room cabin was comfortably furnished. Next to a large bookshelf, a simple wooden bed was positioned against the far wall. From a rustic nightstand a candlestick held a partially melted candle aloft. In the corner nearest the door stood a diminutive, slanted desk, upon which a full inkwell and pen sat ready for use. Several windows let in the natural light. Following Eyoés, Gwyndel shut the door behind, shrugging off her quiver and setting it in a nearby corner with her bow.

"A close friend and I built this place," she explained, noting her brother's interest. "The height keeps the creatures away during the night." The candle flame quivered as Eyoés collapsed onto the bed with a deep sigh of exhaustion. The pain in his shoulder still sent shocks down his arm. Trying to hide the pain in his body and mind, he sat up. Gwyndel removed her boots and set them by the door. Grabbing a nearby chair, she seated herself beside him. For several long minutes, neither spoke, unsure of what to say.

Among his numerous, disturbing thoughts, one in particular harassed him. "How were you separated— from our parents?" he asked, averting his eyes. She paused. Looking through a nearby window, she licked her lips, tense with reluctance. Hearing no response, Eyoés eyed her, noting her hesitancy. She felt his eyes upon her, and glanced toward him.

"It was seventeen years ago, in the middle of the night, when I was seven," she wavered. "I remember being dragged from my bed and forced into Father's bedroom. Men in cloaks seized mother and I and held knives to our faces." The painful remembrance of the frightening incident caused her to look away. "They told Father their client wished to smuggle forbidden goods to the ocean. They gave him three days to prepare a distraction to let the enterprise go unnoticed," Absentmindedly, she reached up to touch the faded, jagged scar on her cheekbone. "They carved their symbol into our faces as a warning of what would happen if he refused. Father struggled against the men that held him because of our distress, to no avail. Without another word, they knocked him unconscious and fled through the windows, vanishing into thin air." The thought of her scar made her cringe. Standing, she leaned against the nearby wall, staring off through the window as though she retold the story to herself.

"The mark proclaimed to all that we were targeted —we would have been outcasts if Father hadn't taken action. Rather than give in to the assassins' threats, he gave mother another name and home, and put a troop of guards around the house. An old friend, Fychan— Commander of the Foresters—owed Father a debt, so I was apprenticed to him for my own protection. The night I was apprenticed, Father embraced me, bidding me goodbye—" Gwyndel stopped, her voice catching in her throat as she unearthed these long dormant sorrows. Her mouth trembled, and she blinked to hide her heartache. She continued, her voice weak. "He warned me to never return home, or the assassins would kill our family," she whimpered, leaning upon the window frame for support.

"The next month, a messenger rode into our encampment and met with the Council. Fychan returned from the assembly with the devastating news

—Father's body was found with a knife in his back. His face was mutilated with the symbol of the Phantom League. Fychan's slack expression and reddened eyes continue to haunt me. As we both grieved together, his expression lightened as he told of mother's pregnancy. I've been a Forester ever since, hoping for the day I could return to Castle Asdale and see mother again—and you."

The pain in his shoulder no longer in the forefront of his mind, Eyoés stood, the bed creaking as he did so. Although aware of his approach, Gwyndel did not move, her longing gaze still wandering among the trees. Not far from her, Eyoés stopped, looking to the floor.

How am I to tell her?

Despite the several beginnings that came to mind, Eyoés shook his head to dismiss them. He *would not* lie to her. He set his hand on her shoulder to draw her attention.

"Gwyndel—" he stammered, searching for the right words. "Mother was killed when I was young." Gwyndel moaned with grief, hiding her face from her brother. Despite her efforts to conceal her emotion, tears stained her cheek. Unsure whether to continue, Eyoés waited for her to gather herself.

"After Father's death, Mother fled to her sister Aványn for comfort. I was just a newborn. Seeing my mother so distraught, Aványn agreed to accompany her home. On the return trip, a pack of Qezul-wolves surprised them. Entrusting me to Aványn, Mother led the beasts away, fighting off the snarling dogs with a branch. She lost her footing at the edge of a precipice. Her body was—unrecoverable," he faltered, lips trembling. Stricken, Gwyndel stared at him, breath hitching in her chest. The news sent her crumbling world into a dizzying tailspin. Stumbling into the nearest chair, she steadied herself.

"AvÁnyn never married. Instead, she took me to Asdale and became my Mother," he continued. "Since childhood, Baron Dányth had been my father's closest friend. Grieved, he assumed responsibility for me, setting aside a portion of his own annual income to pay for my leatherworking apprenticeship and personal needs. All was well until—" Eyoés abruptly stopped and turned away.

With a roar, he kicked the bedframe and briskly turned toward his sister. His flinty gaze made Gwyndel's blood cold. "Avánnyn lied to me! From an early age, she let me assume *she* was my real mother, and told me that Father had been the Baron's *scribe*! It was only when I uncovered Father's journal that I discovered the truth," he spat, eyes watering. "Seeing she could no longer keep the truth from me, Avánny showed me Father's sword. I began to train myself using Father's journal from that day on." Choking down a sob, Eyoés paused.

His gaze softened. "He spoke of you in it, Gwyndel," he remarked, looking away to the nearest window. "I never understood *who* Father spoke of in that note, until now."

Gwyndel said nothing, holding her head in her hands.

How could such tragedy befall our family? Why has this happened?

As Eyoés watched her shoulders droop under the weight of his words, he hesitated.

Should I tell her?

It seemed cruel to speak of it, yet the notion of lying to her repulsed him. "That is not all," he sobbed. "Only a few days ago, Castle Asdale—was burnt to ruins by dragons. Nobody was left alive. Except me." The fresh wound of the loss of his home pained Eyoés as he spoke. His chin trembled. Lifting her head, Gwyndel swallowed, the additional grief for the loss of Asdale evident in the red rims around her eyes. With quaking shoulders, Eyoés tried to step toward his sister, yet the grief in his heart held him to the spot. He hid his face in his hand, and sobs racked his body as the fresh wound was pierced by the arrow of recollection. Despite her grief, Gwyndel stood and approached Eyoés, embracing him in a compassionate grasp.

"I—I saw someone on the back of a dragon," said Eyoés, coughing to clear the tightness in his throat. "Someone planned this." Strengthened by his conviction, Eyoés stepped back, steeling himself and leaving Gwyndel's embrace. "I have vowed to kill whoever is responsible for their blood," he snarled, voice trembling, "or die trying."

Gwyndel took a step back, scrutinizing Eyoés with a skeptical eye. His left arm had just begun to heal, and his body was weak from the starvation that still plagued him. Although she had not seen him attempt swordplay outside of delirium, Gwyndel doubted his expertise. Yet, his determination and willingness to commit to a seemingly impossible task caused her to question her intuition. Wiping the tears from her eyes, she gestured toward the bed.

"Make yourself comfortable," she advised. "You must rebuild your strength if you wish to take on such a quest."

5

Gwyndel took several dried mint leaves from a jar by the window and dropped them into a mortar. Taking the pestle in hand, she ground the leaves into a powder, the crisp scent of mint cooling her nostrils. She sprinkled a few drops of fresh water from a leather pouch into the mortar, mixing the solution into a thick poultice. Once finished, she brought it to Eyoés' bedside and smeared it on his disfigured forearm.

The color is returning to his face. The rest has done him well.

Gwyndel took a fresh cloth and wrapped it around his arm, setting it onto his chest. The cool touch of the herbs would alleviate his pain somewhat. Roused by her treatment, Eyoés opened his droopy eyes and yawned.

Gwyndel smiled. "Wait a moment," she insisted, exiting the cabin. Shutting the door behind her, Gwyndel descended the ladder. She stooped to gather several small, dry basalt stones. The sunlight had already warmed their smooth surface—ever the better for the task at hand. She set them aside, collecting dead branches and placing them into a pile as she withdrew her firesteel and flint. As she struck the two together repeatedly, sparks lit the char cloth. She lifted the smoking material in cupped hands, gently blowing through pursed lips to coax the flame to life, and released it into the gathered tinder. Flames licked upward, weaving through the mass of dry brush. One at a time, Gwyndel placed the rocks into the fire.

She stood, returning with a small drinking vessel and pair of wooden tongs from the cabin. Water sloshed audibly within, rippling as she set the cup by the fire. Smoothed by extensive use, the tips of the tongs were charred by the flames of past fires. Plucking a stone from the coals with the tongs, Gwyndel dropped it into the vessel, the water hissing in annoyance. She placed the tongs by the fireside, retrieving a handful of dried flowers from a leather pouch on her belt. After dropping the petals into the steaming flask, she waited for it to steep.

Hearing Gwyndel return, Eyoés opened his eyes. Removing the stopper from the vessel, she walked to his bedside. Steam rose from the flask in her hand. Eyoés sighed.

Something for me to drink.

He reached out to take it from her. Holding the cup out of reach, Gwyndel shook her head.

"Arnica is toxic if taken internally," she interjected. Taking another clean cloth from a box underneath the bed, she soaked it in the tea. She set the vessel on the nightstand, removing the dripping cloth and tying the compress onto Eyoés' broken arm. Drops of liquid rolled down his elbow as the solution did its work.

"This should help your body reabsorb any bleeding and cut down healing time to a few months," she explained. "Until then, it will have to be immobilized." Taking a long section of cloth, she wrapped it around his wounded arm and tied it behind his head. Eyoés fidgeted with his arm, annoyed by its uselessness. Satisfied with her handiwork, Gwyndel left the bedside, sauntering toward the window, her face pensive. Eyoés felt a pang of regret as he remembered the tears on her face. In a short time, her world had been put into the fire and left to burn.

He sat up, silent as he watched her gaze into the forest. "How long have I been asleep?" he inquired, stifling a yawn.

Woken from her thoughts, Gwyndel returned to his bedside. "Two days," she answered, adjusting his arm sling.

Eyes widening, Eyoés felt a surge of heat rush through his body. He threw the covers aside and slid to the edge of the bed. "The violence against Asdale is going unpunished while I lay here swaddled in blankets! There is no time to lose!" he exclaimed, wincing as he tried to stand.

Gwyndel grabbed his shoulders to restrain him. "You will accomplish nothing if you do not recover your strength. A weak warrior cannot stand against superior foes," she chided. Fiddling with the blanket, Eyoés paused and took a deep breath. Avoiding her knowing look, he propped his pillow up against the wall and positioned himself comfortably. Patting her brother's shoulder, Gwyndel returned to her musings.

Eyoés eyed her, puzzled. An inner voice roused his anger.

Where is her fury for vengeance? Does she not care?

Eyoés rejected the thoughts. The pain in her eyes was real. Eyoés pushed it to the back of his mind. Surely there was something he could do to alleviate her pain. His eyes alighted on the bookshelf. A large, black bound volume caught his eye. Standing from the bed, he strode to the shelf, pulling out the book in question. He flipped it over to reveal its cover. Thin stripes of a dark crimson hue graced the cover as they twisted into sharp triangles at each corner. Gold words spread across the middle of this cover.

"Legends of Alithell," Eyoés muttered to himself.

Overhearing his words, Gwyndel turned, setting aside her thoughts. Upon seeing the book, she gave a slight shudder and flashed a small grin. "Have you read it?" she inquired. Eyoés nodded, sitting in the nearest chair. Leaving the depressing thoughts behind, Gwyndel sat on the bed, eyeing the book with apprehension as Eyoés flipped to the table of contents. She leaned over, reaching out her hand and pointing to one of the later titles. "The Story of the Ashen Specter," she suggested. "When I was younger, I feared the story like the dead. Now, I think of it as an old myth, nothing more."

Giving a quiet chuckle to himself, Eyoés turned to the indicated page. As soon as he did so, the title seemed to jump off the page, the bold, dark script whispering evil tidings. Leaning back into his chair, he began to read aloud…

It has been said that, south of the small village of Tawic, a ghastly apparition has haunted the dark forests. Local hunter Talland first recorded seeing the creature on a hunting expedition with his companion Kálros. Over the course of three days, the pair were unsuccessful in their hunt. In a last desperate move to provide for their families, they split up, Talland going north, while Kálros went northwest. Dusk came, and a wet fog descended upon Talland as he searched for game. Orange leaves coated the forest floor, helping him to cover the sound of his footsteps. Despite Talland's efforts, he found nothing. Having decided with his comrade to meet back at Tawic when their searches had ended, he turned southwards, setting out for home.

A sudden, piercing scream chilled his blood as it echoed throughout the misty forest. Nocking an arrow to his bow, he searched the trees for the origin of the sound. An eerie silence followed, casting doubts as to his sanity. Again, the scream echoed through the wood from the northwest. Fearing for his friend, he sprinted in the direction of the sound. Not far into his run, a movement caught his eye between the dark trees. He stopped, drawing his bowstring. Another scream. This time, a dark shape loomed out of the mist, falling into the leaves—then lying still. Racing toward the fallen thing, Talland released the tension on the bowstring.

Gasping with horror, he knelt by the body of his slain friend. Eyes wide with terror, the body lay in a contorted position, mouth agape. Large claw scratches marked his body. Horrified by the sight, Talland stood, pulling his eyes from the body of Kálros and searching the surrounding wood for sign of his killer.

Standing a short distance away, a phantom arose from the mist, its ashen face like a corpse. Long, white hair dangled from its head, and thick, black armor covered its body. The beast's red eyes stared at him. Talland tried to draw his bow, yet his arms refused to listen. Two large, dark red eyes opened behind the specter, harbingers of death. At a gesture from the pale apparition, the immense creature behind leapt from the dark, tackling Talland to the ground with a deafening roar.

The next morning, herb gatherers discovered the unconscious form of Talland. They brought his mauled body to Tawic to heal. Later that day, he regained consciousness, and told his tale to the people of the village. He insisted he had been attacked by a Whiteblood dragon—even though the species had never been sighted in the area. Although the people spurned the notion of the dragon, they accepted the poor man's belief in the ghost, which they named the Ashen Specter. Since that day, no one dares to venture out into the Northern woods during the dusk hours.

Eyoés closed the book with a shudder. His flippant dismissal of the dark tale's power vanished. A tension kept them seated as their minds swirled with gruesome thoughts. Fearful of the book he held, Eyoés set it aside, turning his head away as he did so. The sight of the book unnerved him. Glancing toward Gwyndel, he saw the fear in her eyes, which she attempted to hide behind a nonchalant expression. Neither one spoke.

Forcing himself from his chair, Eyoés paced around the room. The story hit a strange chord within him. Something—familiar. The terrible realization of his fate dawned upon him, as he ceased his pacing.

Gwyndel turned to look at him, her breath stolen away as she saw Eyoés' pale face. "What's wrong?" she questioned, her voice tense. Eyoés didn't answer. Absorbed in the depths of his thoughts, he leaned upon the bookshelf. He gathered his strength and broke the grip of the nightmarish images. He turned.

"The Ashen Specter," he stuttered. "The Whiteblood dragon—they were there!" Gwyndel abruptly stood, rushing to her brother's side, disbelieving. Seeing her doubt, Eyoés seized her shoulder and stared fixedly at her. His arm trembled with the force of his grip. "They were there! At the burning of Castle Asdale!" he argued. "I stumbled into the dragon's path—that is how my arm was injured!"

As the words sank in, Gwyndel stepped back, looking toward the Book of Legends. "Are you sure?" she stammered.

Eyoés strode to where the book lay, taking it in hand. For a moment, he paused, turning the information in his mind. The flames of Asdale seemed to dance before his eyes. Sweat beaded on his forehead.

It was he who led the attack. I must kill him—avenge their blood.

He turned, shoulders square and posture stiff. His eye caught sight of a map upon Gwyndel's desk, unrolled and held open by several stones. Following his gaze, Gwyndel went to the desk. Eyoés took a seat before she could offer it to him. As he searched for recognizable features, Gwyndel pointed out their location. His eyes locked onto a dark section of the map, covered in mountains lying to the north. Pointing toward this foreboding spot, he gave a sharp nod.

Zwaoi. The dark territory.

"Whiteblood dragons live nowhere else," he asserted. Gwyndel remained silent. Of the territories of Alithell, the name of Zwaoi made the blood run cold. Since the beginning of time, the desolate region of dark mountains and ebony forests had remained untamed by civilization. Fell things carved out a violent existence in the name of survival. Among these flourished tribes of gruesome creatures, known as Hobgoblins to the civilized world. Driven from Zwaoi shortly after constructing a fortress within its borders, dwarves spread the news of the heinous race of creatures living there. Still, none of these Hobgoblins had been sighted outside the Northern borders. Of the other inhuman monsters in this dark realm, the rare, native Whiteblood dragon bested them all. Known for its ferocity, the massive creature's pale hide was enough to freeze one in his tracks at the mere sight of it.

Gwyndel trembled at the thought. "You believe that the Ashen Specter brought this Whiteblood south to Taekohar, and was able to domineer an army of dragons to bring Castle Asdale to the ground?" she questioned, eyes glued to the map.

Eyoés nodded firmly. "I am going to Zwaoi," he said.

Although taken aback by this rash suggestion, Gwyndel knew what she must do. Eyoés' skill with the sword had yet to be proven, and the long journey to Zwaoi would be treacherous. She was willing to accept the quest as well.

"I am coming with you," she announced. Eyoés turned to look over his shoulder. His gaze was approving, although surprised at Gwyndel's acceptance.

Encouraged by this turn of events, he returned to the map. "Very well. We must travel through the southwestern corner of Anehstun first," he began. "We will have to stop at Anedyn to get supplies. Then we will move on to Iostan." As he moved his finger to the territory mentioned, the ridges of the old parchment crinkled under his touch. He noted the semicircle of mountains that took up most of the space. At the bottom of this mountain range, Eyoés noticed a symbol in ink, partly smeared. Below, the words "Fychan's Cabin," were scrawled in rough handwriting.

Seeing his interest, Gwyndel pointed toward the symbol. "Fychan moved to a new jurisdiction around two years ago," she explained. "It *would* make a practical stop on the way."

Eyoés grinned, his quest becoming a reality before his eyes. "We will stop for the night at Fychan's cabin," he declared, tracing the path with his finger as he spoke. "Then, we will journey north into Zwaoi."

Gwyndel tapped a small star not far northwest of Fychan's cabin. "The Caverns of Nubaroz would be a convenient place to replenish our supplies," she added.

Eyoés nodded. "Tomorrow, we will spend the day gathering our supplies and leave the following morning," he declared.

Satisfied with the trail he had planned, he stood from the desk. The sun began to set, casting an orange glow into the cabin's interior. Still tired from his wandering, Eyoés collapsed on the bed. He stared darkly at his sword, which leaned against the corner of the building alongside Gwyndel's weapons. It would not be long until he would have his revenge.

With black thoughts in his mind, he faded into sleep.

6

As the light of dawn crested the tops of the trees, they descended from the treehouse, the sound of birdsong harkening the beginning of a new day. Eyoés steadied himself upon the improvised swing, while Gwyndel eased him to the ground with the rope. As his feet touched the soil, Eyoés stood. Thrown off balance by the uneven weight of his bound arm, he staggered forward. As he considered the wounded arm bound to his chest with an embarrassed expression, Eyoés realized his injury would not be a simple hurdle to overcome.

Would this wound cost me my life in combat?

Taken aback by the extent of his vulnerability, he tried to encourage himself.

Pulling the ladder up, Gwyndel pinned it to the porch to fasten it into place. Once finished with her preparations, she hung from the balcony's edge and dropped. Gwyndel fell into a crouch when she hit the ground, rolling to absorb the impact of her fall. Eyoés adjusted the splint on his arm with a grunt. Picking up her pack where it leaned against the tree, Gwyndel shifted it to a comfortable position. Because of Eyoés' injury, the majority of the supplies weighed upon her shoulders. Nestled inside the pack were just enough provisions to supplement her hunting until their arrival at Anedyn. Eyoés slung a small bedroll over his head and under his right arm, adjusting it to the middle of his back.

The gravity of the journey before them weighed in their minds, and doubts about their own abilities began to surface. Longingly, Gwyndel took in the sight of her home, wondering when the familiar smell of the pine planks would greet her return. Eyoés, standing at the border of the forest, gazed deep into the brush, as the path of their trek played out before his eyes. No doubt dispelled the desire for vengeance that bred in his soul, feeding off the grisly memories that haunted his dreams. He woke from his musings as Gwyndel entered the trail in front of him, examining the terrain for directional guidance. A sense of anticipation drove Eyoés to follow in Gwyndel's footsteps.

There is no turning back.

Ruminating on what was to come, he trailed behind his sister, feeling for his sword to assure himself. Eyoés trekked onward, his expression darkening at the unknown.

The two struck camp upon a sloping hill, weary from three weeks of travel. Twisting through the forest below, the Gywic River flowed outside the border of Taekohar. Eyoés shrugged off his bedroll and leaned against a nearby tree, sliding to a seated position. He sighed, looking out over the wild terrain ahead. At the last curve of the distant river, wisps of smoke rose from cook fires, crowning the town of Anedyn. Gwyndel pulled at two thick blankets stuck inside the pack, the stubborn cloth finally yielding. Laying these makeshift beds out upon the ground, she looked to where Eyoés rested. They were still early on in the journey.

I must be sure of his skill with the sword.

She made her way toward him. "The tree behind you," she indicated, pointing to the conifer he leaned against. "Use it as a pell and show me your swordsmanship." Eyoés stood clumsily. Drawing his sword from its sheath, he turned to the tree, his lame left arm sending him slightly off balance. He hesitated.

This will not be my best drill.

The thought of his inability to do well at the task motivated him to prove himself wrong. He must show her he was strong enough. Planting his left foot ahead of his right, he raised the hilt of his sword and pointed the blade skyward. His eyes narrowed as he readied his mind. Then, with a cry of defiance, he brought the blade down in a diagonal cut, the weight of the weapon yanking his one wrist.

The blade cut a gash into the tree trunk at chest height, halting abruptly in the wood. Anger swelled in his chest at his imperfect stroke. Jerking twice at the weapon with a growl of frustration, he stepped backwards as it gave way. He lunged toward the tree again, cutting another slash at mid-height before bringing the blade around and repeating the entire drill on the other side. He returned the blade to a final guard position.

The drill lasted mere minutes. Leaning upon the hilt of his weapon, Eyoés looked to Gwyndel, hoping for encouragement. In the past, he had been able to execute the warm up drill with lethal efficiency. Now, the inability to use his left arm for support and power made his movements clumsy. Gwyndel approached, her expression hopeful, yet woefully short of the encouragement Eyoés wished for.

"Well done. I didn't expect you to be this proficient with an injured arm," she pointed out. When she held out her hand, Eyoés reluctantly gave her the weapon, scowling to himself. Gwyndel tested the weapon's heft, thoughts of her father rising to the surface. A shiver ran through her arm as she held her father's treasured weapon.

Father, this is for you. I pledge to guide Eyoés as you would—in what matters.

Assuming the correct stance Eyoés had begun the drill with, she gripped the weapon with both hands. Her expression calm and concentrated, she brought the blade down, executing the drill with speed. Her smooth strokes melted into a flurry of movement, leaving wounds in the tree exactly where she intended. Eyoés watched, darkly. The shame at his being bettered after two years of training was revealed in his brooding manner.

My father's journal was very in depth—yet I still have not mastered what he has given me.

When Gwyndel concluded with the final guard position, she turned.

"When you cut, be wary of throwing yourself off balance because of your momentum," she explained. "Leaving yourself open is deadly." She lifted the weapon upright. "Don't grip the handle like a staff," she instructed. Gwyndel held the sword so he could see her grip. Her thumb rested upon the crossbar, touching the bottom of the blade, while the rest of her hand wrapped around the grip. "This position will increase your control of where the blade goes," she said.

With this, she extended the sword's handle to Eyoés, which he seized with the bitterness of his humiliation. He said nothing, instead attacking the tree with a vicious wrath—yet applying Gwyndel's instruction. The feel of the alternative grip seemed to connect him with the weapon, allowing him to sense where it should go. With every stroke, the momentum of the sword was checked by his physical strength. The thrill of improvement ran through him as he concluded the exercise, the defaced tree standing before him as an immovable warrior.

Gwyndel set a hand on his shoulder, nodding in approval. "Much better," she assured him, returning where to their beds lay. Fetching her bow and quiver from the pack, she ventured into the woods to hunt.

Eyoés watched her retreat, stomach growling at the thought of fresh food. Once she left his sight, Eyoés returned to the pell, rigorously practicing what he had learned.

I must not fail Father. I must train until I cannot!

Their entrance into Anedyn three days later went unnoticed by the crowd filing through the streets. The din of conversation around them drowned out the two strangers' thoughts. Wisps of smoke ascended from cook fires, carrying with it the smells of the midday meal. The lattice frames of the houses formed X and V patterns using local timbers, and river stones were stacked tightly in alternating arrangement to construct stable walls. Wooden shingles were haphazardly laid to create a sufficient roof. Each home drew attention to the roughness of the townsfolk, who were mostly fishermen and farmers. Although their coarse nature was quite different from the people of Taekohar, Eyoés could not help considering the town longingly as memories of pleasant afternoons in Castle Asdale returned to him.

Hiding his sword underneath the cloak he wore, Eyoés followed Gwyndel through the crowd. Townsfolk eyed her Forester garb with respect and apprehension, giving both of them a wide berth like a stream around a rock. Occasionally, Gwyndel would stop a passerby, inquiring for the location of certain supply shops. Eyoés ignored the crowd, taking refuge in the safety of his own thoughts. Turning a corner in the street, Gwyndel pulled out of the crowd and turned to Eyoés. A sign reading "Wayfarer's Market" dangled precariously above the door of a nearby shop.

Gwyndel grabbed Eyoés' shoulder. "Wait for me

here," she ordered. "This place entices thieves and others we don't need to attract. The quieter we pass through, the less trouble. We'll make camp outside of town." Without further conversation, she entered the building, leaving Eyoés to guard the entrance for her return. Backing up against the wall to ensure no one would catch him from behind, Eyoés observed the crowd, yet avoided eye contact. It seemed only minutes before Gwyndel returned, her sack full of provisions.

Silently blending into the crowd, they left Anedyn —and any possible source of rescue if something went wrong.

7

Eyoés yawned, eyes wandering across the forest rimming their camp, searching for danger. Around him, the sharp chirps of crickets reminded him of the sleep he would lose on this watch. Shaking the weariness from his mind, he forced himself to stay awake. The center fire burned with a stormy intensity. Eyoés glanced toward the flames, the contrast of the light to the darkness obscuring his vision. The distant hooting of an owl made him start. He reached for his weapon and scanned the forest in alarm. When he recognized the origin of the sound, he relaxed, disgusted at his lack of self-control. Grumbling to himself, he leaned against his pack, the monotony of the night watch setting in. Eyoés settled into a comfortable position as he continued to search the surrounding territory. Dark memories of the Ashen Specter surfaced, triggering an involuntary glance into the darkness.

Could the Ashen Specter—could he still be lurking about?

He curled his lip, shaking his head in disgust at his own fear. "Me, the son of a hero, afraid of the dark," he muttered to himself with a scowl. Seething, Eyoés gritted his teeth and gazed into the fire. The flaming arrows of his hatred had a target. The hideous images of the villain he despised only served to increase his loathing. Still, the frigid presence of fear reigned in the corners of his mind, reminding him of the fate of those who had crossed the legendary apparition.

The stench of rotting flesh wafted to his nostrils, and the hair on the back of his neck rose as he felt the presence of eyes searching for weakness.

Tensely, Eyoés looked over his shoulder, pulling his father's sword partially from its scabbard. A massive, black form withdrew into the dark forest, white eyes gleaming in the darkness—then vanished.

Eyoés froze, glancing to where Gwyndel slept unaware of the chilling sight her brother had beheld. He fearfully glanced into the forest, yet saw nothing. Gathering his courage, he risked being spotted and scrambled to Gwyndel's side. Eyes glued to the darkness, he vigorously shook her shoulder.

Immediately, she sat up and plucked an arrow from her quiver. She needed no explanation. Some—*thing* was stalking them. Casting the blanket off, she scanned the woods for the threat. A low, mournful howl rose from the trees, sending a shudder through their bodies. Drawing his sword, Eyoés readied himself, searching for what was hunting them.

He forgot to look behind.

The creature exploded from the forest with a snarl. Eyoés slashed wildly at the beast's face. The wolfish monster pinned him to the ground, jaws snapping at his throat. Eyoés screamed and thrust his blade upwards. The beast limped back with a howl and tensed for another pounce. Gwyndel's arrows embedded into its neck. Howling in defiance, the beast lunged toward her. Two more arrows stuck in the creature's glistening maw. Mortally wounded, the monster collapsed in a heap. Swiftly bounding toward the fallen creature, Gwyndel drew her dagger and finished it off. She rushed to Eyoés, fearing he had been wounded.

Several holes had been torn in his shirt from the struggle. Eyoés cringed as he felt for injuries, his splinted arm aching from the pressure of the creature's paws. Grasping Gwyndel's outstretched hand, Eyoés stood, eying the carcass of their attacker uneasily. It was larger than any wolf he had read about. Its long snout was curled back in a final sneer, revealing curved fangs. Inky fur blended into the darkness. Dagger-like spines protruded from its shoulders, accentuating the size and power of the beast.

Trembling, Eyoés sheathed his sword, creeping closer to the dead animal. "What sort of fiend is this?" he asked, not daring to look at Gwyndel for fear that the beast would revive.

Setting her bow by the fire, Gwyndel crouched by the dark form, yanking her arrows from the beast's flesh. "Kélak, by the looks of it," she mused aloud, wiping her arrows on the ground before inserting them into her quiver. "They are native to Zwaoi—and they haven't been seen elsewhere that I know of."

Eyoés started, regarding the creature with a new perspective. Upon closer examination, something odd caught his attention. Previously hidden by fur was a thick iron collar. Eyoés reached out to grab it—and noticed the frayed end of a leash. Looking over his shoulder, Gwyndel caught sight of the object he studied. They stared at each other in silence, their thoughts going the same direction.

They no longer held the offensive position—and Eyoés' wound would not heal in time for battle.

The light of noon started its descent into the increasing darkness of evening as they trekked for the third day through the timberland of Anehstun. Nestled among the dense shrubbery, conifers soared overhead. Pebbles crunched under each step. Moss of a deep green hue crawled up the bark of the trees, hanging from long branches over their heads. The moist air refreshed them as they trudged through the underbrush, heading west to Iostan. Beneath the shrubs and fallen branches, the remains of an old trail peeked out to direct the two travelers' passage. Stepping over old, dead limbs, Gwyndel scanned the horizon for movement—any sign that they were not alone in the quiet woodland. Behind, Eyoés trod in her footsteps, his movements far less cautious. Gwyndel's heart leapt into her throat at the snap of a branch.

Spinning around, she gestured for him to be silent, annoyed with his inability to stay focused. Ceasing all movement, they held their breath and waited for any sound of pursuit. Nothing. Confident they were alone, Gwyndel continued, Eyoés following close behind. He adjusted the bedroll on his shoulder, grunting in pain as he accidentally bumped his broken arm. As he followed Gwyndel's path, his mind wandered. Glancing over his shoulder, he watched the ferns sway behind them.

With every step, Eyoés realized aid slipped further and further away. He watched Gwyndel climb over a fallen tree, her feet ripping loose, rotten pieces of bark from the toppled giant. Eyoés hastened toward it, searching the tree for an adequate foothold. As he pushed his foot off a large knob, he swung his body over the tree and dropped to the ground. Shifting his weight to compensate for the momentum, Eyoés regained his balance. Ahead, Gwyndel waited, searching the forest floor for a glimpse of the path beneath the brush. Eyoés returned to the solace of his thoughts. Their vulnerability gnawed at his nerves, suggesting possible attackers with every rustling of a bush. His sheltered childhood never exposed him to the tension that now tied his stomach in knots. Eyoés shook his head to dispel the thought.

I will be ready.

Studying his father's journal had not been a waste of time. When attackers came, he *would* triumph. His eyebrows furrowed as he considered Gwyndel's criticisms of his swordsmanship. Clenching his good hand around the hilt of his weapon, Eyoés stared daggers at Gwyndel's back. Two years of sweat and blood had gone into his training.

She thinks I would fail.

The very thought woke memories of his crushed dreams of heroism. His face contorted in sorrow as he recalled the fates of Aványn and Baron Dányth. When his dream collapsed in smoke, it brought them down to the grave with it. He slowed his gait unconsciously, as he contemplated the loss, fury building within him. His muscles tensed and he looked to the trail ahead. Somewhere, in the northern mountains of Zwaoi, the Ashen Specter hid, the debt of his wrongs yet unpaid. A low growl escaped him, his voice breaking as a tear stained his cheek.

He has stolen my chance to prove myself a worthy heir to my father. I will use him as a new opportunity.

Still, past failures would not leave him alone. With Gwyndel's instruction, he had improved—a sign his capabilities had fallen short. Would he accept further teaching? He wiped away the traces of his grief. Realizing he had fallen behind, he pressed on, thoughts coming to an abrupt conclusion. He would *prove* that he could meet the challenge, and would use whatever necessary to overcome—even if it came from Gwyndel's hand. Satisfied with this resolution, he withdrew from his thoughts. The loud snap of his foot breaking a nearby branch caused him to freeze. Turning to her brother for the last time, Gwyndel bared her teeth in a frustrated manner. Eyoés couldn't help a small grin.

As night fell, the once beautiful forest transformed into a foreboding lair, the darkness hiding whatever lurked in its shadows. Tree limbs twisted above their heads, the glow of the moon lighting the forest floors with an eerie blue. Calls of nocturnal birds echoed throughout the wood, the location of their origin unclear. The two ventured further in, all the more vigilant to the surroundings. Side by side they walked, not daring to whisper. Eyoés had insisted they get as close to the border of Iostan as possible before resting. Initially, Gwyndel had objected to Eyoés' insistence to continue on, due to the late hour. When he had argued its potential to save rations, however, she gave in to his demands. Now, as they trekked on, Eyoés wondered if he had made a wise decision.

He forced every footstep forward into the gloom, as the dread of what lay beyond warned him to turn back. Hand grasping the hilt of his sword, he glanced toward Gwyndel. Fingering her nocked arrow, she searched the path for hidden dangers. Ahead of them, the trail widened into a small field, covered in flowers and thick grass. They kept to the forest edge, avoiding contact with the brush.

A sudden whippoorwill's call caught them off guard. Eyoés drew his sword from its scabbard. Hands shaking, they scoured the forest for the enemy.

Nothing. Gwyndel hurried to leave the exposed ground. Sheathing his weapon, Eyoés moved to follow.

A deep, guttural growl rumbled from the small field off to his left. Eyoés stopped.

Gwyndel turned. The look of foreboding on her brother's face urged her on. Silently, she hastily gestured for him to follow.

An arrow hissed past her head, embedding itself in a nearby tree with a thud.

9

Gwyndel pulled her bowstring, unsure where to aim. Eyoés drew his sword, searching for the threat with wild eyes. Three tall, dark forms burst from the trees with guttural cries of fury. Lit by the moonlight, the fearsome creatures charged, formidable weapons raised over their heads. Eyoés was shocked by their haggard, disfigured faces glaring maliciously at him. Their tailored leather pauldrons sat arrogantly on their bulky shoulders in stark contrast to the filthy rags they wore. Eyoés could not help being repulsed by their hideous expressions.

"Hobgoblins," Gwyndel said. One of the attackers fell into a heap at the twang of her bowstring, an arrow protruding from his heart. Cries of horror and anger rose from the creatures as they witnessed their comrade fall and drop his bow. Spurred into a rage, they pressed on. Gwyndel turned to flee with her brother—only to see him instead spring into action, charging the attackers with zeal.

"For Taekohar and Asdale!" he screamed, the battle cry of his father bringing tears to his eyes as he rushed to the fight. The Hobgoblins shrieked in reply to outmatch their foe in ferocity.

Now is the time to prove my worth.

Eyoés met the oncoming attack with a yell of

passionate rage. Dodging the blade of the nearest Hobgoblin, he lashed out in retaliation. The creature collapsed with a cry, clutching the fatal wound in its chest. The young warrior's eyes widened.

My training is proving itself now that I've met real combat!

He dropped to his right knee at the hum of a rushing blade. Parrying the blow aimed for his neck, he swatted it away and struck, hoping for a decisive victory. Eyoés' face fell as the Hobgoblin stepped back. The tip of his blade passed harmlessly before its midsection and left him open to attack. The advantage was lost.

Eyoés desperately attempted to regain the advantage. The Hobgoblin slammed its axe into his sword, wrenching it from his grip and into the air. The force of the blow sent Eyoés sprawling, knocking his breath away as he hit the ground. His head throbbed. A savage sneer exposed the Hobgoblin's pearly fangs as it closed in for the kill. Eyoés closed his eyes in resignation. The energy to rise and fight again no longer came to his aid, and hot tears spilled from the corners of his eyes as he contemplated his fate.

I've failed. My life has been a waste. Father would have been ashamed of me.

He awaited the final death blow. Screams and the thudding of arrows startled him from his stupor. Shafts bristled from the Hobgoblin's chest. Dropping its weapon, the beast collapsed, its screams cut short by the hand of death. Bewildered, Eyoés rolled onto his side, searching for the origin of his rescue. Gwyndel had already nocked another arrow. The sprawled corpse was still. Assured they were safe, Gwyndel replaced the arrow in her quiver and threw her bow aside. Kneeling next to Eyoés, Gwyndel felt his head for signs of injury.

Eyoés moaned as a dull pain resulted from her probing. "I'm fine. Stop waving your two fingers in front of my eyes," he growled as Gwyndel tested for the limits of his head injury.

Sighing with relief, Gwyndel removed a small, clean cloth from her pack, dabbing the abrasion on the back of his head. "The King must be watching over you. You nearly split your skull open on a rock!" she exclaimed. "This should heal in a matter of days." Hearing the verdict, Eyoés stared deep into the night sky, the endless stars covering the expanse. Blinking to drive away the dizziness, he replayed the scene in his mind, realizing how narrowly he had escaped death. Yet, the fact he had been overpowered was a deeper wound. As Gwyndel tended him, his mind drifted, considering the likelihood of further failure. Eyoés closed his eyes and lifted a silent prayer.

Don't let me fail. Let me live to see it finished.

10

The light of dawn glowed amid the dying night, as morning worked to dispel the evils lurking in the forest. Perched among the leaves, birds sung in response to the appearance of the sun. Underneath the boughs of the trees, shadows hid, trembling at the presence of day. Leaning against a nearby oak, Gwyndel shifted her position uncomfortably. Eyes darting over the shadows, she clutched her bow, tense at the memory of the earlier ambush. The image of Eyoés lying helpless on the ground was burned into her memory. The hope of reuniting with her family had withstood years of separation and the news of her father's death. During the time of separation, she had turned to the King for her identity, rigorously following his guidance. With the news of her mother's passing, Gwyndel had poured her passion for her lost family into care for Eyoés, binding his wounds and joining his journey. Shivering from the cold breeze, she glanced to where Eyoés slept, wrapped in a thick blanket.

She joined the quest out of kindness to her long lost sibling and pity for his plight. Her eyes alighted on the sword lying in the grass next to him. Initially, she had thought only his honor to be at risk. Now, after their near brush with fate, it was obvious more was at stake than Eyoés' pride.

Sunlight began to stream through the boughs of the trees. An inner prodding proposed a way out. If she continued on with Eyoés, the chances of their death increased with every passing mile.

If I left now, I could disappear before Eyoés wakens. It is foolish to lose my life for someone else's pride.

Gwyndel clutched her bow, fastening her quiver over her shoulder. Casting a final glance toward her sleeping brother, she disappeared into the tree line. Squinting in the sunlight, she avoided an overgrown stump in her path. She stopped, turning back. The realization of her actions settled into her thoughts.

I am about to leave the last of my family.

The likelihood of Eyoés surviving the journey on his own was slim, despite his confidence. Pursing her lips, Gwyndel fingered the string of her bow. She swallowed the lump in her throat, recalling her old dreams of reunion. Resolutely, she retraced her steps.

I cannot take any more loss.

Eyoés squinted as he opened his eyes, the morning sunlight at full strength. Mustering the energy to sit up, he cursed under his breath as his wounded arm protested. He threw aside his blanket with his good arm. Retrieving his sword and belt next to him, he stood and wiped the dew on his shirt. The vivid recollection of his encounter with death grew stronger with contemplation. A heaviness weighed his body down as he relived his defeat. Rubbing his hand in the wet grass, Eyoés wiped his face to relieve the fatigue, to no avail. He glared at his bound arm as he thought of yet another strategy which would have turned the tide in his favor.

I should have died. Why didn't I?

Gwyndel's words preyed on his thoughts.

The King must be watching over you...

Pressing his lips together in a slight grimace, Eyoés sighed through his nose. His life had been in constant upheaval since its beginning. The death of his parents, Aványn's lies, the destruction of Asdale, and his inability to defend himself. How could Gwyndel say such a thing? Eyoés rejected her absurd notion.

If he's watching, he clearly doesn't care. I have to watch out for myself. I must make things right because nobody else will.

Even with this resolution, the disappointment at his failure remained. As Eyoés paced across the span of their camp, he noticed Gwyndel emerge from the trees, eyes locking onto his position with suppressed surprise. During his musings, he had failed to notice his sister's absence. He began to speak.

"Couldn't find any small game for our breakfast," she explained, cutting her brother off.

Shrugging, Eyoés returned to where the night's supplies lay and pulled out a portion of dried fruit. "I don't understand how I could be defeated like that," he pondered aloud. "With my training, I should have conquered!" Forcefully, he stuffed his night blanket into Gwyndel's pack. Dark circles under his eyes revealed the discouragement within.

Seeing her brother's plight, Gwyndel stepped forward and set a hand on his shoulder. "Your wounded arm could not be helped—thank the King you survived Asdale's destruction," she replied.

Eyoés ceased his preparations and diverted his eyes. He recalled the many nights he had dreamed of heroism. Until the destruction of Asdale, those dreams had gone unchallenged. Now, at the first opportunity to avenge the deaths of those dreams, he had failed the test.

A bitter smile crossed his features. "Conquered by a brutish creature. Twice. I can think of many ways I *should* have defeated them. How will I prevail in the next battle?" he ranted.

Shaking her head, Gwyndel gestured to the sword that lay next to the pack. "You can't win every battle. Defeat keeps you humble and sharp. Learn from your mistakes and use that knowledge to improve," she responded. "Our power is limited."

Eyoés remained silent as he mused over Gwyndel's words. The realization of his insufficient skill dawned upon him. He couldn't bear to meet Gwyndel's eyes. "I feel like I have failed Father," he confessed, voice thick. "I wish he were here to guide me."

Gwyndel laid a compassionate hand on his head. "Many times, I am uncertain too," she answered. "You must not always look backwards. Move on from your mistakes. Leave them in the past."

Eyoés looked into Gwyndel's eyes.

It is not over yet.

He nodded, kneeling on the bag and cinching it tight with his free arm. "Very well," he declared, standing. Picking his sheathed weapon from the ground, he extended it to Gwyndel. She nodded and fastened it around his waist. Eyoés watched Gwyndel's hands furtively, frustrated at his inability to do it himself. When she stepped back, he relaxed. As Gwyndel hoisted her pack onto her shoulders, Eyoés put his bedroll securely onto his back. Orienting themselves northwest, they set out for the border of Iostan. Soon, he would have use of the arm.

He had only to be patient.

11

Eyoés emerged from the brush as the sun reached its zenith, with Gwyndel not far behind. Leaving the steep slope of thick scrub behind them, they ascended to the hilltop. A meadow of thick, spongy shrubbery blanketed the summit, the groves of evergreens like a tower's spires. Above their heads, a cloudless sky stretched far to the horizon. Hills topped with forest rolled in every direction. Sprawling valleys yawned below them, covered with green velvet. Approaching the nearest copse, Gwyndel shrugged off her pack with a sigh, leaning against a tall conifer.

"Let's rest for awhile before moving on," she suggested.

Eyoés removed his bedroll, tossing it onto the soft ground. Sweat dotted his forehead, and burrs clung to his shirt. Ignoring his weariness, he searched for an adequate place to train.

No sense in wasting time.

He caught sight of a bare tree, its wood faded by years of weathering. Casting an eye toward Gwyndel, he drew his sword. He reviewed her teaching under his breath, adjusting to the correct grip. Honing his attention on the tree before him, he began his drill, a series of clear thuds echoing for miles in the open air. With each stroke, the suppressed disappointment of his defeat faded as he noticed improvement. Captivated, he pressed harder, his already weary muscles cramping with overuse. In minutes, his shirt clung to his sweaty skin.

Gwyndel watched as his strokes gradually weakened and his legs trembled. "Stop!" she shouted, darting toward him. Jarred from his concentration, Eyoés glared at her, pausing for only a moment before returning to the pell. Gwyndel seized his shoulders before he could strike, pulling him from the tree. Surprised, he fell backwards, sword dropping to the ground. Gwyndel took a step back. Catching himself, Eyoés whirled around to face her. As he stared her down, the muscles of his neck tensed. Gwyndel gestured toward the tree with obvious alarm.

"You are driving yourself to exhaustion!" she exclaimed. Eyoés barely heard her through the blood pounding in his ears.

Nostrils flaring, he jabbed a finger into his chest. "If that is what it takes for victory," he roared, "I will do it!" Breathing shakily, Eyoés clenched his fist as Gwyndel shook her head.

She cannot understand.

Her stare fixed on Eyoés, Gwyndel sought for a way to stop him. Since the beginning of their journey, it was obvious his notion of grandeur was consuming him by degrees. "I understand your pain—but this quest was unnecessary," she insisted.

Eyoés' eyes widened at the accusation. He advanced, laughing spitefully. "This fate was forced upon me," he hissed. "Do you think I *chose* for my home to be destroyed? All those people slain?" Eyoés halted, lingering as he considered his next move. Gaze locked on her brother, Gwyndel took another step back, fingering the bow slung over her shoulder. Before she could speak, he leapt to where his sword lay and reached for the handle. He withdrew his hand as an arrow thudded into the ground between him and the weapon.

"You only aid me because you see me as weak!" he yelled, refusing to look her in the eye.

"You *are* weak!" Gwyndel screamed in reply, bow drawn for another shot. "But I do not intend for you to stay that way!" Eyoés bit his tongue, silencing himself. Only the whisper of the wind filled the silence. His expression twisted in anger, Eyoés stood, retrieving his sword. Regarding Gwyndel with narrowed eyes, he thrust his weapon into its sheath. Without a word, he sat under the shade of a nearby bough with a grunt. Gwyndel released the tension on her bow, shaking her head in frustration. Turning from the scene, she plunged into the brush, leaving Eyoés to his thoughts.

Gwyndel ducked underneath a low hanging branch, her hair brushing the leaves. A gentle breeze blew through the trees growing on the hillside, the swaying of the leaves ebbing and flowing like the ocean's waves. Pine cones dotted the ground. Hiding behind a mass of tangled brush, Gwyndel drew an arrow from her quiver, eyes scanning the forest for sign of game. The solitude of the woodland soothed her anxiety. Clenching her jaw, she ran her finger up the arrow's fletching.

How can he be so blind? His weaknesses are obvious.

She scratched the back of her neck, muttering under her breath. Why wouldn't Eyoés acknowledge his shortcomings and ask for help? She had not been there on the night of Castle Asdale's fate, but she understood the consequences well enough.

A nearby rustling in the bushes caught her attention. Silently, Gwyndel moved closer. She pressed herself against an old tree stump, peering around it. A deer weaved among the branches, unaware of her presence. Several hours of patience had paid off. Gwyndel drew the bowstring to her cheek, lining her sights with the creature's vitals. When the buck stopped to graze, Gwyndel let fly. Springing in reaction to the unexpected pain, the beast fled deeper into the forest. Gwyndel slung her bow onto her shoulders and followed the trail.

Even as she traced the animal's tracks through the underbrush, her mind raced with frustrated thoughts. Before long, she would have to return to where Eyoés waited. Taking a deep breath, Gwyndel listened for sounds of the buck's retreat, instead hearing only birdsong and wind. She plunged into the forest, eying the ground below as she dodged a patch of brush. Amid the cluster of trees and bushes, a craggy boulder overshadowed a small patch of open ground. Lying askew beneath the overhanging rock, the carcass of the buck awaited. Gwyndel stepped over a large branch and removed her dagger. She crouched by the fallen animal and began to clean it.

Eyoés is striving to be like someone he has never met. Father died before Eyoés was born.

She paused, glancing skyward. The orange hue of evening tainted the deep blue sky. Day was fading.

Redoubling her efforts, Gwyndel hurried to return to camp.

12

The last stray rays of light withdrew from the lush, green meadow. Eyoés noticed Gwyndel emerge from the brush as the sun began to set on the horizon. He stared at the tree in front of him, refusing to look toward her. Gwyndel shook her head, seeing her brother's gesture of scorn. She adjusted the bag of backstrap thrown over her shoulder. As she neared the grove of trees crowning the hill, Eyoés gave a quick glance in her direction.

"So, you've returned to find fault with me again?" he questioned, raising his chin high.

"No," Gwyndel replied, loosening her shoulders. "I've only returned with dinner."

Furtively, Eyoés watched her shrug the bag onto the ground. His stomach growled in anticipation as he considered the evening meal. As a result of their quarrel, lunch had been forgotten. Eyoés stood, adjusting his belt. Gwyndel said nothing as she went about her task. Although the bite of her accusations still held fast, his convictions remained.

I am doing what is necessary to avenge the honor of my father and the deaths of the people.

Removing the strips of silver from the meat, Gwyndel gathered these scraps into her hands, tossing them off the edge of the hill into the forest below. "Help me start a fire. The sooner we eat, the less of a chance predators will come prowling," she reasoned, washing her hands in a small puddle of water. With a nod, Eyoés scoured the grove, bending down to grab fallen branches and foliage. He muttered angrily to himself as a thorn pricked his finger. Struggling to keep his emotions in check, he breathed deeply, continuing to gather kindling and fuel wood. After multiple trips for firewood, Gwyndel lit the campfire, the flames stark against the dying light of the sun. She carved up the thick bands of venison, shoving each piece onto a stick before repeating the process. Pondering, Eyoés stared into the fire.

You are weak!

He stood, paced about the camp, then sat again as he wrestled with Gwyndel's statement.

What if she is right?

He ran his hand through his hair, afraid to consider the answer. Wrapping his cloak about him, Eyoés found himself trapped by a possible truth he feared to believe. He inhaled through his nose and released a pent-up breath.

I've come too far to consider such foolishness. Her words mean nothing.

Kneeling by the fire, Eyoés watched the flames repeatedly curl over the burning logs, stretching upward only to die in sparks.

Unlike these tongues of flame, my passion will not die out. I will rise from the ashes of my life like the phoenix.

Gwyndel set a makeshift spit over the hungry flames before leaning against a tree. She glanced toward her brother, mulling over what to say to him. Because of their argument, it would not take much to stir his emotions. Gwyndel mustered her courage.

"Father was a noble man," she remarked, watching her brother for his response. "But you never *knew* him."

Eyoés stiffened, his eyes fixed on the flames. Was the statement an insult or a revelation? Seeking to rebuff her statement, he examined his past—only to realize she was right. He ran his hand through his hair. The Baron's brief statement about Élorn had been the only link to his father's true character for years. The journal's pages had not revealed his father's nature. Eyoés said nothing, fiddling with a piece of grass. Gwyndel hesitated, unsure whether his silence indicated anger or thought. Hearing nothing, he gestured for Gwyndel to continue.

"Father—he was kind and patient." she gazed up into the evening sky, watching the stars brighten with the sun's fall. "I remember how frustrated I was over learning to spell. When I began to cry, he would cradle me in his arms and tell me 'Learning takes time. Don't rush. Be patient and you will succeed.'" Eyoés followed her eyes to the sky, the brightness of the flames still etched in his vision. Lost in memory, Gwyndel continued. "Whenever he was insulted, he would never fly into a rage, but forgive," she thought aloud. Looking back toward her brother, Gwyndel watched as Eyoés rubbed the back of his neck, face reddening.

I cannot stop now. He must hear this.

Watching his sword hand, Gwyndel rotated the spit, preparing to tell the truth. "Father also knew when to push on—and when to stop," she concluded. Eyoés sprang to his feet, striking the nearest tree with his open palm, silent. He struggled to keep his emotions in check. Heat rushed through his body as he considered her statement. Although anger clouded his thinking, one thing remained clear—his own notions were at odds with the reality of his father's character.

Would he have approved of this quest?

Eyoés shivered, unsettled. Shaking his head, he turned back to the fire. He pulled a skewer of meat from the flames, eating in silence without a thought for his sister. Gwyndel reached over and pulled a skewer from the fire for herself. The savory venison didn't compete with her troubled thoughts. The moon bathed the valleys below in a peaceful white light. Listening to the chorus of crickets in the grass, Gwyndel glanced toward the dark thicket behind them. Her lips pressed into a pensive frown as leaves fell to the ground, shaken by the night wind. The weeks had flown over the course of their travels.

Winter draws near. We must hurry to Fychan's.

Finishing his meal, Eyoés tossed the stick aside, and moved to where his bedroll lay. Gwyndel watched him pull his blanket free, too troubled by his musings to speak to her. Without a word, he enfolded himself and settled down for an uneasy sleep.

Biting the inside of her cheek, Gwyndel stood and

disappeared into the grove of trees. She returned with a collection of forked sticks. As she kneeled by the fireside, she glanced to where her brother lay. Despite his anger and hate, she pitied him.

He never had a chance to learn what honor really means—that kindness, not heroic deeds make a man noble. He is guided only by his fanciful dreams.

After planting them around the fire, she fetched some nearby branches and laid them horizontally across each pair of forks to improvise a grate. Although she had compassion for him, she struggled to foresee a change.

His pride is holding him captive. It may never release him.

Gwyndel retrieved a small hatchet from the supply bag and unfastened the leather sheath. Again, she returned to the grove.

Several minutes later, she returned, dragging three tree limbs behind her. She looked toward Eyoés, watching his chest steadily rise and fall. Setting the wood beside the fire, she sharpened the bottom end of each with her hatchet.

Do I have the strength to stay at his side to this journey's end?

She stopped mid-stroke, several shavings curling away from her hatchet. Looking fixedly into the fire, she envisioned the days ahead, plagued by strife. Closing her eyes, she muttered a prayer.

Please strengthen me. There is much ahead and I fear I might not endure.

Gwyndel finished whittling and stood, setting aside

her hatchet. With a heave, she rammed each pole into the ground at an angle to create a tripod. Retrieving the freshly skinned deer hide, she sliced off a small band and lashed the posts together with it. Then, she draped the hide over the tripod frame to trap the smoke within. Smoothing the front of her shirt, she cut thin strips from the remaining meat.

This venison will be finished just in time for our early start tomorrow.

Gwyndel pushed aside the hide flap and placed the meat over the branches laid across the pit. As she closed the hide covering, she gazed northwest with a sigh.

They would not reach Fychan's cabin quick enough to escape winter's bite.

13

The landscape morphed from forest to plain as the two lonely figures traveled. Together, yet lonely. Behind them, the path was clearly beaten down, betraying their passage. Sparse groves of trees dotted the meadow, strongholds of green amid a sea of flaxen grass. Sweeping back and forth, the tall grass danced in the whistling wind, yellowed in anticipation of winter. Despite four days with no sign of danger, Eyoés continued to scan the horizon for sign of an enemy. The green of Gwyndel's attire stood out starkly against the yellow background, and the lack of trees and large hills provided little shelter from prying eyes. He adjusted his belt as it chafed against his side.

No danger in sight.

Eyoés turned his attention to Gwyndel. Since their argument, the tension between the two of them had lessened with time. Yet, a strong feeling of unease remained over the conversation about his father's character. Multiple opportunities had arisen for the ashes to be kindled to flame, which had narrowly been avoided. Waking from his thoughts, Eyoés moved to Gwyndel's side. The monotony of their travels had begun to wear his patience thin.

"We are moving over the border to Iostan," Gwyndel declared, guessing at her brother's

restlessness. "We'll be at Fychan's cabin in two days."
Surprised, Eyoés' eyes brightened. Looking out to the
grassland ahead, he grinned.

Another step toward fulfillment.

"Tell me about Fychan," he ventured, hoping to
mend their differences. His image of the experienced
Forester thus far had been formed solely from his
knowledge of Gwyndel's past. He knew little besides
her apprenticeship to Fychan. It was reasonable to
learn about the man he was about to meet.

Gwyndel stopped, withdrawing the curled map
from the side of her pack. Pointing to the next
mountain range on the map, she scanned the horizon.
Faded in the distance, a range of mountains could be
seen on the right side of the plain, correlating to the
location on the map. Replacing the map, Gwyndel
continued on, glancing over her shoulder toward
Eyoés.

"In a sentence, Fychan is a man of discipline and
boldness. He is not afraid to speak his mind—a strange
characteristic in such a kind and friendly man," she
explained, smiling to herself.

Eyoés followed her at a walk. "What was it like,
growing up with him as your mentor?" he inquired,
eyes averted. "Did he ever—lie to you?" Awaiting her
reply, Eyoés forced himself to keep up with her pace in
an effort to appear nonchalant.

Gwyndel shook her head, giving him an
incredulous expression. "Of course not!" she replied.
"Fychan *always* told me what I needed to hear. Lies
disgusted him." Backing her confident statement with

wide steps, she gestured for Eyoés to follow.

Hurrying his pace, he muttered to himself.

Why couldn't I grow up with a truthful parent like everyone else?

He shoved his thoughts away as Gwyndel continued.

"As for my growing up, it was far from normal. Not long after I was committed to his care, Fychan began to train me with the bow. I learned the weapon quickly, and was soon one of the top apprentices," she commented with a bright gaze. "Every day began and ended with rigorous training in the skills of a Forester. Fychan's disciplined manner and attention to the slightest detail pressed me to the limits of my abilities. I began accompanying him on his outings and learning what it took to keep the forests of Alithell safe. Over five years ago, I was assigned to the mountains and forest around Castle Asdale, along with several others. However, the distance makes it difficult for us to communicate."

Eyoés stepped over a rock embedded into the ground, the heel of his boot scraping the rough surface. In Gwyndel's warm manner of speaking about Fychan, it was clear he was more than a mentor. The fact that Gwyndel had spent her youth vigorously training for a specific skill struck a familiar chord. She too had felt the exhaustion and satisfaction of a hard day's training.

Have dreams of heroism occurred to her as well?

Eyoés sighed to himself. She seemed too practical for such heroic imaginings. A tall pine stood in their path, surrounded by swaying grass. Ducking under a low limb, Eyoés scratched at his bound arm with his free hand. By this time, the pain had become much more bearable and infrequent. He was eager to rid himself of the hindrance and use his left arm again. Ahead, Gwyndel paused, checking their course with a small compass. Built in a palm-sized box, the device had been originally devised by the Foresters to aid their navigation. When news of the creation had spread, replicas began to fill the shops across Alithell. Now, the tool was widely used. Aligning the compass north, Gwyndel traced the direction with her finger. She nodded.

Satisfied with her findings, she returned the compass to its place. Eyoés stepped ahead of her, eyes locked on the mountains. Gwyndel followed behind, hurrying to keep up with her eager sibling. As they approached the peaks, trees began to appear more often amid the grasses. Above them, the sun stretched their shadows across the ground. Birds darted from one tree to the next. The deep green of the trees darkened the horizon of yellow, overtaking the plain one foot at a time. Eyoés held in a sneeze as the pungent scent of tree sap stung his nose. The ground ahead began to rise and fall in an uneven rhythm as the land transformed into forest. Exposed by rain, boulders were visible in eroded soil. The branches wove into a tapestry of green, limiting the sun's light. Thick moss sprawled over the bark of evergreens and bare rock.

As the sun gave way to clouds heavy with rain, the two travelers trekked further northward into unfamiliar lands.

14

They spotted the cabin at the bottom of a hill the
next afternoon. Over a month had passed since their
departure from Gwyndel's home. Throughout the trials
of the journey, the convictions of either traveler
repeatedly aroused tension. The thought of Fychan's
company drove them forward.

Snow blanketed the underbrush like dust, yet failed
to hide much of the brown grass. The icy breeze bit
through clothing like thorns, heralding the arrival of
winter. The cabin below would prove a safe haven
from the weather.

Dark moss clung to the rusty brown log walls,
attempting to reclaim the tamed land. Eyoés watched
his feet, carefully stepping over exposed roots in the
steep hillside. Behind him, Gwyndel earnestly scanned
the forest for sign of Fychan, searching for even the
slightest disturbance in the trees. A section of ground
gave way underneath Eyoés, and his free arm shot out
to the nearest tree for stability. Despite his firm grip on
the limb, he struggled to keep upright. Loose dirt and
snow slid down the hill, stones knocking against each
other. Steadying himself, Eyoés continued with
caution.

When he arrived at the bottom of the slope, he
stopped, hearing Gwyndel ease down the hill behind

him. The cabin seemed empty. Eyoés staggered forward, unable to bear the weariness in his legs any longer. Briefly glancing to the surrounding forest, he set his foot upon the first porch step.

An arrow shot past his shoulder, burying itself into a post next to the steps. Leaping back, Eyoés reached for his sword, managing to jerk it halfway from its sheath before Gwyndel seized the weapon's pommel and shoved it back into its scabbard.

"Don't be so hasty!" she whispered. Glaring at her, Eyoés looked to the forest line. A man came out of a group of trees near them, his dark green garments accentuating his tall and muscular form. A dark hood shadowed his face. Moss and snow clung to his clothing. He scrutinized Eyoés curiously. Shifting his gaze to Gwyndel, his face brightened, a smile tugging at the corners of his mouth. A deep laugh rose from his chest as he approached.

"Well! What a pleasant surprise, Gwyndel," he chuckled. "I missed you at the last Council meeting!" Leaning his bow against the wall of his cabin, Fychan embraced Gwyndel, left hand cradling the back of her head. Released from Fychan's arms, she gestured to Eyoés.

"I would like to introduce you to my brother, Eyoés," she announced.

Fychan turned toward Eyoés, eyebrows raised. He regarded the young man's bound arm and dirty appearance with pity. "It is a pleasure to meet you, son of Élorn," he declared, clasping Eyoés' uninjured forearm. "Your father was a good man." Gathering his weapon, Fychan gestured toward the door of his dwelling. "Come. I will prepare an afternoon meal for you," he said, ascending the steps and pushing open the door.

A cold stone fireplace was inset in the opposite wall. Two rocking chairs sat before it. To the right, a door to the bedroom was left ajar. The cracks between the rich brown logs were chinked with moss and dried mud. A locked door to their left lead to a lean-to. Searching for a place to rest, Eyoés entered the bedroom. Only a well-made bed, closet, and simple nightstand occupied it. Eyoés began to slip off his bedroll when he felt Fychan's hand on his shoulder.

"You and I can sleep in the main room," he whispered, glancing toward Gwyndel. "She is not particular to this kind of treatment—but we are gentlemen nonetheless." Eying the hard wood floor with distaste, Eyoés reluctantly withdrew from Gwyndel's new lodgings. He tossed his bedroll next to the wall closest to the door, sinking into one of the chairs with eyes closed. Fychan directed Gwyndel to her room.

Holding the door ajar, she gestured for Fychan to follow her. Glancing over his shoulder toward her resting companion, Gwyndel quietly shut the door and leaned against it.

Her expression was grave. "This was not a simple visit, Fychan," she whispered, slipping her bag off her shoulders.

Taking it from her, Fychan set it on the bed. "I can tell you have traveled far—and by the mud caking your boots, by foot," he replied, turning and regarding her steadily. "What happened?" Gwyndel covered her mouth, looking to the roof above Fychan's head.

"Castle Asdale was decimated by a mass dragon attack last month," she sighed. "Eyoés was the only survivor." Fychan's eyes widened as he glanced to the door behind her.

He took a step toward Gwyndel, lowering his voice. "Asdale has fended off an attack by a dragon before, and the Guard has been more than adequate," he whispered.

Gwyndel shook her head. "Not like this one," she insisted. "From what Eyoés told me, more than five torched the castle at night before the garrison could take action. He saw an armored rider on the back of one monster."

Visibly reeling at the news, Fychan steadied himself against the wall. "You suggest war?" he wondered aloud. Images of the mauled dead lying twisted upon the ground were burned into his memory —the aftermath of skirmishes he'd stumbled upon.

Gwyndel set a comforting hand on his shoulder. "If it is, it is being undertaken covertly. I fear someone has their eyes set on bigger things," she worried.

Fychan collected himself, eyes narrowing. "Could it be the Phantom League?" he inquired. Gwyndel stiffened at the mention of the group responsible for her father's death. The thought *had* occurred to her.

She shook her head. "It's not their way. No amount of Phantom Leaguers could bring down that many creatures—and they harbor a particular dislike for dragons. Someone else is responsible." Baffled at the puzzle, the two Foresters fell silent. Both knew the demise of Asdale would haunt them tonight. Looking toward the door, Gwyndel heaved a sigh.

Of all the tragedies and possibilities, her brother's fate worried her the most.

15

Skreon's grim stare struck terror into the Hobgoblin officers under his command.

"The southern detachment reported *possible* casualties?" he inquired, the growl in his voice withering the Hobgoblins' resolve. "Humor me and explain."

Avoiding his gaze, the beasts cowered before Skreon's menacing form. "A squad of our troops went on patrol several weeks ago and were found dead in a nearby field by a scout, Kóenar," stammered the taller of the two creatures.

Skreon locked eyes with the one who spoke. "The bodies—how were they slain?" he hissed. Silence. He bared his teeth in rage, taking a step toward the trembling creatures. Skreon watched them flinch with spiteful mirth. His hand fell to the dark sword at his waist.

"Two were shot by arrows, while the other was deeply cut in the chest," they whimpered, eyes glued to their master's sword hand. Skreon began to pull the weapon from its sheath, letting the moment of dread linger. He thrust himself forward, red eyes gleaming with wrath. Pressed against the door to the chamber, the two Hobgoblins diverted their gaze.

"Look into this matter," Skreon snarled, waving his

hand toward the door in a dismissive gesture. Giving a hasty bow, the two creatures fled the chamber. As the door slammed behind them, Skreon released the hilt of his weapon. He stroked his chin, stepping away from the door and retreating further into the room. At the beginning of his campaign, he had sent battalions of Hobgoblins throughout the land to sow fear and confusion. As he had planned, their talent for living unseen by human eyes had proved a useful tactic in many surprise raids.

From the evidence given by his troops, the skirmish had been quick and decisive. He mused on the identity of the warrior. A skilled archer was undoubtedly responsible. The Foresters' skill in the brush would prove an equal match for his troops. The Hobgoblins had evaded their watch thus far.

Merely a trifling matter. A single Forester does not concern me.

Loosely holding his hands behind his back, Skreon turned toward the iron door. With each step, the sound of his boots clicked on the polished black floor of his chamber. A grin creased his face at the memory of the burning ruins of Castle Asdale. Memories of the smell of burning flesh and smoke soothed his unease. Ordered for the specific task, a regiment of his troops had subdued dragons from nearby territories and accompanied him to the costal territory to obey his orders. The capital of Taekohar was brought to its knees—and the Western Coast was now clear of prying eyes. He slipped through the door, thrusting a key into the lock and turning it with a click. Skreon knew better than to trust the Hobgoblin tribes. War and deception were staples of their existence—only their fear of his power and their dread of the Norzaid kept them in submission.

Skreon strode down the dark hall, the torchlight reflecting off of his pale skin. As he entered the antechamber, the two double doors came into view, a mighty reminder of the sinister aspirations of its lord. Hot breezes wafted through the tunnels connecting to the Hobgoblin barracks, carrying the sounds of conversation and work to his ears. Stiffly standing on either side of the double doors, Hobgoblin guards each clutched a spear in hand. When Skreon entered the chamber, they lifted their spears in a brisk salute. The albino ignored their sign of loyalty, intent on surveying his troops.

One of the guards turned, beating against the entry with its fist. In response, the double doors swung wide, letting the light of the overcast sky stream into the dark antechamber. The howling wind greeted his appearance on the mountainside, blowing chalky dust into the antechamber. The gruff battle cries of his troops warred against the roar of the wind as they drilled.

Skreon scrutinized the Hobgoblin ranks, noting their vigor. The slam of the doors behind him announced his arrival.

Ceasing their drills, each soldier set aside his weapon, kneeling in the unnerving presence of their sovereign. "Urez na Kóenar!" they chanted, their beastly voices in perfect unison. Skreon swept the ranks with his piercing gaze. He suppressed a grin at being addressed as Sovereign. Faces turned to the ground, the Hobgoblins motionlessly awaited the signal to rise. Letting the silence hang in the air, Skreon made his authority known. A movement to the left caught his eye. Sitting on the terrace ledge, one of the Hobgoblins fiddled with his knife, oblivious.

Seething, Skreon barely controlled his indignation. "Na Kóenar ur lavd," he bellowed, voice unsteady. As soon as the words left his mouth, the Hobgoblins rose in unison, returning to their drills with increased zeal. Skreon's deathly glare settled upon the idle Hobgoblin, who still remained seated, not bothering to stand. The albino grimaced at the act of treason.

This scoundrel will not acknowledge his Sovereign.

Approaching the creature, Skreon seized the hilt of his sword. He stopped before the idle soldier, his shadow causing the creature to look upwards. The beast's eyes widened at the sight of his impending doom. Absentmindedly, one of the nearby Hobgoblins glanced toward the end of the terrace and caught sight of the impending bloodshed.

"Rá nu váz! Rá nu váz!" the beast cried at the top of its lungs. Distracted by this sudden exclamation, Skreon spun on his heels. The creature struggled against his comrades as they held him back. Skreon glanced back toward the beast at his mercy. The words spoken by the protesting soldier were true then.

The pitiful creature is deaf. A weakness.

Ignoring the continued cries of the other soldier, he drew his blade. The Hobgoblin threw himself at the

Kóenar's feet in supplication.

Expression steeled, Skreon slew the creature. Horrified cries from behind him attested to the unpopularity of the act. With a swift kick, he sent the Hobgoblin's remains plummeting into the canyon below.

Turning to face the infuriated troops, Skreon sheathed his weapon. Those holding back the struggling Hobgoblin now rallied to the same cause, gathering their weapons. Quenching the rising fear within, Skreon glanced toward the caves in the mountainside.

His thunderous shout echoed off the rock face, silencing all the Hobgoblins present. All eyes turned toward a jagged scar in the mountain to the side of the drilling yard. A savage roar shredded the silence that hung in the air, answering the master's call. The Norzaid had spoken.

Covering their ears to repel the dreaded sound, the Hobgoblins turned back toward their leader, trembling.

The edge of the cliff where Skreon stood was vacant.

Screams of horror ran through the ranks as the creatures fell to their knees, searching for the Kóenar with bulging eyes. A deep, spiteful laugh erupted behind them. The troops whirled around to watch Skreon turn away in mockery, doors closing with a thunderous slam. Once again, his power had baffled the weak minds of his army.

Rebellion was *not* an option.

16

Watching Fychan return from the shed with ingredients in hand, Eyoés tried to quiet his growling stomach. The elder Forester set the armload onto the nearby table. He drew his dagger from its sheath, washing it in a bowl of warm water and drying it with a clean cloth. Laying several vegetables horizontally on the counter, he chopped them into small pieces.

"Are you partial to stew, Eyoés?" he inquired. Eyoés took a seat by the newly lit fire. The chair creaked loudly as he sat.

"Yes," he replied, gazing into the fire in thought. With the many days passed on the trail, the longing for someone connected to his father had grown strong. The very presence of a man who had known Élorn comforted him. Eyoés adjusted himself in his seat. "Where are you from, Fychan, and how did you meet my father?" he inquired. Fychan heaved a pot of chopped vegetables and other ingredients onto the table with a grunt.

He glanced to where Eyoés sat. "I was born and raised in Edeveros. Didn't move to Taekohar until I was well into adulthood," he answered, continuing his cooking duties. Chuckling to himself, he brought the heavy pot to the fire. "I met Élorn not long into my service in Taekohar. I was heading northwest toward

Asdale to respond to a rumor of outlaws along the main road. After traveling by horse for almost an hour, I rounded a bend and found myself amid the ranks of bandits," he recalled, hooking the pot onto a long pole inside the fireplace. "As I attempted to fight off the ruffians, your father appeared and valiantly joined the fight, evening the odds before I could be overcome by such a superior number. When the thieves fled, I introduced myself to Élorn. In thanks, I declared my debt to him—the least I could do to acknowledge his courage." Fychan returned to the table, wiping the stew off his hands. Scratching his beard, he returned to his seat, examining the young man's bound arm from a distance.

"How long has your arm been immobilized?" he asked, sitting opposite.

Eyoés glanced toward his arm, eying it with distaste. "A month and a half," he replied, scraping at an itch underneath the cloth.

Fychan stood from his chair and stood next to Eyoés, untying the knotted fabric over the young man's shoulder. "It's been there long enough," he declared, pulling the sling away and setting it onto the floor. "Gwyndel told me about your injury. You were lucky she found you. Those treatments she gave you shortened your recovery time."

As Fychan pulled the last of the cloth from his wound, Eyoés rolled his shoulder in an attempt to diminish the strange lightness in his left arm. The feeling of unbound freedom in his arm had become a distant memory. He stood from his chair, testing the motion of the limb. A thrill of excitement went through him as he realized he was no longer at a disadvantage. As if he knew Eyoés' thoughts, Fychan shook his head, putting a hand on the healing arm.

"The pain often stops before the bone is completely healed. You will need to regain your strength slowly," he advised. "Lift rocks every day. Don't push yourself too much but allow your arm to strengthen with each lift." Eyoés nodded absentmindedly, grasping the handle of his weapon with his freed hand. Fychan stood, throwing the old cloth into a nearby basket. "Your sister also told me about Asdale's doom," he remarked, looking down at his hands.

Awakened from his thoughts, Eyoés winced. He attempted to appear unconcerned. "What of it?" he retorted, keeping his eyes from the Forester. Despite Eyoés' best efforts at concealment, his sorrow would not be hidden. Setting his hand upon Eyoés' shoulder, Fychan ignored the tightness in his own throat. The young man attempted to shrug away the Forester's hand, without success.

"The news grieves me as well," Fychan admitted. Releasing his sword, Eyoés turned toward the Forester and opened his mouth to speak. The sound of Gwyndel's footsteps ended the conversation. Gwyndel closed the door behind her, eyebrow raised questioningly toward her mentor.

Glancing toward Eyoés, Fychan gestured to the pot of stew dangling over the fire. "The food is almost ready," he announced, crouching by the fire and stirring the stew with a long wooden ladle.

Swallowing the last of the stew from his bowl, Eyoés sighed, leaning against the back of his chair. The meaty taste lingered in his mouth as the warm stew settled in his stomach. Gwyndel finished her meal and began to gather the bowls together. Standing from his chair, Fychan took the bowls from her and set them in a bucket of dishes to be washed. Reluctantly, Gwyndel let her mentor take the responsibility.

"It has been quite some time since I've heard from you," she acknowledged, standing and walking over to the fire. "I've heard rumors of your stepping down."

Fychan wiped his hands on a nearby towel. "It was about time for the next generation of Foresters to step up," Fychan declared, gesturing for Eyoés to take a seat by the fireside. With a nod, the young man left the table. "I've heard this was a particularly bad year for poaching," the elder Forester inquired.

Gwyndel absentmindedly fingered her wavy hair. "I have been able to fulfill my duties well. Your training has prepared me more than enough," she replied.

Fychan chuckled to himself. "It is better to train rigorously for something you may never experience than be in dire need when the time comes," he said, leaning against the stone mantle. Gwyndel couldn't help grinning.

He hasn't changed.

Eyoés folded his arms and studied the two Foresters. He hadn't expected Gwyndel's attachment to her mentor. Rubbing his chin, he recalled Aványn's constant tenderness and motherly love. It was because of her lies that he had believed in her affection. Fychan was not related to Gwyndel by blood.

How can she treat him as a father?

Eyoés narrowed his eyes as he attempted to understand. As he considered the reasons, he watched the two Foresters speak, ears deaf to what was being said. Gathering his courage, he broke in.

"What was it like, working together?" he inquired, pulling at the neck of his shirt to cool himself.

Although interrupted, Fychan set aside his thoughts to answer the young man's question. He grinned. "It could be quite interesting at times," he replied, pulling one of the dining chairs to the fireplace. "It always seemed that the most intriguing incidents in our careers occurred during our time together. I still remember our second mission."

15th *of Biarron, 2186 S.E.*

Gwyndel ducked below an overhanging branch, suppressing her irritation as pine needles poked through her dark green garb. Watching the trail ahead for movement, she grimaced at the needles' sharp tips. She searched the sea of green and bit her lip.

Where has Fychan gone?

Wrinkling her brow, she hesitated and fingered her bow. Her mentor was nowhere to be seen among the evergreens and underbrush. Gwyndel mustered her courage, trying her best to disregard the panic rising within.

Surely I did not lose him.

Boldly, she stepped out from cover, nocking an arrow on her bowstring. She began to stand, opening her mouth to whisper for him. A hand shot out from the nearest bush and clamped firmly over her mouth. Instinctively, Gwyndel drew her knife in retaliation.

"Think before you act, Gwyndel," Fychan whispered, eying the forest with suspicion before removing his hand. "Never reveal your cover. Whenever we are on a mission, I am not far. Don't panic." Releasing a sigh of relief, Gwyndel sheathed her dagger. The assurance of Fychan's help was comforting. Watching Fychan glide into a clump of underbrush, she gathered her senses. Her eyes locked on his last known position. Quietly, she darted behind the nearest tree, tracing her mentor's path.

Soundlessly mouthing his admonitions, Gwyndel painstakingly stepped between the underbrush and fallen branches in her path. Two vagrants had been sighted on the local farmer's land, harassing and killing his livestock. If Fychan was correct about their location, silence would be essential. Gwyndel tensed at the thought of being seen.

What would they do to me?

Pushing away violent imaginings, she pressed on,

seeing Fychan dart across a small patch of empty ground. She stepped over a fallen log, emerging from the forest at the bend in the path. Peeking around the corner, she hid behind a dead bush. The sudden chirping of a songbird erupted over her head. Gwyndel started, brushing loudly against the dead branches she hid behind. Holding her breath at the sudden noise, she looked over the top of the bush to assure herself she had not been heard.

In response, a glitter of metal hurtled through the air toward her cover. Dropping to the ground, Gwyndel heard the throwing knife sail over her back with a hum and clatter onto the hard-packed ground of the trail. Fychan burst from the bushes across the path and pulled her up. Wide-eyed, he seized her shoulders. Seeing his concern, Gwyndel shook her head, trembling. Fychan rubbed his face with the palm of his hand, sighing in relief.

Loud, raucous voices exploded from the other side of the bushes. Despite the near death of his student, Fychan gestured for Gwyndel to follow him and slipped into the bushes. Gwyndel hesitated, eying the fallen knife with a shudder. Drawing her dagger from her belt, she followed suit, the brush closing behind her.

As the two Foresters soundlessly approached the origin of the threat, the voices became more distinguished. "You missed!" one voice exclaimed, wavering unsteadily. From within the cover of the bushes, Gwyndel pursed her lips, eyebrows furrowing in thought.

They aren't very careful to conceal their conversation.

She emerged from the bushes behind her mentor, scanning the small grassy knoll for signs of their quarry. Faltering voices continued to argue loudly, drifting in and out of incomprehensible mumbling. A large movement among the tall grasses attracted their attention. Overhanging boughs concealed the two Foresters in shadow, allowing them to draw their weapons unseen.

Fychan raised his finger to his lip in a gesture for silence. Staying as close to the ground as possible, he crept up the knoll to surprise the trespassers from behind. The whispering wind covered the sound of his advance. From the concealment of the trees, Gwyndel watched him move through the grass like a serpent, avoiding obstructions liable to give away his position. Silently, he disappeared over the top of the ridge, the grass waving ever so slightly behind him. Assuring herself that the side of the knoll was unwatched, Gwyndel crouched and followed Fychan's path. The tall grass tickled her skin as it brushed against her face. Resisting the urge to scratch, she moved on, the crest of the small hill coming ever closer. Despite her care to remain unseen, she watched the ridge with unease.

I am not invisible. All it takes is one careless look over the edge.

Gripping her bow, she looked over her shoulder, seeking any unseen foes from behind. The explosion of wild voices on the other side of the knoll arrested her attention, propelling her over the ridge without further consideration.

Fluidly drawing an arrow from her quiver and nocking it to the string, she dropped onto a small plateau on the side of the hill. Standing next to the remnants of a pitiful campfire, two vagabonds staggered back from the unexpected attack. One closest to Fychan attempted a clumsy swing at the Forester's jaw. Stepping away from the pathetic fist, Fychan seized the man's arm in an iron grip and pulled him off balance. With a cry, the man fell into a heap at Fychan's feet. The other, seeing his comrade's demise, broke into an awkward run. Gwyndel fired an arrow ahead of the man's feet, bringing the fugitive to a dead stop.

"Kneel and keep your hands raised where I can see them—*now*," she commanded. Trembling, the vagrant obeyed, his tattered hair obstructing his face.

Bow drawn, Fychan eyed the two disheveled men, and a partially eaten carcass of a sheep. "These are the two harassing Farmer Glyn's livestock," he declared. As he shifted his position, his boot accidentally knocked an earthenware jug into sight. A pool of dark maroon liquid spilled onto the ground. Glancing at the criminals with distaste, he kicked the jug into the forest below.

"They're drunk," he growled, bow aimed at the nearest crook. The confusion of the past few minutes now made sense. Gwyndel intently watched the kneeling criminal, flicking her bow toward his comrade in a gesture to move. Eyes bouncing back and forth between the two Foresters, the man stood, tripping over his own feet as he hastened to his comrade's side. Seeing Gwyndel's bow drawn, Fychan returned his arrow to its quiver. Questions needed to be asked.

And these men better have good answers.

He stood in front of the huddled vagabonds, his expression carved in stone. "Tell me—why did you send a dagger spinning toward my apprentice's neck?" he inquired, his voice sharp. To the Forester's surprise, the man frowned, eyebrows creased in an expression of confusion.

"What? We never threw anything at you," he stuttered. "That man Glyn's prized cow somehow got out this morning. Would've made one feast of a meal, would it not?" At this comment, the two vagrants burst into laughter, the alcohol on their breath causing Fychan to wrinkle his nose. Eyebrows raised incredulously, he noticed Gwyndel holding back a grin.

Briefly glancing toward the two criminals, Fychan noted her mud-smeared clothing. "You don't look like a cow to me," he remarked, a smile breaking through his attempt at solemnity.

17

Fychan and Gwyndel chuckled at the tale's conclusion. Despite his musings, Eyoés found it difficult to keep back the smile tugging at the corners of his mouth. It was clear a bond had formed between the two during their years together, not only in the home, but on the field as well.

I never had that chance.

His expression darkened at the thought of his father's death and his own past. Because of the lies, the bond that had formed between himself and Avànyn had burned. Now, his quest would fill the open wound. He was sure of it.

Any hole can be filled, whether by dirt, stone, or water. Why should this be any different?

Leaving his musings until a more opportune time, Eyoés rejoined the conversation as the laughter died away. An idea struck him. Once all was quiet, he made his move. "Speaking of stories," he began. "Gwyndel and I have discovered the author of Asdale's destruction." All fell silent—one intrigued, the other knowing the dark things that would be spoken of. Fychan stroked his beard, nodding toward Eyoés. Once sure of Fychan's attention, Eyoés related the story of the Ashen Specter, the Whiteblood dragon, and the armored figure spotted during the fateful night. Fychan said nothing, lost in his thoughts.

After several painful seconds, he spoke. "Possibly," he answered, voice pensive, yet tightly wound. "If the Ashen Specter has indeed emerged from the legends of old, we have reason to be afraid."

"I do not take kindly to ill news," Skreon snarled, seizing the Hobgoblin's throat. Helpless in the albino's grasp, the creature attempted to strike out, terror in its eyes. The weak blows did nothing to improve the situation. Lips curling in a grim smile, Skreon drew a dagger with his free hand and set the edge to the Hobgoblin's cheek. Eyes gleaming with malice at the Hobgoblin's helplessness, he drew the blade across the creature's cheek, opening a wide gash. Too afraid to cry out in pain, the Hobgoblin winced as black blood trailed down its face. Skreon's smile faded. Muscles rippling underneath his dark robe, he threw the soldier across his chamber with a roar.

Slamming against the wall with a crack, the creature fell into a still heap. Skreon spun toward the window in disgust. Following the public execution of a deaf soldier, several of his troops had dared to desert from his forces. Fearful for their lives, several squads had taken the fugitives captive. Already irritated by the growing disorder in the ranks, the report of this act of rebellion brought the Kóenar to a boiling point. Skreon shoved his knife into its sheath. The sound of footsteps demanded his attention. His eyes narrowed as he turned to the source.

A lone Hobgoblin passed through the open entryway. Fastened around the neck, a grey fur cape covered the creature's entire left side, as if to conceal a hidden danger. Thin hair grew from the back of the creature's scalp. Twisted in a permanent scowl, the Hobgoblin's grotesque face boasted countless scars.

"Makulazai, I see you have answered my summons," Skreon declared, his voice cold despite his feigned friendship. The Hobgoblin strode toward the albino, his bulky form equal to the height of his superior. Unconsciously letting his hand drop to the pommel of his sword, Skreon eyed the Chief of the Hobgoblins with disdain.

Makulazai cast a disinterested glance toward the corpse by the wall. "What do you wish to speak of, *Kóenar*?" he growled, contemptuously mocking the given title. A glint of hot fury burned in Skreon's red gaze, and he took a step toward the chief. Makulazai glared in response, unflinching at this show of hostility.

"You must control your own people, Makulazai," Skreon snarled through his teeth. "Next time you catch deserters in the act, do not come and report to me—*kill* them." The Hobgoblin chief strode toward the window, dark stare lingering. A sneer of scorn exposed his blackened fangs. Skreon stiffened, catching a glimpse of movement underneath Makulazai's cloak.

The Hobgoblin turned away from his superior. "For centuries, my family has ruled these mountains," he hissed, his voice hoarse and airy. "Do not command me." A dangerous silence settled between the two warriors at this blatant breach of loyalty.

The shriek of metal on metal pierced the stillness as Makulazai turned, yanking his sword from under his cloak.

The room was empty. Wide eyes darting around the room, the chief stepped back. The dark walls of the chamber seemed to advocate his doom.

The rumors of his evanescence are true.

A shadow danced to his right. Involuntarily, Makulazai started, swinging his sword through empty air. A deep laugh rang from the silence.

"Is rebellion still your choice?"

Makulazai's dark skin turned pallid. Holding his sword at the ready, he opened his mouth to speak. A powerful blow sent his sword clattering onto the hard stone floor, the weapon skidding far from Makulazai's reach. Reeling, the Hobgoblin recovered his balance, searching for the origin of the attack. Before his eyes, the white form of Skreon materialized from the air.

Skreon's sword was held to the Hobgoblin's throat, poised to kill. The albino's red eyes felt like a burning knife.

"I am a Gahrim—you only see me when I so desire," he declared, his voice poignant.

Backing against the windowsill, Makulazai gasped for breath, squeezing his eyes shut. "I am your servant, Kóenar," he stuttered, voice cracking.

Letting the tip of his weapon rest precariously on Makulazai's throat, Skreon paused—then returned the weapon into its sheath. "Prove it to me," he commanded. Vanquished, the Hobgoblin edged toward the door, trembling. Without a word, Makulazai fled the chamber, his footsteps echoing on the stone.

The corpse of the Hobgoblin soldier remained where it had fallen.

18

Eyoés woke. Fighting off the bonds of sleep, he sat up, breaking the moonlight entering the window. The songs of crickets and owls filtered through the cabin walls. Shadows lingering in corners of the building twitched as the boughs of trees swayed in the wind. Eyoés started to lie down, shaking his head at the inconvenient rousing.

"On your feet, Eyoés," a voice whispered from one of the shadows. Throwing his blanket aside, the young warrior started, gripping the weapon beside him. From the corner nearest the window, Fychan thrust his hand out, commanding immediate silence. Releasing his sword, Eyoés frowned in agitation. The opportunity for a proper night's sleep was dashed. Irritated, he began to retort. His breath hitched as low, bestial voices joined the night's song. Heavy footsteps plodded through the underbrush around the cabin, and the light snow crunched underneath thick boots. Eyoés crept toward the window, glimpsing dark, hulking forms slinking through the brush.

"How many?" Fychan inquired, voice low.

Eyoés ducked beneath the windowsill. "Five, possibly more. It's difficult to make them out in the darkness," he replied. Brow furrowed, the Forester hesitated before approaching the window. Gazing into the black forest, he caught sight of the creatures in a beam of moonlight.

His head cocked to the side. "I've never seen such brutes before," he muttered to himself, squatting below the window.

"Hobgoblins," Eyoés replied. "We've been rushing to stay ahead of them."

Fychan's mouth slackened. Instinctively, he slipped one of his knives from its sheath. "Impossible. Not this far south," he insisted, shaking his head in disbelief.

Eyoés tightened his mouth into a thin line. "Believe it," he said, creeping beneath the window on his way to the side door. Taking one last glance toward the window, Fychan followed suit. Eyoés slipped his hand over the door handle, opening it a crack before Fychan grabbed his wrist. The Forester gestured for the young man to wait. Opening the door just enough to slip his body through, Fychan disappeared into the shadows. Eyoés scowled.

This is not battle—this is cowardice.

Dreams of glorious combat demanded he burst out of hiding and attack his foes in the open. He began to draw his sword.

"No," Gwyndel whispered into her brother's ear. "There could be a larger force not far off. Silence is key."

Eyoés jumped, eyeing Gwyndel with irritation. He held his tongue despite the anger boiling inside. The weakness in his arm and the scab on his scalp silenced his objections. The chances of their winning a large battle on their own would be slim. Muttering to himself, he released his weapon. A gentle thump from within the lean-to heightened their awareness.

Gwyndel drew her bowstring to her cheek, arrow centered toward the doorway. She flinched as Fychan stepped back inside the cabin. Eyoés reached for his sword. Drawing his mouth into a frown, the Forester shook his head. He removed one of his daggers from its sheath and handed it to the eager youth before disappearing behind the door again. Shifting her weight to the balls of her feet, Gwyndel set aside her bow and drew her knife. Noiselessly, she also disappeared into the lean-to.

Immersed in the silence of the impending ambush, Eyoés studied the dagger with distaste. His father would never have attacked his enemies in stealth.

Maybe that's what got him killed by the Phantom League.

He recoiled at the thought—there was no honor in fighting an enemy from behind. Still, he hesitated.

My enemies don't <u>care</u> about my honor. If they see me in the open, they will surround and kill me.

With a heavy sigh, Eyoés unbuckled his sword, the worn metal buckle leaving the scent of steel on his hand. Setting the weapon by Gwyndel's bow, he entered the shed and quietly shut the door behind him.

Moonlight streamed through a small window, illuminating the interior of the shed with enough light to see by. The crisp fragrance of dried herbs permeated the room. Spiderwebs laced the rafters, and various tools stood in corners of the building. Eyoés spotted the exit to the left. As he stepped forward, his foot bumped against a fallen obstacle. The still form of a Hobgoblin lay crooked on the packed dirt floor, its blackened mouth spread wide in a grimace of pain.

Fychan's work.

Pulling his eyes away, Eyoés stepped over the body. He plowed into a shelf of pottery, sending shock of pain coursing up his shoulder. He froze, eyes fixed on the shed door as the clay pots swayed precariously, the clatter seeming to break the silence in two. Heavy footsteps approached the shed. Gripping his dagger with his sweaty palm, Eyoés crept toward the door, examining the floor for potential obstacles. The door swung open.

Eyoés dove at the creature, tackling the Hobgoblin and knocking it to the ground. Dodging a clumsy punch from the dazed beast, he hastily ended the creature's life. Assured he was not seen, he grabbed the beast by the ankles, dragging it through the doorframe and into the darkness of the lean-to.

Stepping outside, Eyoés closed the door behind him, still shaken by the sudden encounter. Carefully sweeping the disturbed snow with his boot, he erased the signs of the struggle. He edged toward the corner of the cabin with knife in hand, ignoring the clamminess of his hands. Eyoés paused, searching the forest's edge for sign of the attackers. His eye caught sight of a still heap peeking out from behind a clump of snow-whitened bushes. Gwyndel and Fychan had done their part. If his estimate was correct, only two of the beasts remained alive. He pressed up against the wall, glimpsing another Hobgoblin step onto the porch from around the corner. He pressed himself against the wall and started toward the cabin porch. A narrow strip of shadow cast by the overhanging roof masked his advance.

His eyes were riveted to the place the creature was last seen. The inability to see his foe amid the darkness sent his heart racing. He paused at the wall's edge, picturing his massive target lying in wait for him. He squeezed the handle of his dagger. His previous victory had come due to the element of surprise. Since the beginning of his quest, fate had not been kind to him. What was to say that the advantage was still his?

And what if it is? Am I not prepared to risk all for an opportunity for retribution?

Gritting his teeth in determination, he leapt around the corner and dashed up the porch steps, clutching his knife in a reverse grip. He stopped short at the bottom of the veranda. Gwyndel yanked her dagger from the creature's heart, struggling to keep the carcass from falling on her. Tucking his knife into the waist of his pants, Eyoés rushed to her side, slipping his arms underneath the creature's shoulders. Gwyndel nodded in thanks and pushed open the door, allowing Eyoés to drag it into the quiet recesses of the cabin.

Leaving the door ajar behind him, Eyoés drew his dagger from his makeshift sheath. "Did Fychan slay the last of them?" he whispered, searching for movement in the darkness.

Gwyndel's shoulders slumped. "I saw him edge around the other side of the cabin. I haven't seen him since," she replied.

Before her brother could ask more, she dove into the night, rounding the left corner of the cabin with her weapons drawn. Eyoés followed her path into the moon-lit gloom. The sound of a struggle quickened his footsteps. As he rounded the corner, he caught sight of the elder Forester locked in a tense struggle. The edge of the Hobgoblin's short sword pressed dangerously close to Fychan's neck, kept away only by the Forester's iron strength. With a growl, the Hobgoblin leaned forward on the blade, letting its body weight drive the weapon ever closer. Fychan leaned backward, using both arms to deter the attack. His dagger blade glinted in the moonlight, lying on the grass out of his reach.

Eyoés dashed forward, overtaking Gwyndel and slamming into the Hobgoblin's side. Fychan fell to a knee as the blow knocked the beast off its feet, sending up a cloud of snow. The Forester dove toward his fallen dagger. As his hand wrapped around the weapon, he hurled it toward the fallen creature, hitting the mark with lethal efficiency. Clutching at the wound, the Hobgoblin attempted to sit up. Its eyes widened in pain as an arrow buried itself into the middle of its chest. With a rattling breath, it fell to the side, still. Pulse pounding in his skull, Eyoés paused, listening raptly for sign of further attack. Only the whispering breeze answered. Gwyndel released the tension on the bowstring, slipping the arrow back into her quiver.

Fychan sheathed his dagger. "Let's put these bodies out of sight. I'll take the first watch tonight," he declared, his voice low. Eyoés and Gwyndel grasped the closest Hobgoblin's ankles. As they pulled the body to the forest's edge, Fychan followed them with his gaze.

Someone's looking for them.

19

The morning sun pierced the mist hovering above the powdered ground, painting the snow gold. Straying from the canvas of underbrush, several beams brightly colored the table through the window.

They ate in silence. The ambush weighed heavily on their minds—yet each kept his thoughts to himself. Downing the last of the leftover stew, Eyoés wiped his mouth with his sleeve and looked at his two quiet companions. He absentmindedly massaged his aching shoulder, while carefully lifting a rock with his recovering arm.

Fychan stroked his coarse beard, reclining against the back of his chair. "How did these Hobgoblins get on your trail?" he inquired, opening the topic for discussion.

Gwyndel pushed away the hair from her face, her forehead wrinkled. "A small party of them attacked us not far into our journey. They would have prevailed over Eyoés had I not been there," she replied. "Another group must have discovered the bodies and sent a hunting party to follow our trail." Eyoés scowled at his sister.

The elder Forester leaned against the table, chin in hand. "How many are there?" he questioned, eyes probing.

Eyoés hesitated, glancing toward his sister before drawing himself up against the back of the chair. "Surely, their numbers are of no concern," he declared, tilting his head back.

We will be out of reach long before more of the creatures reach this place.

Despite his confident boastings, Eyoés wasn't so sure. He set the rock on the table.

Fychan clasped his hands tightly upon the table, scrutinizing Eyoés with a frown. "Always assume your enemy outnumbers you," he chided. "It is better to find yourself prepared for something larger than what is really at hand." With a nod, he leaned back into his chair, folding his arms on his chest. "You will have very little time to leave and stay ahead of these Hobgoblins. If they press on through the night, you might be caught unawares."

Gwyndel stood, striding toward their bags piled by the door. "Is there a way that leads north that will give us an advantage?" she asked, looking to Fychan. Eyoés stood as the Forester left his seat and stooped next to the table. Grasping a small knob, he pulled outward, revealing a small drawer. He pulled out a weathered map, the parchment scratching against the wood.

As he stood and shut the drawer with his knee, Fychan splayed the map open on the tabletop. "The crags and harsh wind of the mountains will buy you precious time. We can ride there on horseback," he speculated, affirming Gwyndel's hopes. Eyoés glanced over at the map as he hastened toward the packs. He lifted his bedroll from the pile, but Gwyndel pulled it from his grasp and swung it over her shoulder. She gestured toward the heavy sack of supplies. With Eyoés' arm healed, there was no need for her to carry all the load.

Muttering to himself, the young man begrudgingly shouldered the pack. As he adjusted the straps for comfort, Gwyndel passed him his sword, the metal belt buckle clinking against the scabbard. Stepping around the two travelers, Fychan pulled the cabin door open, letting a draft of cold wind inside. He gestured for them to follow after. Making several last minute adjustments, they followed the Forester at a jog, each footstep crunching the snow dust below.

At the forest's edge, Fychan took a narrow trail, weaving through the trees and brush like a serpent before disappearing behind a group of boulders. Driven by the thought of pursuit, they doubled their efforts.

As they rounded the bend in the trail, a small corral appeared underneath the overhanging rock. Small, trimmed pine logs served as fence posts, bare wood gleaming in the morning light. Two horses trotted to the side of the corral at the appearance of their master. Fychan jogged toward the fence, lifting one of the rails away with a grunt.

Setting it aside, he nodded toward the horses. "Both of you, grab the reins," he commanded. Planting her hand on one of the rails, Gwyndel swung herself over the fence into the corral. Eyoés vaulted neatly over the barrier and into the enclosure with a grin. Gwyndel grabbed the reins of both creatures, extending one set toward her brother. Grasping the leather in his hand, Eyoés admired the black steed tugging at the strap. A shock of white streaked through the beast's mane and across its back.

With a neigh, the horse tossed its head and yanked the reins from Eyoés' hand. Startled, he fumbled for control of the beast, seizing the reins while they were still within reach. A deep laugh from Fychan caused the blood to rush to the young man's head. Once he threw the last fence rail to the side, Fychan stepped into the corral and gently took his horse's reins from Gwyndel's hand. Quickly mounting the chestnut brown mare, he tapped the beast's sides with his heels. He guided the creature out of the corral and disappeared around the mound of boulders.

Gwyndel took the other reins from Eyoés. Using the fence as a ladder, she swung herself onto the black horse's back, leading it partially out of the enclosure. She gestured to the rails. "Step up and get on behind me," she insisted. Eyoés grimaced at the notion—yet knew that time forced it upon him.

Using the fence as a ladder, Eyoés stepped up, the wood creaking with his weight as he climbed to the top. He wobbled precariously as he turned toward the steed, clumsily extending his arms for balance. With a grin, Gwyndel offered her hand. Eyoés shook his head, eyebrows furrowed in concentration. He leapt toward the creature—only to miss his target and fall to the ground.

Pulling the reins backward, Gwyndel brought their horse to a stop.

Fychan dismounted from his steed and gestured toward the cabin. "There is one thing I would like to give you before we depart," he said, quickly jogging inside. Perched atop the black steed, Eyoés clutched at Gwyndel's shirt to balance himself upon the uneasy beast. Gwyndel suppressed a smile.

Fychan exited the cabin, cradling a long object wrapped in cloth. Eyoés gratefully accepted the bundle from Fychan's outstretched hands. As he unfolded it, his dry hands caught on the silky fabric. Eyoés sucked in a quick breath as last flap fell away.

The dark, nutty brown recurve bow fascinated him. Thin strips of gold intertwined with the wood grains. Carvings of vast forests graced the sides of the weapon, so fine the very needles of the boughs were starkly visible. A golden symbol of an owl in flight crowned the top limb of the weapon. Arrows traced with gold nestled snugly inside a solid wood quiver, which was adorned with carved knotwork. Etched in inlaid turquoise, two unnerving sentences caught his eye.

Walk in the light,
and I shall be the King's beacon.
Walk in the darkness,
and I shall be your downfall.

Eyoés shook his head in wonder. "Where did you get a weapon of such beauty?" he stammered, eyes entranced.

"It was passed down to me from my father. During the war of Adrógar, my ancestor Eryndál received it from the King himself as a reward for his selflessness on the battlefield. Even then, he remained humble," he remarked, drawing his shoulders up. "It is named Fóbehn—meaning 'blessed' in the High Tongue."

Fychan extended his hands toward the weapon. Pulling his eyes away from the magnificent gift, Eyoés reluctantly set the bow back into the elder Forester's hands. "Hand me one arrow and remove all the others in the quiver," Fychan instructed. Eyoés obeyed, handing the Forester an arrow while keeping the rest of them bound in the cloth. Nodding in thanks, Fychan nocked the arrow and drew back, letting the string slip from his fingers. With a sharp whistle, the arrow sped toward a nearby tree—punching through the wood and out the other side, spraying splinters of wood across the brush. It thudded firmly into the tree behind. Before their eyes, the arrow vanished.

Eyoés went rigid at the sight. He looked toward Fychan, unable to speak. Letting the bow drop to his side, the Forester gestured toward the quiver. The young man shifted his gaze to the empty wooden quiver.

Inside, a single arrow awaited another shot.

"In battle, you will never run out of arrows," Fychan revealed, handing the weapon back.

Eyes wide, Eyoés received it with awe, hands shaking as he held the mighty frame of the weapon. "What sort of magic is this?" he muttered.

Fychan chuckled to himself. "Magic? No, magic

belongs to the darkness. What you have seen is only a small portion of the King's power to bless. There are other things more blessed than this," he declared. "Its power is potent—use it to protect and defend, not maim and destroy."

Eyoés marveled at the power and elegance of Fychan's gift. A tear ran down the side of his cheek.

I am a coward and disgrace to my father. I do not deserve such a gift.

Wiping his face in embarrassment, Eyoés peered at Fychan with a troubled gaze. "Why are you giving me this?" he asked, attempting to hide the weakness in his voice.

Fychan's pointed stare prodded his thoughts. "I believe that the King has another plan for your quest. You need not fear the bow because of the past," he replied. "It has been held by unworthier hands." A moment of silence rested upon the three as Eyoés wrapped the weapon in its cloth, along with its quiver and arrows.

While the two siblings remained in thought, Fychan mounted his horse. He loudly cleared his throat. "We must depart before the day is lost," he spoke, grabbing the reins. With a whistle, they took off at a gallop into the forest.

They dismounted at the forest's edge, sheltered by

the hulking form of the mountains. Sheer crags ascended into a low blanket of fog. Eyoés eagerly hopped off the black steed, landing shakily. His face burned with embarrassment.

No real man rides behind a woman.

Adjusting the heavy pack, he turned toward the mountainside, following the treacherous mountain path with his gaze.

Gwyndel dismounted, passing the reins to her mentor. "Tell the Assembly I was called away on an urgent business. I do not want them to misunderstand and think I am lax in my duties," she added, tightening the buckle of her quiver belt across her body.

Fychan nodded, tying the reins of both horses together. "Eyoés, you have the bow?" he inquired. A brief smile crossed the young man's features as he patted the pack on his shoulders in confirmation. The Forester's expression turned grave. "The wood will never break," he announced, lowering his voice. "It must *not* be lost. If it falls into devious hands, it *will* be used against you."

Eyoés gave a firm nod.

This weapon will not leave my sight.

The elder Forester glanced toward the overcast sky. "Your wisdom and skill will serve you well," he sighed. "The King be with you." With a smile and nod, he galloped back into the forest, leading the other horse alongside. The two travelers waved their farewells as they resumed their northward trek. As the trees raced past, Fychan glanced over his shoulder, watching the distant figures hurry up the mountain path before a curve in the trail obscured them from view. His expression turned pensive as he uttered a quiet prayer.

May he not share his father's fate.

2◊

The wind whistled over the sheer crags of rock, tossing Eyoés' hair back as he struggled to maintain his footing on the narrow trail. Scattered pieces of broken rock crunched with each precarious footstep. He pressed himself against the wall to his right, looking fearfully across the valley below to the opposite side of the canyon. Several rocks tumbled over the edge. Swallowing, he forged on, eyes locked on Gwyndel's back to keep his thoughts from the empty air below. Scrubby trees sparsely clutched to the mountainside, offering temporary respite from the wind. Crowns of white topped the peaks. A curve ahead brought them to a small widening of the path. With a sigh, Gwyndel leaned against the rock face, flexing her feet to release the cramps in her calves. Shrugging the pack of supplies from his shoulders, Eyoés set the bag on a shelf of rock. He wiped the sweat from his forehead.

Since their departure from Fychan's two days previous, his thoughts had run rampant. In the immediate aftermath of the ambush, the Hobgoblins had seemed no more than unfortunate enemies seeking only vengeance. Now, he checked himself.

There must be a reason for their appearance. Why are they this far from Zwaoi?

His passion for his quest had ruled his thoughts,

hiding the larger picture fighting for his attention. Eyoés frowned.

Every action has some reason behind it.

His thoughts fell into place at the sight of a fiery-red bush growing inside the recess where they rested.

Do these Hobgoblins have something to do with Castle Asdale?

Eyoés shook his head.

Gwyndel noticed his unfocused gaze. "What is it?" she inquired, moving to his side.

Unwilling to look her in the eye, he lowered his head. "How could I not realize this?" he wondered aloud. Gwyndel drew her eyebrows together in confusion. Hearing no response, Eyoés looked up at her. "These Hobgoblins—they're somehow connected with Asdale. I did not see it until now."

Her nod surprised him—apparently she had come to the same conclusion before him. She opened her mouth to answer, but was cut off by a gut-wrenching crack below.

The ground beneath Gwyndel's feet gave way. She desperately snatched at the edge, only for her fingers to slip and catch a smaller shelf at her brother's feet. Pieces of rock crumbled and fell to the canyon below. Biting her lip as the jagged stone pricked her fingers, she strained to keep herself up. Stunned, Eyoés hesitated. Lying flat on his stomach at the edge, he extended a hand, watching her legs sway over the chasm below. Gwyndel seized her brother's hand.

As soon as her position shifted, the small shelf she gripped broke away, tumbling to the valley below.

Gwyndel screamed. Eyoés grimaced as her full weight yanked on his wrist. He quickly extended his recovering arm and grasped her free hand. Ignoring the strain, he heaved her upward onto the stable ledge. With a sigh, he released her hands, rubbing his sore arm. Shoulders shaking, Gwyndel rose to her feet.

Eyoés wrapped his arms around her, shaken by the sudden brush with fate. Past arguments were forgotten. "What have I done, bringing you here? You could have been killed," he thought aloud. "You are the only family I have left. I cannot bear to lose you." They lingered.

"Danger does not always mean we've made a mistake," she finally replied, her voice choked. She wiped a tear from her eye before brushing the dust off her clothing with a brief smile. Her brother's show of endearment was unexpected. "Let us move on," she declared. Gathering their senses and their packs, they warily edged across a small ledge of undamaged rock, avoiding the chasm.

Gwyndel adjusted the quiver on her back. The theory about the Hobgoblins' connection to Asdale was not new to her. From their first encounter, the beasts' appearance far from home had aroused her suspicion. Although the details remained hidden, it was obvious that the disaster and the Hobgoblins' arrival were somehow intertwined.

A shriek ripped through the black veil of Eyoés' sleep. Sitting up, he tossed aside his blanket, sending up a cloud of ash from their dead campfire. He searched for the handle of his sword. The fear of hearing the sound again seemed to root him to the spot. As he peered into the darkness, another cry split the night, echoing across the rocky peaks. The high-pitched, metallic rattle sent him into a cold sweat. Panic seized him as he fumbled to locate his father's weapon. Unwilling to pull his eyes from the dark valley, he continued to grope about. His hand touched smooth fabric.

The bow.

The poignant memory of Fóbehn's demonstrated power reassured him. Whatever should come, he would be ready. Another roar pierced the stillness, then fell silent. Pulling the bow and quiver closer, Eyoés returned to a fitful sleep.

They were not alone in this wilderness.

21

Skreon drew the edge of his sword across the whetstone's gritty surface. Intent on his fine work, the albino hardly noticed the howls of midnight prowlers drifting through the window of his personal chamber. The light of two candles lit the blade with a fiery glow. Powdery iron shavings collected in mounds around the heavy whetstone. Skreon's arms swayed in a smooth arc as he sharpened the blade to perfection. The process soothed his nerves, allowing him precious time to relax his guard. A distant smile creased the corners of his mouth. The stillness of the night assured him that his troops lay asleep in their barracks, unaware of his moment of repose. As his muscles adapted to the monotonous task, his mind drifted to the conquests of the past.

Ebony boughs twisted above the heads of the Hobgoblin escort. Intimidated by their prisoner's bearing and spectral appearance, the warriors avoided openly staring at the pale figure marching among their ranks. Strangely, he had yielded his weapon to them without violence—and his calm and confident demeanor breathed an icy fearlessness they had never seen before.

Regarding the silent beasts, Skreon watched as the path ahead opened into a clearing. Tents of branches and animal hide dotted the open ground, and small cook fires sent pillars of smoke curling into the overcast sky above. The eyes of the repulsive villagers widened at the entrance of the prisoner. Gathering near the strange albino, the Hobgoblins gawked at the dark iron armor offsetting his pallid skin, talking among themselves in their discordant tongue. A smug grin from Skreon sent the crowd back. A large tent stationed in the middle of the encampment drew the albino's eye.

The hide walls of the tent were covered in paintings of violent conquests. Standing on either side of the entry flap, a Hobgoblin warrior stood rigid, weapon in hand. One by one, members of the escort departed from the ranks, finally leaving Skreon standing alone before the central tent. Weapons at the ready, the sentries pushed Skreon through the entrance, the hide flap brushing against his face.

As his eyes adjusted to the dim light, the albino noticed the elders seated in a circle around the interior. Their crossed arms and dark expressions did not make him feel welcome. Positioned across from the entry, a robed chief waited in silence, his broad physique endangering the creaky chair beneath him. With a bow to their leader, the guards stepped back from their prisoner, tossing the prisoner's sword into a pile of weapons at the tent's entrance. Skreon locked eyes with the Hobgoblin chieftain, the dark gleam in his eye drawing a frown from the creature. The beast growled something in his native tongue. Cocking his head, Skreon sarcastically lifted an eyebrow.

One of the elders stood from his place among the others. "Master Kral demands you bow," the creature stammered clumsily. Skreon nodded with a smirk.

Some of these creatures know the Common Tongue. Impressive.

With a chuckle, Skreon turned his red gaze to their leader. "I will not bow to one who sits upon a throne of twigs," he snarled.

Looking at the newcomer with shock, the elder hesitated, then relayed the bold statement to his leader. Kral tensed, fangs glistening as he gave an arrogant laugh. He spat an insult in his native tongue. "You have no scars, and no weapon! What do you have to prove yourself—prisoner?" The elder translated, enjoying the insult as much as his leader.

Skreon's eyes darkened, the sarcasm gone from his expression. A growl rose from within his chest. "Do not call me prisoner," he hissed, vanishing before their eyes. A cry of terror rose from the elders as they jumped to their feet, wildly searching for the missing captive. A shriek from the throne arrested their attention.

Writhing in his seat, Kral scraped at his neck, ragged breaths racking his body as he struggled for air. They rushed to their chieftain's side and attempted to pull him from his seat. Two of the Hobgoblin warriors were tossed backwards by an unseen enemy, daggers plucked from their belts. One knife sailed over the elder's heads and ripped through the side of the tent. The pale form of Skreon materialized behind Kral's throne, holding the remaining blade against the chief's neck.

"I offer to fulfill any task you present to me—if your tribes join me in war," he growled. Trembling, the elder repeated the offer in the native tongue, his voice quiet. Skreon waited, jaw clenched. The silence pricked at his confidence and he forced himself to relax.

They will accept. Their respect for violence and power will assure it.

Kral whispered in the elder's ear, gesturing toward a thick, diamond-shaped object hanging from the armrest by a strap. With a nod, the elder backed away, poorly disguising a grin. Standing, Kral pushed the knife away from his neck. He turned with a smug smile, the strange object dangling in his grip.

"For years, a dragon has attacked our villages, slaying our people in droves," the elder declared, gesturing to the scale in the chief's hand. "It is called the Norzaid. Subdue it, and we will follow you."

Skreon snatched the scale from Kral's hand, the pale sheen catching the light from the roof opening.

Whiteblood species. This will not be easy—but it is not impossible.

He tossed the relic toward the chief with a nod. "I accept your terms," he conceded, throwing the dagger to the ground. Striding toward the pile of weapons by the exit, Skreon retrieved his sword. Silent, he plowed through the tent flap, squinting as his eyes adjusted to the light again. He glanced back toward the chieftain's tent, recalling his sudden disappearance amid the council.

Have I given away my advantage?

Shaking his head, he buckled his sword around his waist.

I have seen generations forget the sacrifices of their fathers. In time, they will forget what they have seen.

The clang of an anvil aroused him from thought. With an iron mallet, a burly blacksmith beat a rod of iron on a flat boulder. Sparks flew with each strike on the red hot metal, dissipating in midair. Absorbed in its work, the creature failed to notice Skreon approach. The albino caught sight of a pile of metal upon a nearby stump. Keeping an eye on the blacksmith, he edged toward the stump. Among the useless crooked rods and circles of iron, two large, jagged shards of metal attracted his eye. The uneven surface of the scraps reflected odd shadows as he took them in hand. Skreon flinched as one of the sharp edges pricked his hand through his leather glove.

These scraps might prove useful.

Turning to leave, Skreon noticed a small weed by his foot. Pausing to examine its black needles, he uprooted the plant, watching it wither and dry in his hand. "Deadnettle," he muttered to himself, "A temporary cure for pain." Secretly tucking the plant under his belt, he left the smithy behind him, holding the shards in his hand.

A piercing roar shook the Hobgoblin village. Skreon leapt to his feet and drew his sword. A hulking white mass burst from the dark trees, swatting a nearby Hobgoblin into the forest. Several warriors hurled jagged spears toward the beast. Diving to the side, the creature released a column of fire from its massive maw, the red frills behind its skull flaring in rage. The villagers disappeared into underground tunnels to escape the onslaught. In their hurry to safety, crowds formed at the tunnel entrances. They inwardly willed the destruction of their primeval adversary, yet their distrust for the albino stranger fueled a desire for his death.

Leaping over the twisting, burning mass, the beast clamped its jaws around the struggling escapees, scattering the bodies around the camp with a thrash of its neck. Skreon smiled with admiration at the sudden slaughter and seized a nearby axe. With a growl, he hurled it at the pale fiend. The blade chipped the beast's tough hide before clattering to the ground. With a snarl, the Whiteblood fell back, eyes locking upon Skreon with hatred. Gripping his sword, the albino dashed toward the dragon with a roar, bracing himself for impact.

The beast sprang forward with a screech, catching the air underneath its wings. Skreon fell flat to the ground and evaded the dragon's claws. The dragon's tail whipped downward, cutting a furrow in the packed ground with the knife-like spikes on its tail. As the creature whipped around for a second attack, Skreon sped across the camp and vanished into the forest with the Whiteblood hot on his heels.

With a roar, the dragon burst into the small forest clearing, knocking several trees over in its path. With frenzied, blood-red eyes, the beast scoured the surroundings for its elusive prey.

The glade was empty.

Wings folded by its sides, the beast stalked through the underbrush, baring its black-stained teeth. Its head snapped to the right at the sound of rustling bushes. Closing in on the target, the beast opened its mouth, an orange light glowing in the back of its throat.

Materializing behind the beast, Skreon fingered the shards in his hands.

The back of the skull is unprotected and vital. That is where I will strike.

Clutching the metal in his hands, he leapt onto its back and wrapped himself around its neck. The dragon thrashed its head, flaring its red frills. Seizing the opportunity, the albino shoved one of the shards into the flesh behind its frill. With a shriek of pain, the creature scratched furiously at the side of its head in an attempt to alleviate the agony. Skreon mustered his strength to keep from falling off.

You are mine now—and so are these brutes.

With zeal, he rammed the remaining scrap of metal behind the other frill. Overtaken by its torturous wounds, the Whiteblood collapsed into a heap, too weak to attempt retaliation. Skreon leaped from the beast's neck, crouching by the dragon's eye. A wicked smile spread across his face.

You hate me, but soon you will think otherwise.

Clutching a jagged axe, Kral exited one of the tunnels, emboldening the villagers to follow behind. Forced to the ground by the pain in its skull, the Whiteblood stared darkly at the Hobgoblins, lying still.

Skreon gestured toward the fallen beast. "Here is your tormentor," he proclaimed. "Now fulfill your oath."

As the elder translated the order, Kral eyed the stricken Norzaid with wariness. Compelled to kneel, he extended his axe toward the albino with head bowed. The villagers followed his gesture of obedience. "Kóenar," he said, through gritted teeth. Skreon gave a crisp nod, reaching to take the axe from his subjugate.

Sudden cries of defiance erupted from the forest behind. Spinning on his heels, the albino watched as more Hobgoblins burst from the trees, brandishing their weapons as they charged. Skreon's features contorted in fury.

So this is how you thank me.

Turning back toward the chief, Skreon watched Kral rise from his bow with a smile. He jerked the axe from Skreon's hand. A malevolent stare from the albino wiped the triumph from the Hobgoblin's face.

Skreon removed the deadnettle from his belt and crushed it in his hand. "So be it," he hissed, voice shaking with outrage as he locked eyes with the stricken beast. He lightly tossed the crushed dust in front of the dragon's face as the creature took a deep breath inward.

The Whiteblood's head shot up. As Skreon snapped his fingers, the creature stood, gaze riveted on him. He released a primal shout, pointing toward the oncoming attack. The beast awaited no further instruction.

Tucking its wings, the dragon pounced, an explosive barrage of fire bursting from its jaws. Before the Hobgoblins realized their peril, half of their number lay sprawled upon the ground, charred by flames. The Whiteblood spread its wings, swerving to the right as it raked the Hobgoblin ranks with its tail. Screams rose from the ambushing party as they attempted to flee in vain, swept away by its wrath. Only corpses remained in its wake.

Terrified by the dragon's sudden resurrection, Kral swung his axe toward Skreon's neck. With a laugh, Skreon ducked beneath the blade. He seized the handle and pulled it from Kral's grip. Seeing the attacking Hobgoblin, the dragon screeched and charged. Skreon wrapped his arm around the chief's neck and restrained him in front of the dragon. With a hiss, the Whiteblood slowed to a walk, blowing Kral's hair with its searing breath. The Hobgoblin chief stared fearfully at the beast's teeth, the whites of his eyes opposing his dark skin.

"Do not cross me again," Skreon commanded. This time, Kral understood perfectly.

22

The sun now crested its peak, towering directly above the grey mountain path the two warriors traversed. Ahead of them, the path widened several feet, allowing easier passage. With each step, their breaths came raggedly, mixed with the jingling of the supply pack. A gentle breeze graced the land, providing a welcome relief from the sun's rays and the sweat of travel. Distracted by his own musings, Eyoés remained silent, his dark eyes speaking of dark thoughts. The monotony of travel wore down his determination. Zwaoi seemed much more distant, as if it fled their approach with every step they took. Scowling, he increased his pace.

How much longer? Where does this path lead?

Gruffly, he shoved his hand into the side pouch of his pack, withdrawing the abused map. Setting his finger upon the map's face, he searched for anything that might lie in their path. He stopped at a large mountain range, roughly shaped as a half-circle. On the map, it seemed but a small mark on the entirety of the world. From where they stood, it seemed like the land stretched on for an eternity. A symbol nestled amid their location on the map caught his eye.

The Caverns of Nubaroz. Such a small mark on the map, yet if we do not reach it, we will starve.

Jolted by a sudden collision with Gwyndel, he stopped, map still in hand. He opened his mouth to reprimand her—then stopped. Gwyndel had halted in her tracks. Before them, the mountains to their right caved inward, forming a large dent in the mountainside. A majestic, carved entrance towered over them. Rimmed with various geometrical designs, the diamond-shaped entryway led into a black, plunging darkness deep in the mountain. Taken aback by this imposing structure, Eyoés fingered the hilt of his sword.

Gwyndel's eyebrows raised in silent respect for the builders. "The Caverns of Nubaroz," she declared. Without another word, they approached the entrance, appreciating the masterful work. Mustering his courage, Eyoés stepped into the deep darkness. Enveloped by an eerie silence, he squeezed the handle of the sword at his side as his eyes adjusted to the darkness. Eyoés stopped, straining to see any sign of movement. Something felt wrong.

Spinning on his heel, he moved to draw his sword. "Let's get out—"

A boot slammed into the back of his knee, causing him to fall forward. Before Eyoés could recover and draw his sword, two powerful arms forced him to the ground. His scabbard clattered awkwardly on the cold stone. Surprised by the sudden attack, Gwyndel leapt backwards, narrowly avoiding the same fate. She reached for her dagger.

"State your name and business, or I break his arm," commanded a deep voice, echoing in the dark hall.

Gwyndel let her hand drop to her side.

Eyoés gritted his teeth in fury, unable to break his attacker's iron grip. "I am Eyoés. Son of Élorn the Protector of Taekohar!" he shouted, his pent up anger evident in his tone. The grip upon his wrists lessened.

"And I am Gwyndel, daughter of Élorn. Forgive our impetuousness—we are in desperate need of supplies," Gwyndel said, confirming her brother's claim. A dark silence hung in the air. Eyoés' attacker gave a gruff growl before releasing his captive. The mention of the legendary Élorn's name warranted interest.

Grunting, Eyoés stood, adjusting his sword belt. From within the darkness, the scraping of flint on steel summoned flame to several torches. Revealed by the orange glow, a band of dwarf guards sheathed their weapons. The sharp edges of their plate armor accentuated their sturdy frame. Locks of hair draped over their shoulders like capes, some braided in the fashion of their families. Eyoés sheathed his sword, regarding their captors with a confident air, despite his face being flushed in both anger and embarrassment. One of the dwarves stepped forward, his fitted armor making little noise as he moved. His thick blonde hair was caught in small intertwined braids, and beard stubble could be made out in the dim light. The sharp edges of his face gave him the appearance of weathered stone, and light brown eyes inspected the newcomers in momentary silence.

Flicking his torch deeper into the mountain, he gestured for them to follow. "Welcome to Nubaroz," he spoke coldly, his churlish voice dripping with mistrust. Without another word, he plunged into the darkness, followed by several of his company.

Unsure whether to follow, Eyoés remained standing. Gwyndel glanced toward them, then nodded in the direction their guide had taken.

Reluctantly, Eyoés followed his sister.

23

The darkness of the drafty tunnel was pierced by shafts of white lantern light, revealing a turn in the chamber ahead. Following their guide's footsteps, Eyoés and Gwyndel watched as the light of the torches blended with the chamber's ethereal light. The sound of their footsteps in the tunnel was joined by the commotion of civilization as they rounded the bend. Carved neatly away, the shaft opened into an immense cavern, stretching for several miles in a multitude of directions. Several giant pillars supported the mountain above. The windows of houses glowed, and some lodgings were carved directly into the stone walls. Illuminated by so many white flames, the underground city shone with a clarity that rivaled the light of the sun.

Thousands of dwarf folk went about their daily lives, some gathered around each other, engaged in delighted conversation. Sloping down from the entrance into the city, a wide road twisted through the mass of houses. Taken aback by the sight, the two travelers halted, their mouths agape in awe. Unaware their captives had stopped, their guide—accompanied by several of his dwarf sentries—continued on, their eyes blinded to the magnificence of their home.

Snapped out of his stupor, Eyoés bounded down

the sloped road, his lack of civility attracting the eye of some of the folk. Gwyndel followed in pursuit. Eyoés and Gwyndel caught up to the small party of dwarves. Their arrival was no longer unnoticed. Crowding to the sides of the wide road, dwarves of all ages gaped at the two outsiders. The dwarf children were amazed at the sight, while older dwarves wore expressions tinged with shock and distrust. Giving the best smile he could, Eyoés attempted to appease the masses. Several civilians wrinkled their noses at the detestable intruders.

Noting the crowd's growing attention, the head of the dwarf escort glanced over his shoulder toward his captives, a slight grin twisting the side of his jaw. "You've become quite a spectacle, children of Élorn," he chuckled, letting his hand drop to the hilt of his sword unnoticed. "Not that it's a good thing." Before either of the newcomers could speak, he gestured toward the crowd and ordered them back. For a moment, they hesitated—then left the gathering to return to their business.

Like a winding river, the road continued to twist through the underground city for several minutes before widening into a large courtyard. Extravagant gemstone mosaics decorated the expanse, glittering in the light. The escort increased their pace, forcing the two travelers to continue at a rapid walk. Before them, a set of stairs ascended to a magnificent gate, built upon the side of the cavern. The doorway was narrow, yet compensated for its lack of width with immense height and skillful craftsmanship. Beautiful artwork twisted up the door, and a handle carved of marble was mounted at the average dwarf height. Emblazoned upon this magnificent doorway, was a diamond and pick.

Three guards stood like statues in their path, unflinching at the approach of the small party. Each warrior held the weapon of his choosing and boasted exquisite armor. Without a word, the company ascended the steps, the dwarves' faces grim.

Immediately, the guards stepped forward, leveling their weapons toward the oncoming captives. "On what mission do you enter Lord Ardul's hall, Ardul?" they inquired in unison, their voices low and commanding.

Looking on with uncertainty, Eyoés reached for his sword. Gwyndel's hand seized his shoulder, inducing Eyoés to turn. As soon as she had caught her brother's eye, she fiercely shook her head, her lips tightened. Biting his tongue, Eyoés returned his hand to a neutral position. Their appearance in this underground society had already caused visible disruption. Eyoés turned back toward the guards, his forehead wrinkled.

These people are not eager to welcome us.

The leader of their escort stepped toward the trio of guards, giving a slight bow as he did so. "These two attempted to enter the gate bearing arms. I bring them to Lord Ardul for a full questioning," he replied. Eyoés held his breath. Their guide, Bról, gestured toward them as he spoke, causing the guards to darkly regard the two from underneath their helms.

The guards hesitated for a moment before the leader of the guard gave a sharp nod. "Very well," he declared, his eyes riveted to the subjects of interest. "We are eager to know Lord Ardul's judgement." They stepped back in unison, returning to an alert stance. Bowing once more, Bról seized the ornate door handle with an eager fervor.

Gruffly, the dwarves behind Eyoés and Gwyndel pressed them forward. Caught unawares by the sudden force of the armed escort, Eyoés stumbled and quickly caught himself. Now was not the time for mistakes.

As they hastened through the tall doorway, their footsteps were cut off as the door closed them inside the mountain.

24

Eyoés flinched as the door locked behind them like a trap. Seeking solace from the tension wringing his gut, he let his gaze wander across the hall. Despite its considerable lack of decoration, the large room lured his curiosity. The walls were smooth, entirely carved of a slate that reflected blue light onto their clothing. Thick, square pillars rose above their heads, before widening into a flowerlike blossom that seamlessly melded into the stone above. Lined against the walls in a stiff, motionless line, robed guards probed at the confidence of those who entered, their eyes as emotionless as the stone itself.

The throne asserted itself among those present. Positioned on the far wall, it sparkled blue, inlaid with bold lines of silver. Carved above the occupant's head, an imposing silver disc drew attention to the one seated there. Squinting his eyes as much as he dare, Eyoés began to make out the throne's occupant as they advanced. The dwarf's regal posture bespoke strength and control. His tawny hair was neatly combed, complimenting his lightly shaven beard. He wore no armor, and instead was draped in elegant robes. As they came within several feet of the throne, Eyoés clenched his jaw and locked eyes with the Lord of Nubaroz. The forest green eyes of the ruler forced Eyoés to look away. They stopped.

"Lord Ardul," Bról declared, his voice reverent as he clapped his fist to his opposite shoulder while bowing. "These two entered the main gate bearing arms. I've brought them here for questioning." Gesturing for Bról to rise, Lord Ardul turned his gaze upon Eyoés and Gwyndel.

"May the King bless you," he welcomed.

Eyoés noticed the sword that leaned against the side of the throne, ready for action—yet not actively threatening. Opening his mouth to speak, he began to step forward. Gwyndel's hand stayed his approach. A reproachful glance made it clear that careful words were of the essence. Although incensed at her presumption, Eyoés kept still, eyes riveted on Gwyndel as she approached the throne in his place. Having noted the dwarves' etiquette, she bowed, bringing her fist to her shoulder. Unconsciously, Ardul nodded in approval.

"Lord Ardul. I am Gwyndel, daughter of Élorn, Protector of Taekohar and earnest follower of the King," she addressed, gesturing next to Eyoés. "This is my brother, Eyoés. We congratulate you on the thriving civilization you have ardently protected for so long." With a slight grin, Ardul gave a civil nod toward the young elf. Emboldened by the Dwarf Lord's kind attitude, Gwyndel pressed on. "Yet I fear that there might soon be a threat to that peace," she declared.

Lord Ardul stiffened, gripping the armrests of his throne with a shocking vigor. "Do you bring fell news, or do you bring threats?" he inquired, his voice tense.

Gwyndel extended her hands in a peaceful gesture, the tension mounting with the possibility of violence. "I bring no threats, Lord Ardul," she hastily assured him. "But I do bring dark news. Castle Asdale—capital of the Territory of Taekohar— has been destroyed, and the memory of the venerable Élorn disgraced with innocent blood." Casting wary glances at the guards lining the walls, Eyoés wiped away the sweat beading on his scalp. Restraining himself from speaking out of turn, he took several deep breaths to calm down.

Lord Ardul released his grip on his throne, resting his chin on his hand. Vacantly, he stared at the walls. "What does this mean for the Caverns of Nubaroz?" he questioned.

Hoping to regain some of the fragile ground she had lost, Gwyndel struck a confident air. "We have set out to put an end to this menace. We simply ask for shelter and food for the next three days," she said. Ardul glanced toward Gwyndel, his face pensive.

Reclining back upon his throne, he dismissed the thoughts spinning through his mind. "Very well. For the sake of security, however, I will post two guards outside your lodgings," he announced. "May your journey be—"

Eyoés boldly stepped forward, giving a nod toward the Dwarf Lord. Shocked by this sudden show of audacity, Gwyndel stepped to intercept her brother, her eyes staring daggers.

"Lord Ardul, this journey is not one we can travel alone," the young man reasoned, his eyes alight with passion. "Our enemy is strong and the trail long and unclear." Turning toward his captive, Bról moved to retaliate.

Lord Ardul held up his hand for silence, his face clouded with embarrassment at this breach of etiquette. "Calm yourself, Eyoés, son of Élorn. I will forgive this rude interruption—for now. Outsiders cannot be expected to follow our ways," he boomed. Bról immediately backed down, his gaze less understanding.

Excitement checked by the Dwarf Lord's reprimand, Eyoés gave a deep bow. Hope in a new strategy still burned brightly in his mind. Despite this, it was now apparent to him that his rash move had put them in a dangerous position. "F—Forgive me, Lord Ardul," he stuttered. Glancing upwards from his bowed position, Eyoés waited to rise until bidden. Graciously, the Dwarf Lord gestured for him to speak. Eyoés arose, inching ever closer to Lord Ardul. "This threat that I desire to avenge, threatens you also. Guide us along the trail and help us bring this evil to its knees!" he said, his voice assertive.

Gwyndel, watching from behind, bit her tongue. It was inevitable that the words spoken would reopen an old wound. The jawbone of Lord Ardul tensed as he gritted his teeth. For once, the guards in the chamber dared to stir and talk among themselves. Ignorant of the history that provoked this astonishment and anger, Eyoés locked eyes with Lord Ardul, demanding an answer. After several seconds, the Dwarf Lord reclined into his throne in a decisive manner.

"No," he avowed. "The dwarves of Nubaroz will have nothing to do with your vengeance. You must fare on your own!" Utter silence filled the chamber. Gwyndel held her breath, eyes riveted on her brother. The excitement of duty that had radiated from Eyoés' eyes twisted into a scowl of pain and rage. The dark hair that loosely dangled over his forehead emphasized the wrath in his eyes.

His hand gripped the handle of his sword, yet he didn't draw the blade. "Do you care nothing for the lives that burned that night?" he hissed. The bluntness in his voice chilled Gwyndel. Lord Ardul said nothing, his face set like flint. Infuriated by the silence, Eyoés stepped closer. "Your lack of zeal—is *pitiful*," he spat. Without another word, he turned, his dirty boots leaving marks on the polished floor.

Breaking away from their escort, Gwyndel sprinted after her brother. The guards surrounded the two intruders and roughly escorted them out. The doors swung open, allowing the buzz of the city to enter the chamber.

With the decisiveness of fate, the doors slammed on their heels—leaving Lord Ardul to his thoughts.

25

The wooden door of their temporary lodgings bounced upon its hinges as Gwyndel slammed it shut. Turning at the sudden sound, Eyoés watched her face darken with a cutting glare.

"You cannot let your zeal run rampant!" she insisted, voice sharp. "Lord Ardul has reasons for refusing your impetuous demand!"

Eyoés gritted his teeth. "There was no other reason besides his own self-interest. He would rather sit on his chair and assure his own comfort than aid me!"

Gwyndel marched toward him, shoving their baggage out of her way and putting her face mere inches from her brother's. "Why would Lord Ardul *owe* you anything? You've shown yourself to be a fool!" she snapped.

Eyoés pushed her away, raising his chin and looking down upon her with his cold eyes. "I am the one destined to avenge Asdale—the only one who cares enough to act!" he roared. "Ardul could both have aided me *and* saved his people, had he consented. I only asked him to lead me out of these mountains."

Gwyndel gestured toward the door, and the dwarves living beyond it. "You asked for him to lead an army to fight your battle for you—a battle in which the allegiances are unclear to him. Did you not think of the hundreds of families that would be destroyed because of your *war*? I know you did not want just *guidance* through the mountains," she retaliated.

Eyoés stiffened. "You dare suggest that I would put others in a position to be killed solely for my—"

Gwyndel abruptly drew an arrow from her quiver and pointed it at Eyoés' throat. "*Silence!*" she shouted. Eyoés opened his mouth to speak, then, eyeing the arrowhead, held his tongue. Gwyndel sighed, recovering her patience. "It is time for you to learn about the Draed. The Dwarf Civil War," she declared, returning the arrow back to her quiver. Gwyndel sat at a small table in the corner of the room, underneath a window carved in the stone wall. Eyoés took the other seat, anger momentarily eclipsed by curiosity. He had never heard of this war during his schooling in Asdale. Quietly, he waited for Gwyndel to speak, concealing his alarm at her sudden, violent outburst. She paused. Her bleak expression dampened his curiosity.

"During the first era of our world, before the War of Adrógar began, Llumiael—the Rebel—visited the dwarf capital of Arbundur," she began. Eyoés stared off through the window.

Aványn spoke much of the War—how it defined not only the kingdom, but the hearts of the people themselves.

The mention of the fallen Gahrim Llumiael made him shiver. He repulsively pushed the memory from his thoughts.

Gwyndel continued her tale, staring blankly at the table. "With his cunning tongue, he offered the dwarves power, riches, and freedom to do as they please—if they would join in overthrowing the King himself. Seeing through the Gahrim's speech, Lord Ladur the First rejected the offer outright, demanding Llumiael leave his halls. Had Ladur's scribe been trustworthy, the news would not have entered the public mind.

As the word spread, a faction of dwarves arose in strong favor of Llumiael's offer. Efforts to bring the faction back to the truth were in vain. Tensions between those following the King and those allied with Llumiael heightened, eventually becoming so strained that battles broke out within the entire territory of Qelezal over the subject. In a final show of defiance, the faction left Arbundur outright, forming their own colony in the Caverns of Nubaroz. Over the course of the War of Adrógar, brothers and fathers ruthlessly murdered each other for the cause they believed in."

Eyoés pictured dwarves hewing down their own families on the battlefield.

"After the war ended, the dwarves of Nubaroz returned home, their numbers cut in half and their spirits utterly crushed. For months, they had no hope— until the King himself paid them a visit and showed them his mercy. Because of this, the dwarves returned to the King's side, taking his teachings to heart once again with fervor," Gwyndel said. Eyoés watched with uneasiness as a pained expression haunted her features. "But when they approached the King's other followers with an apology, they were shunned. The others were too resentful over their kin's betrayal to forgive them the way the King had.

King Fohidras grieved because of their disunity. Hurt by the treatment of their fellows, they retreated into Nubaroz, shutting themselves away from the outside world in an attempt to keep evil from seeping into their homes—and to protect themselves from further pain," she concluded, turning to look her brother in the eye. "It is said that Lord Ladur the First died of a heart broken for his rejected people. The Draed is considered one of the most tragic events of the War of Adrógar. *That* is why Lord Ardul refused you."

Standing from his seat, Eyoés walked toward the far wall, shoulders sagging. He leaned against the cold stone, shrugging off the feeling of heaviness. The more he recalled the words he had spoken to the Dwarf Lord, the more he came to realize his mistake.

I openly mocked their zeal for virtue and insulted their ruler without knowing the pain behind their actions.

Eyoés glanced over his shoulder to where Gwyndel sat. He considered revealing his regret to her, then rejected the idea. Admitting his wrong would only bring humiliation. Still, a prodding within told him to apologize. Shaking his head, Eyoés turned toward Gwyndel. He needed time to himself.

"I'll go buy the supplies for dinner," he muttered, stepping over their gear heaped in the middle of the floor. Seizing the door handle in an eagerness for time to himself, he threw it open, slamming the door behind him as he left.

Weaving through the crowd, Eyoés searched for a sign indicating a market among the many crowded buildings, muttering to himself. "She called me a fool. For being passionate about my people? Years with those bushmen has hardened her heart to what matters," he mumbled. He moved like a giant through their midst as he examined the surroundings. Each structure was built of skillfully cut stone bricks, mined from the heart of the mountain. Many homes boasted large gardens, grown upon beds of sod. Lamps dangling from poles in the ground surrounded the gardens, illuminating them with brilliant white light. Through the glow, Eyoés could see a flaming heap of turquoise stone powder in each lamp. Intrigued by the strange sight, he advanced toward a garden fence. Tending the vegetables with care, a lone woman kneeled in the moist soil. Eyoés leaned against the fence next to one of the lamp posts.

"Excuse me. How are these lamps lit? Never in my lifetime have stones ever burned," he inquired. The dwarf looked up from her work, pushing her single red braid of hair behind her shoulder. Raising an eyebrow, she nodded toward the lamp, eyeing the stranger with misgiving.

"You won't see anything like it elsewhere—except in Arbundur," she declared, spitting the name of the Dwarf capital that carried a bitter taste. "Gesadith is mined not far from here. When ground into a powder, it becomes flammable. It acts as a false sun for the plants and provides a good light." With a nod, she returned to her farming. Sensing the tension, Eyoés stepped back. The tragedy of the Draed still plagued the people's hearts. He returned to the crowd.

The darker tones of their clothing melded into a strange, melancholy canvas that did not give justice to the nature of the people. A burst of uproarious laughter erupted between two dwarves at the road's edge over a game of cards. Their smiles faded at the sight of the towering man in their midst. Eyoés looked away, taking a deep breath of the warm, damp air. Recalling Gwyndel's earlier impatience, he shook his head, recognizing his own rage in her actions.

She's no better than me—and has no right to scold me for my anger.

He stopped amid the crowd as his eyes caught sight of a mining crew across the cavern. Crews picked away at the sides of a newly opened tunnel. Eyoés tensed. The other miners struggled to control groups of bulky dragons by their reins. Thunderous percussions boomed in the immense chamber as the dwarves mounted the creatures and, with a flick of the reins, sent them headfirst into the stone wall. Their thick skulls sent dust into the air with each hit. Eyoés laughed to himself.

It seems the dwarves themselves are as thick-headed as their dragons.

Even from where he stood, the roars of the creatures could be heard above the noise of the crowd. Involuntarily, Eyoés stepped back, attempting to hide his unease at the dragons' presence. A deep laugh from behind made him jump.

"They're not as vicious as you think," a brawny dwarf declared jovially, nodding toward the mining dragons. "Tamed at birth they are, and exercised outside these halls every fifth day to keep them flying."

Giving one last glance back toward the hulking beasts, Eyoés nodded in thanks. "I just won't get in their way," he joked through a forced smile. With a hearty chuckle, the dwarf disappeared among the throng. Nudged by the crowd, Eyoés continued on. He frowned to himself as he sought for a market in vain. Mustering his courage, he tapped the nearest dwarf on the shoulder.

"Excuse me," he interjected, clearing his throat.

The wizened dwarf turned, momentarily taken aback at the sight of the tall stranger. He quickly recovered. "What do you want to know, lad?" he inquired with a thick accent.

Eyoés paused in an attempt to understand the man's brogue before answering. "Where is the nearest market or shop?" he asked. Noting the stranger's weathered appearance, the elder gestured down the street to where a side road ventured further off into the town.

"See the road over to the right? Head down there and look for the Hammer and Chisel. There's a sign— you can't miss it. Plenty of goods and the finest drinks in Nubaroz," he declared with a smile. Eyoés gave a thankful nod and returned the smile. Turning back toward the road ahead, he pushed through the throng of dwarves. At the side road, Eyoés left the crowd and ventured within. He spotted a large wooden sign not far into the alley, boasting the image of a crossed hammer and chisel.

I am not a fool. Gwyndel had no right to threaten me.

The door to the establishment opened. A tall figure emerged from within wearing a white cloak, his cowl obscuring his features. Shutting the door behind him, he ventured down the alley toward the main road. As the man passed, he bumped into the young man's shoulder. Two penetrating blue eyes gazed intently at Eyoés from under the white hood.

Fools always justify themselves.

The foreign thought struck Eyoés like a blow to the jaw. Puzzled, the young man furrowed his eyebrows at the stranger. He shook his head. The stranger gave a firm nod, affirming the unthinkable. Eyoés opened his mouth to speak.

The cloaked figure looked away, vanishing into the crowd and leaving Eyoés to wonder.

26

Eyoés woke, momentarily confused by the absence of the rising sun. Glowing through the windows in the stone walls of their room, the strange white light of the Gesadith lamps reminded him of the blinding reflection of the sun on water. He sat up and cast aside his blankets. In the other bed beside him, Gwyndel's chest rose steadily in a light sleep. Stretching his sore muscles, Eyoés bent to slip on his boots.

The baggage at the foot of his bed had been tampered with.

Rushing toward the large sack, he rifled through its contents. His mouth fell open.

Gwyndel woke at the clanging of their camp supplies. "What is it?" she asked, her voice raspy from sleep.

Eyoés feverishly dug among the bags. "Fóbehn!" he exclaimed, his voice raising in pitch. "The bow is *gone*!" With a gasp, Gwyndel sprang from her bed. The unconscious forms of the two dwarf guards could be seen through the window, lying in the middle of the street.

"Are you sure?" she questioned. Eyes wide, Eyoés lifted the large bag and dumped its contents on the stone floor. Only supplies. With a roar, he threw the empty bag into the pile. He stood, fists clenched.

"Lord Ardul," he muttered.

The doors of the Dwarf Lord's chamber were thrown open. Lord Ardul leapt from his throne at the clamor. Sword buckled haphazardly around his waist, Eyoés marched through the maze of pillars. The two guards at the entrance rushed to apprehend the sudden intruder. Regarding the newcomer with unease, Lord Ardul held up his hand. With a salute, the guards retreated, still within striking distance of the unwelcome visitor.

"My bow—it has been stolen from me!" he cried.

Lord Ardul raised an eyebrow, returning to his seat. "How does this concern me, Eyoés? I know nothing of this," he inquired, voice calm despite the tension.

Eyoés stepped closer, a dark stare blackening his features. "It is no ordinary bow," he hissed. "And I believe treachery is involved!" A silence smothered the hall at these words. The guards lining the wall of the round chamber tensed, expressions grave.

Lord Ardul slowly stood from his throne, glaring at Eyoés. "Do you call me a *liar*?" he questioned. With the loud shriek of metal, the guards simultaneously drew their weapons. Blinded by the haze of his anger, Eyoés drew his sword, surveying the guards with a scowl. He assumed a ready stance.

"Your recklessness is a disgrace to your father's name, son of Élorn!" Lord Ardul shouted.

Eyoés went rigid. The fog lifted from his mind as he stared at his weapon in horror.

I've offended them twice. I am belittling my father's noble character with my anger.

Biting the inside of his lip, the Dwarf Lord stroked his chin, stubble scraping against his fingers. With a wave of his hand, the guards sheathed their weapons. "You are forgiven," he consented, sitting. "Your loss is unfortunate. It grieves me that there are thieves within my jurisdiction. With the King's aid you will find this weapon—I am sure of it."

Eyoés stood, giving a courteous bow of embarrassed thanks. Not daring to speak again, he turned to leave, escorted by guards out of the chamber.

I must find Fóbehn.

As Gwyndel ventured toward the towering gates of Lord Ardul's hall, she didn't notice the crowd around her. Her blank features disguised her private thoughts.

I should not have threatened him. I was not setting an example of self-control.

She shook her head with a dejected sigh. Memories of the moment of anger had replayed in her mind throughout her sleep, leaving her wasted.

If Eyoés had learned to control himself, I would not have been driven to such an extreme.

Her eyes dulled at the thought of her brother's wild behavior. For months, she had watched his anger drive him closer to the brink of failure without any lasting sign of remorse.

Will he ever change?

To Gwyndel's surprise, she doubted he would ever regret his actions. She was powerless to act, despite her fear for him. Amid the bustling crowd, she closed her eyes.

I am inadequate to change him. Only the King can lead him to change.

Turning, she gazed back in the direction of their lodgings, then looked ahead toward Ardul's hall.

I am finished with this quest. It will come to nothing. I must make amends for the uncontrollable boy I have brought to their home and the shameful treatment they received after the Draed.

Gwyndel pulled her sagging shoulders up, trying her best to hide the despair within. Emerging from the crowd, she ascended the steps. As was protocol, the guards barred her path. Gwyndel raised her hands in a truce. Eyoés' shameful treatment had not yet faded from their memory.

"I come alone to speak with Lord Ardul," she announced, pulling at her pockets. "I am unarmed and wish no harm upon him. Is he currently occupied?"

The guards eyed each other with apprehension, recalling the tumultuous confrontation of the past hour. "Lord Ardul is presently strolling in his personal garden—we will escort you to him," one of them declared in a low voice, allowing Gwyndel entry.

Lord Ardul strolled through the labyrinth of colors, his slow, heavy footsteps uneven on the garden path. His pensive gaze paid no heed to the beauty around him, and instead fixed on the ground at his feet. Mouthing the accusations of the young guest, he shook his head.

How could such foolish words arouse such an ancient wound?

A hand lightly touched his shoulders. Lord Ardul looked up from his musings and gave a brief smile.

"I thought the past was behind me," he sighed, shaking his head. "Now one impetuous guest has brought it back to life." Removing his hood, the cloaked stranger revealed himself.

"Pride dies a hard death, and exacts a costly price," he replied, looking keenly at the Dwarf Lord.

Ardul turned to face his companion. "Why has he come to us? This youth tears open old wounds and does nothing to help," he groaned.

With a smile, the stranger shook his head. "Consider this, my friend," he reasoned. "Could you feel compassion for one who is walking the road you suffered on?"

Lord Ardul looked to the ground, frowning as he contemplated his companion's convicting words. Removing his hand from the dwarf's shoulder, the cloaked visitor vanished.

The two guards escorted Gwyndel to the far chamber wall, their reflections in the polished stone floor distorted by the grain of the stone. As they approached, the guards lining the chamber watched her with disdain at the memory of her previous appearance. She was glad Eyoés was not with her. The two guards halted in front of a large entryway. Sweet, herbal scents wafted through the entry, and Gwyndel caught glimpses of colorful blossoms from within. Gwyndel glanced over her shoulder toward her escort.

She turned toward the guards, bowing. The two dwarves glanced at each other, unsure how to reciprocate the unusual gesture of thanks. Awkwardly, the two bowed before returning to their posts. With a warm smile, Gwyndel stepped through the entryway.

Her breath hitched as a bright, flourishing canvas of flowers welcomed her entrance. The garden grew upon thick layers of sod, which covered the expanse of the inner chamber. She noticed a steady stream of water running through stone drains alongside the plant beds to provide a steady supply of water for the garden. Below her feet, an intricate mosaic path led further into the maze of color. Gwyndel walked down the pathway, focusing on the task ahead. She rounded a bend in the path.

Lord Ardul turned at the sound of her footsteps— eyes hardened. At the sight of her, his expression relaxed. "I thought your brother returned to challenge me," he speculated, gesturing for her to walk alongside him.

Gwyndel strode to the dwarf's side as he returned to his stroll. "I apologize for Eyoés' impetuousness. He cannot control himself," she admitted with a clenched jaw.

Lord Ardul clasped his hands behind his back. "He returned again not less than an hour ago—accusing me of thievery. I am sure you did not send him," he mused aloud, looking at her from the corner of his eye.

Gwyndel gasped, legs stiff as she continued to walk by the Dwarf Lord's side. "I *did not* send him," she replied, voice strong as she stared at him gravely.

The tension in Lord Ardul's bearing visibly shifted. "He is young and has not yet learned to keep his outrage within," he declared, lifting his chin to assert his statement. "Perhaps my forgiveness will prevent him from wandering from the King the way my people did."

Gwyndel's heart sank as the dwarf blinked back tears. She set a hand upon his shoulder. "Your people were treated shamefully after the Draed," she said.

Silent, Lord Ardul pushed her hand from his shoulder, turning toward her. "You were not there—did not see the hate in their eyes as they rejected us!" he snarled. "I know my people have done wrong in the past. We admitted our mistake. *Still*, they turned their backs!"

Gwyndel looked Ardul in the eye. "It was wrong," she replied. "Oftentimes we treat those who have fallen as less than ourselves. We forget that *all* mistakes are the same in the King's eyes—including our own." The Dwarf Lord's eyes softened. It was clear she meant no harm by the statement.

He turned away. "The King provides for our every need because we have committed ourselves to him. Entering the world again only invites deceit into our homes," he sighed. Gwyndel once again set a hand on the dwarf's shoulder. This time, Ardul allowed the comforting gesture.

"There will always be evil in this world. You can attest to this," she urged. Regretfully, Lord Ardul nodded. She continued, "The King will never let us be overcome by evil. We decide whether to give in or not."

Still, the Dwarf Lord shook his head. "They treated us like outcasts," he insisted.

Gwyndel stopped. "What a person does to you does not indicate what the King thinks of you," she protested. "The King remembers your mistakes no more." Removing her hand from his shoulder, Gwyndel flashed a bright smile as she returned down the path.

As she disappeared around the bend, Lord Ardul paused, fingering the hem of his garment with a bowed head. Finally, he lifted his head, an expression of determination chiseled into his features.

No longer will the past define us.

Sitting at the bar, Eyoés carved a chunk from his meat and impaled it on his fork with vigor. He furtively eyed the door with a dark expectancy, jaw set. Once dismissed from Lord Ardul's presence, he had inquired of several locals as to the criminal acts around their lodgings. Most ignored the stranger's request. Only upon further prodding did one of them provide useful hints about a criminal named Dárig. He had been spotted with a suspicious bundle underneath his arms the previous night. For many, the Hammer and Chisel proved a comfortable place to trade stories and wares. Dárig was known to frequent the place, and his guard would be down. Eyoés scowled and looked toward the door yet again. It seemed as though days had passed with no reward.

He'll be wishing he'd never wandered inside this place.

Shoving the meat into his mouth, Eyoés examined the interior of the tavern and shop. Behind him, poorly-made shelves strained to hold the weight of labeled sacks of goods. Past the storerooms, a hallway ventured further into the building where the owner and his family lived.

The spice and smoky juice of the meat barely registered.

If this Dárig is coming to eat or drink, he'll be forced to sit at the bar.

The door to the establishment opened. At the entry of the newcomer, the tavern's patrons turned to look, some too full of drink to see through bleary eyes. Trying to appear inconspicuous, Eyoés shoved another morsel into his mouth. The door closed with a thud. Eyoés listened intently as the customer's footsteps made their way behind to the stool beside him. He glanced toward the dwarf as he sat upon the stool.

A badly trimmed beard covered the front of the dwarf's throat, as if to make up for the lack of hair upon his bald head. Eyoés laughed inwardly in triumph as he spotted several whitened, jagged scars wrapping around the side of the dwarf's neck. Some said he acquired the scars while murdering his own brother. Others insisted he had been strangled in a drunken feud. Although fresh out of prison, rumors circulated that he had returned to his past ways. Eyoés felt a sense of satisfaction at the sight of Dárig. Nonchalantly, the thief glanced toward Eyoés.

Baring his teeth, Eyoés seized the dwarf's burly arm. "Dárig," he growled. "I believe you have something of mine."

Caught off guard, the dwarf sized up Eyoés with a frown. "And what would that be?" he retorted.

Eyoés stood from his stool, pulling the dwarf closer. "A bow," he uttered in a scathing tone. Dárig's frown faded. Shoving Eyoés back, he leapt to the ground, running toward the door and throwing it open. Eyoés staggered backwards, nearly collapsing into the laps of the other patrons. Swerving through the bewildered customers, he dashed toward the door as Dárig leapt from the steps. His heart sank as the thief shot into the alley. Rushing out the door, Eyoés searched for sign of the guilty dwarf.

The alley was empty.

27

"Gwyndel!" Eyoés exclaimed, leaning against the frame of her bed. Startled, Gwyndel leapt up, disoriented by the light coming from the open door. At the sight of Eyoés, she sheathed the dagger clutched in her hand. He had been gone all night.

"Where were you?" she shouted, stifling a yawn.

Eyoés couldn't contain a wide grin. "I've recovered his trail! We can get Fóbehn back if we hurry!" he yelled, gesturing for her to come.

The heaviness in her heart dampened her enthusiasm.

I must tell him. I cannot continue on this reckless journey.

Seeing the elation on her brother's face only worsened her guilt. She knew this would be the last time to speak to him if she left him to continue on his own. It seemed cruel to leave him to die—but the futility of his mission could not be ignored.

Gwyndel rose, securing her knife belt to her waist. "I can't come with you," she answered with an empty stare.

Eyoés rolled his eyes. "It will not take long. Follow me," he nagged.

Gwyndel opened her mouth to protest. Hurrying out the door, Eyoés left their quarters and dashed into the streets of Nubaroz. The sound of his footsteps on the cobblestone began to fade. With a growl, Gwyndel slipped on her boots and rushed out the open door, shutting it behind her. Although sickened by the thought of prolonging the inevitable, she sprinted after him. Her departure would have to wait.

I will tell him after we recover the bow.

Eyes intently searching for his enemy, Eyoés drew his sword and stepped into the alley. A stack of old broken crates crowded the pathway. Shadows masked the alley's dark recesses like a somber shroud, daring him to enter. He started at a footstep from behind, turning to confront the possible threat. The sight of Gwyndel put him at ease. If a predicament arose, she would cover his back. Gripping his weapon, Eyoés continued further down the path.

He approached the stack of crates from an angle to peek behind the obstacle. A rat scurried further into the dim light. A twitch of movement caught his eye from the edge of another small alley entrance branching off to the right.

There he is.

Eyoés felt a tap on his shoulder. "Where are we?" Gwyndel whispered, eyes constantly scanning her surroundings.

Eyoés kept his gaze riveted on the path ahead. "This thief, Dárig, lives somewhere in this alley—and from what I've heard, he's not used to visitors," he replied. Eyoés inched past the crates, with Gwyndel in tow. In an attempt at silence, he slowly applied his weight with each step. He struggled to maintain his balance with this strange form of walking. With a smug smile, Eyoés complimented himself on his secrecy.

Dárig won't see us coming.

The creak of a taut bowstring behind him stole the smirk from his features. "Knew you'd ask around," Dárig sneered. "Eventually someone would lead you here." Eyoés spun on his heels to confront his attacker.

He must have trailed us here.

Drawing her dagger, Gwyndel stepped forward— only to plant herself to the spot.

Dárig grinned as he pointed Fóbehn toward them. His biceps strained against the bow's strong limbs. The golden owl emblem seemed to scowl at the two. Eyoés gritted his teeth as the dwarf released a derisive chuckle. "On your knees—*now*," Dárig ordered through his teeth. "And put your hands behind your head." Sheathing her knife, Gwyndel kneeled. With a fevered stare, Eyoés stood his ground. The dwarf pointed the weapon toward the young man's chest, pulling the bowstring farther back. Silent, Eyoés grudgingly complied. Eventually, the dwarf would weaken his guard.

Dárig gave a triumphant smile as he stepped toward them. He gazed at the weapon in his hands with admiration. "This bow suits me," he jeered. The dwarf didn't see Eyoés bring his hands down from his head.

Eyoés grabbed Dárig's ankles and yanked him off

his feet. As he fell, the dwarf accidentally released the bowstring, sending an arrow racing toward Gwyndel's head.

A hand shot out of the darkness and seized the arrow in flight. Gwyndel flinched at the sight of the arrowhead mere inches from her face. The suddenness of the brawl had found her unprepared. As she realized the gravity of the event, tears formed in the corners of her eyes. Trembling, she looked toward her unexpected savior.

The hair rose on her neck when she recognized the white cloaked figure from the stories of her childhood. A strangely ethereal kindness inhabited the man's gaze. Snapping the arrow in his grip, the cloaked man gently grasped her wrist with his free hand. With a smile, he pulled her up from her knees. A strange comfort seeped into Gwyndel's mind as he released her wrist. Hearing the thump of blows, the figure's smile faded.

Too caught up in the fight, Eyoés failed to detect the stranger's arrival. Dárig grabbed Eyoés' shirt and pulled him to the ground. Quickly pushing himself up, Eyoés grabbed the dwarf's shoulders and drove a knee into his stomach. Gasping for breath, the thief fell to the side. Eyoés snatched an arrow from Fóbehn's fallen quiver and stabbed at Dárig's heart.

A burly hand snatched the dwarf out from under Eyoés. With a clang, the arrowhead hit bare cobblestone. Infuriated, the young man looked up. The fury left him at the sight of the cloaked figure. A sudden dizziness swept over the youth as the stranger gave a stern frown.

This vengeance will destroy you if you refuse to lay it down.

Reeling, Eyoés fell to the ground, too faint to dismiss the thought. Gwyndel drew in a sharp breath at the sight of her stricken brother. The cloaked man turned toward her, setting his free hand on her shoulder. His strong gaze compelled Gwyndel to look him in the eye. A peace put her fears to rest.

He will be alright. Do not forsake his quest—for on it he will find the truth. Eyoés will not be the same man when he returns.

Removing his hand from her shoulder, the stranger continued to clench the struggling dwarf. Like a silent wraith, he fled into the adjacent alley with Dárig helpless in his grip. The dizziness in Eyoés' head lifted. Wearily, he stood, leaning against the alley wall for support. Gwyndel picked up the fallen bow and quiver and shrugged them onto her shoulder. It was time to gather their things and continue on.

Adjusting the shoulder straps on his pack, Eyoés accustomed himself to its weight. After cleaning their lodgings, they had acquired fresh provisions at the Hammer and Chisel for the quest ahead. He furrowed his brow at the sight of the steps to Lord Ardul's hall. Watching the reluctance in her brother's demeanor, Gwyndel slowed to a stop. Her brother refused to look her in the eye.

"We must bid farewell before we leave," she explained, voice strained. "You must apologize for your actions to Ardul." The muscles in Eyoés' jaw tensed.

It is the right thing.

Despite his inner conviction, admitting the foolishness of his past actions was too embarrassing to consider. Silent, he averted his eyes. Gwyndel shook her head at her brother's iron will, considering what to say.

"Gwyndel, may I speak with you privately?" a quiet voice inquired behind her. Gwyndel turned.

Standing at the edge of the road, Bról, Captain of the Guard, quietly awaited her response, hands clasped behind his back.

Leaving Eyoés to ponder his apology, Gwyndel approached the somber dwarf. "You seem torn," she noted, her tone uncertain.

Shaking his head, Bról indicated for her to sit beside him on a short wall. "I was in the garden when you spoke to Lord Ardul," he revealed. "You've destroyed my perspective—challenged the way I see things."

Gwyndel narrowed her eyes. "I—I don't understand," she stammered.

With a sigh, Bról looked her in the eye. "I was there, during the Draed. I was there when our penitent people were rejected," he explained, hanging his head. "I remember the hate in their words as they told us we were traitors." Looking away, Bról struggled to compose himself. "No matter how hard I tried, I could

178

not forgive them. I hated them for their words and could not do otherwise. Soon, I even told myself the King did not care about our suffering—and that his followers reflected the King's thoughts toward us," he spat, unable to look toward her. "You reminded us of the truth." Bról wiped his face with his sleeve before turning toward her with bloodshot eyes. "Have our past mistakes truly been forgiven?" he questioned, his voice weak.

A warm smile spread across Gwyndel's features. "Yes, the King remembers them no more," she declared. "Until the end, evil will always be in this world—nobody can escape it—but the *King* has no evil in him. He is our lantern."

With a nod, Bról stood, composing himself in an attempt to hide his emotions. "Then I forgive them for what they have done," he concluded. Bowing, the dwarf began to walk away.

"Bról," Gwyndel called, standing. "How did my father earn such a reputation with your people?" Bról paused, looking over his shoulder.

"Élorn's grandfather was the only one to forgive us that day," he answered. "Your father himself brought medicinal herbs and a group of healers to our doors during a great plague. His selflessness healed not only our sick, but our burdened spirit. We have not forgotten the family of Élorn." With a final bow, he entered the bustling crowd in the street.

As the doors to Lord Ardul's hall swung open, Eyoés gritted his teeth. Restraining the impulse to leave, he followed behind Gwyndel as they strode toward Ardul's throne. At the sight of the impetuous youth, the guards tensed, loosening their weapons in their scabbards.

Gwyndel pulled Eyoés closer. "Do *not* speak until I clear my throat," she whispered in his ear. At the throne, she released her brother. Lord Ardul watched Eyoés with an eyebrow raised, seeming to question his motives for returning. Gwyndel bowed. Clenching his jaw, Eyoés followed her example.

"We have come to bid our farewell, Lord Ardul," Gwyndel announced. "We thank you for your generous hospitality." Lord Ardul smiled in return.

Eyoés clenched his fist.

He's eager to see me leave this place.

"May the King guide you on your journey," the Dwarf Lord replied. Eyoés heard Gwyndel clear her throat. His pride battled against this call to humility. He fought to maintain his composure. Silence. Gwyndel gave her brother an icy glare.

Eyoés looked up with an answering scowl, opening his mouth to deliver one last parting jeer.

This vengeance will destroy you if you refuse to lay it down.

The hate fell from his eyes as the cloaked stranger's words again permeated his thoughts. Mustering his strength, he inhaled a deep breath. "I have treated you wrongly, Lord Ardul. Please accept my apology. I do not want to leave this place without being on good terms with you and your people," he acknowledged.

For an instant, Ardul's eyes widened in surprise before the ruler regained his composure. "You are forgiven, Eyoés son of Élorn. It seems you have learned much during your stay," he said. "May the King guide you on your *own* journey." With a half-smile, Eyoés bowed in thanks.

Standing, Lord Ardul gestured for several of the guards to come forward. "My forces shall escort you out of the mountain," he proclaimed. "We will meet again." With a bow, the several guards left their posts and strode to the sides of their guests. Turning away from the throne, Eyoés and Gwyndel marched down the hall with their escort.

As the doors closed behind them, the two considered the journey ahead with expectancy—and fear.

28

The choked afternoon sun struggled to shine through the dreary grey sky as a harsh wind swept the mountainside. Wrapping his cloak around him, Eyoés pressed on, careful of his footing on the narrow path. He glanced behind him, watching Gwyndel follow with her hand pressed against the stone mountain for guidance. A tense silence hung between them. Although his controlled words of parting to Lord Ardul had visibly encouraged them both, the gravity of Gwyndel's near death at the tip of an arrow preyed upon their minds. Eyoés reached over his shoulder, assuring himself the powerful weapon was with him.

Gwyndel noticed the action. "Are you more worried about losing the bow than losing me?" she snapped.

Eyoés' face reddened. Staring at the path ahead, he hurried his walk. Truth be told, the incident unnerved him more than he wished to reveal. Lowering himself by admitting his mistake was not an option. "I didn't lose you," he replied with a strained voice. "That's what matters."

Gwyndel stared off across the valley. Once again, silence claimed the mountain as they rounded a bend in the path.

Eyoés halted, cocking his head as he turned. "The

strange man in the white cloak," he mused. "Who is he?"

Pausing, Gwyndel considered what to say. She knew the man's identity. His words returned to her thoughts.

He will be alright. Do not forsake his quest—for on it he will find the truth. Eyoés will not be the same man when he returns.

Eyoés would have to discover the man's identity on his own. In time, the stranger would return to speak with him.

"I know for certain he is not of the race of men," she vaguely replied. "No human could have stopped that arrow in midair." Pursing his lips, Eyoés turned back to the path. His questions remained.

As the two travelers rounded the bend in the mountain trail, a band of green forest weaved through the valley below, tainted with a light, powdery snow. At the sight, they pressed on, eager to settle themselves under the shelter of the trees.

Embedding the hatchet partway into the piece of wood, Eyoés lifted it above the rotting stump. He brought it down on the cutting block, twisting the blade as he did so to split the wood cleanly down the middle. Wiping the sweat from his forehead onto his pants, he fetched the last piece. Unanswered questions about the cloaked stranger would not leave him alone.

I must have imagined him speaking in my own thoughts.

Setting the wood upon the block, he secured it onto the blade. With a sigh, he mustered his strength and brought it down with a growl. Splinters of wood flew into the snowy grass.

"Finished," he sighed. He set the hatchet aside. Standing, he seized several chopped pieces and tossed them into the middle of an unfolded blanket. Eyoés sighed to himself as the hollow knock reminded him of the early mornings spent cutting wood for Aványn. At the thought of her, a pang of loss surprised him. Strangely, her deception seemed irrelevant now—only a former memory that had lost its sting. She had loved him as a mother, despite the sacrifices. A trickle of salty sweat dripped into his eye. Squinting and blotting his eye with the collar of his shirt, he subdued the prodding questions for another time. He took a piece of jerky from his pocket and chewed on it. It was a savory addition to their rations from the Hammer and Chisel.

The sweeping sound of wings arrested his attention. Seizing the fallen axe, Eyoés searched wildly for the source. Bloody recollections of Asdale's destruction resurfaced as he searched for an escape route.

My sword—I left it with Gwyndel. If I choose to flee, I would be caught before I reached camp.

Flee. The word put a bitter taste in his mouth. Violently shaking his head, Eyoés refused to give in.

My father would never flee. Now is the time to face my fear.

The rustling of bushes further into the forest identified the direction of the unseen creature. Gripping the axe with both hands, Eyoés forged his way toward the sound. He compelled himself to slow his steps and take an indirect route to buy time to appraise the threat. The frosty grass crunched under his feet. Constantly analyzing the terrain, Eyoés ducked under an overhanging branch and entered the forest.

Thick brush hid him from prying eyes, and yet challenged Eyoés to traverse the land without making noise. Stumbling upon the hidden beast wouldn't be difficult. Eyes darting back and forth, Eyoés pushed further into the brush. His heart leapt into his throat as a nearby bush loudly rustled against his leg. Silence.

Have I been spotted?

Fearing the worst, Eyoés took another step forward. As he lifted his foot, he failed to notice an exposed tree root.

Leaning forward against the unexpected resistance, he lost his balance and dove deeper into the forest. In a desperate attempt to catch himself, he put his hands forward and released the axe. To his surprise, he tumbled out of the thick brush, coming to a stop at the edge of a frigid creek. Sitting up, Eyoés wiped the hair from his eyes. He froze, hand on his forehead.

Two piercing eyes peered down at him from the opposite side of the creek. Cocking its bird-like head, the creature swayed its long, feathered tail. The reflected light off the water danced on the golden fur covering its body. Folded above its back, two immense wings awaited the next wind. Each long, golden feather intricately folded over the next, forming a quilt of gold. Sweeping backwards off its head, long feathers angled over the creature's massive neck. From within this golden crown, two short ears twitched toward the fallen warrior. The creature's bulky forearms were armored with dark blue scales. Slowly, Eyoés let his arm down, eyes riveted on the beast. He recognized the creature from the books of old. The drawings had failed to capture its magnificence and massive frame— the creature dwarfed even the stoutest working farm horse.

A griffin.

Curiously, the creature took a step toward him, folded wings raking through the boughs of the trees. Eyoés leapt backwards to the edge of the thick brush, an involuntary shout escaping his lips. Thrusting his hand into the brush, he fumbled for his axe, watching wide-eyed as the griffin approached. The beast released a deep chirp, eyeing the strange newcomer with interest. Unable to locate his weapon, Eyoés abandoned the search. According to the books, stories of the creatures harming humans were rare, despite their known identity as a pest to livestock.

Slowly, he stood, keeping a wary eye on the beast he faced. "Stay back," he pleaded, extending his hands in front of him as a barrier. For a moment, the griffin seemed to consider Eyoés' command.

Gwyndel burst from the brush, bow drawn. Leaping backwards, the griffin released a piercing roar as it prepared to defend itself. In a reflex movement, the creature's wings spread wide, breaking several branches.

"Wait!" Eyoés demanded, seizing his sister's arm.

Gwyndel watched the beast with apprehension. "I heard you shout. Are you alright?" she questioned, stepping in front of her brother.

Eyoés released his grip. "I'm fine," he replied, pushing the bow away while observing the griffin's behavior. As the weapon moved away, the creature paused—then took a step toward the two with folded wings.

Gwyndel cleared her throat as she watched a grin form on her brother's features. "Are you suggesting—" she began, watching with unease as Eyoés inched toward the creature.

Gesturing for Gwyndel to wait, he inserted his hand into his pocket and removed a small piece of bread from within. At the sight of the scrap, the griffin came several steps closer. Swallowing the lump in his throat, Eyoés cautiously extended his hand toward the creature's black, hooked beak. With a warble, the griffin snatched the bread. Eyoés involuntarily pulled his hand backwards, fearful of losing his fingers. Wide-eyed, he examined his hand and found no sign of injury. Swallowing the meager portion, the griffin waited with an expectant cock of its head. Eyoés nodded.

"This is our way out of the mountains. Gwyndel, return to camp and tear up some bread," he quietly ordered. "I'll lead the griffin back to camp."

29

Offering another piece of bread to the griffin, Eyoés stepped backwards into their camp. He edged further out into the center of the clearing. The griffin peeked out from the forest's edge, intent on acquiring the morsel in Eyoés' hand. Tilting its head to the side, it left the protection of the trees. Eyoés gave a cocky smile as he tossed the morsel to the ground in front of him. The griffin darted toward the fallen bread. Picking it up with its ebony beak, it swallowed the meager portion with elevated interest.

Gwyndel stepped from behind her brother, opening the small sack in her hand. Her features tightened as she dropped a couple of biscuits on the ground.

We must train this creature, or these provisions will have been wasted.

Gwyndel knew that convincing Eyoés to give up the idea would be impossible. At the sight, the griffin leapt forward, its wing knocking Eyoés to the ground in its rush. The griffin gave a peal of delight before feasting upon the bread.

Eyoés cleared his throat and sat up, rubbing the back of his sore neck. As he watched the creature devour the food, he stood.

Now is the time to make my move.

Creeping toward the side of the unsuspecting beast,

188

Eyoés held his breath. He leapt onto the creature's back behind the wings. The griffin abruptly lifted its head with a roar, thrashing its body backwards and throwing Eyoés into the grass. With a cry, Gwyndel rushed to where her brother lay face down. Expecting the worst, she knelt by him.

Eyoés rolled onto his back, laughing. Gwyndel sat back upon her heels, surprised. In their time together, laughter had been distant. Biting remarks had taken its place. Gwyndel smiled. Laughter was a welcome change. She clasped her hand around her brother's wrist and helped him up, as their laughter came to an end. Sighing, Eyoés rubbed his back, considering another way to tame the creature.

Finishing its meal, the griffin watched him with suspicion. Eyoés hesitated and stepped backwards. Gwyndel stealthily pulled another portion of bread from the sack and slipped it into his hand. "It seems to learn by association," she whispered in his ear. "Show him this before you mount."

Eyoés used both hands to obscure the bread. Swallowing, he approached the wild beast. The griffin turned to face him, keeping its back away from the young man's reach. Eyoés looked steadily into the creature's eyes as he drew closer. Backing away from the oncoming man, the griffin let out a low rumble of warning. Eyoés revealed the hidden biscuit in his hand. The reluctance in the creature's eyes wavered. Extending the bread with one hand, Eyoés circled around to the creature's side. The griffin longingly stared at the extended bribe. Eyoés chuckled to himself as the griffin watched the food rise while he mounted the beast's back. Once he had secured a comfortable seat, he tossed the bread toward the beast. The griffin snatched the biscuit from the air.

Gwyndel bent over the campfire, mixing the ashes and coals with a nearby stick before shoveling soil over the dying embers. Shoving the rest of the supplies into their large sack, she cinched the opening and dragged the bag to where the griffin watched, curious. Eyoés leaned over and grabbed the sack from Gwyndel's uplifted arms, setting it into the deep depression between the griffin's wings. She tossed him a bundle of rope.

Tying one end to the bag's cinched opening, he dropped the loose end to the ground. Speaking quiet words of comfort to the creature, Gwyndel threaded the rope underneath the griffin's front legs and passed the rope upwards to her brother over the left wing. Taking the rope in hand, Eyoés hitched the bag in place once more to secure it. Unaccustomed to the weight on its back, the griffin fidgeted, attempting to alleviate the itching of the rope rubbing against its chest. Calmly stroking the creature's fur, Gwyndel removed another biscuit from her pocket and offered it to the beast. Once assured the bindings were secure, she jogged to the side, ducking underneath the griffin's wing.

Extending a hand down to Gwyndel, Eyoés pulled her onto the griffin's back. Gwyndel seated herself behind her brother and secured her belt to the second rope. Eyoés looked over his shoulder toward her.

"Now—we fly," he declared. The beast did not

seem to need any prodding.

Spreading its wings wide, the griffin violently pushed off from the ground, shooting upwards with a screech. The blasts of wind from the creature's massive wings came close to knocking the two riders off its back. Gwyndel gave a scream of terror, while Eyoés clung to the griffin's back with a death grip, wide-eyed. A tingling seized his extremities as they soared upwards. White tufts of clouds sped past, glowing with the afternoon sunlight. Clinging to her brother's cloak, Gwyndel squeezed her eyes shut. Below them, the valley shrank into a thin, green carpet. The griffin leveled out its flight among the clouds. Eyoés released a gasp.

Before he could regain his composure, the creature pulled its wings inward, plunging downwards toward the mountains below. A shout of fear slipped from Eyoés as a rising sensation seized his stomach. The carpet of green rapidly transformed into the hard, unforgiving ground. In desperation and terror, Eyoés punched the griffin's shoulders with both hands. Instinctively, its wings popped open, bringing their descent to a screeching halt. With shallow wingbeats, the creature opened the wide fan on the end of its tail, tucking it underneath its body to suspend itself in the sky. The jolt almost sent Eyoés off the griffin's back.

Trembling, he shoved his hand inside their supply pack. He tore another coiled rope from the rest of their supplies and untied it in a rush. Eyoés grabbed both ends, flicking the rest over the griffin's head and yanking backward. The griffin roared in protest as the rope jammed between its beak, shaking its head to throw off the offending reins. Gritting his teeth, Eyoés fiercely regarded the creature, jerking the griffin's head backward.

"You devil!" he muttered under his breath. The griffin determinedly stared over its shoulder at Eyoés.

If we are to survive this flight we must assert ourselves over this creature.

Gwyndel released a long breath. Leaning past Eyoés, she stretched her arm out and scratched the back of the creature's head. With a warble of defeat, the griffin indicated its submission.

"Elves must have quite a way with such wild creatures," he commented dryly. Once Gwyndel had retracted her hand and situated herself behind her brother, Eyoés gave a flick of the reins. To his relief, the griffin began to descend at a reasonable speed. Below, the forest came into sharp definition, the stiff boughs shading the ground below. Orienting himself in the right direction, Eyoés guided the creature toward the tall, grey peaks.

The cold mountain breeze coursed through the griffin's feathers like waves in a sea of gold. As they rode the drafts of wind, the griffin's deep eyes scoured the terrain ahead. Eyoés contemplated the dark summits against the backdrop of sunset. Only in books had he ever visited these lands. The thrill of discovery

Sword and Scion

lured him further north. His eyes fell to his father's sword, tied among the baggage.

I must not forget the purpose of my quest. I did not come here to admire mountains.

Dismissing the childish thoughts of discovery, Eyoés focused on the journey ahead. He patted the griffin on the side.

"Gibusil," he declared. "That is what I'll name you." Hearing no response from Gwyndel, he looked over his shoulder. She had turned in her seat, gazing to the land behind rather than the unknown land before them.

Silent, Eyoés let her think in peace as he searched for a place to land for the night.

30

The whipping wind abated as the overcast sky cleared above them the following day. Glistening in the afternoon sun, the sheer rock face of the grey Iostan mountains coldly observed the travelers flying past. Eyoés loosened the cloak around his neck. Below them, the lush valley faded into an empty gorge, carved into the mountain range by rain, wind, and snow. The previous night was spent away from prying eyes, underneath the trees in the valley. Now, there was nowhere to hide—nowhere to flee from the shrieks in the night.

Shivering, Eyoés wearily searched the barren landscape for peril.

Danger cannot not hide on a bare mountainside.

The strange territory hemming them in refused to back his claim. Ahead, the mountain range bent at an odd angle, as if the earth had accidentally nudged the peaks from their intended place. Flicking Gibusil's reins, he urged the griffin forward. The beast spotted a lone bird close by. Swerving to intercept the bird, Gibusil plucked it from the sky.

Eyoés stuffed the reins into his left hand, loosening his sword from its sheath with his right hand. The last time he felt this apprehension, he had not been prepared.

Gwyndel leaned close to Eyoés, startling him. "According to the map and compass," she shouted, competing with the sound of the air rushing past, "We will be out of these mountains by tonight."

Whether the sounds in the night had awoken and scared her, Eyoés could not tell. He guided Gibusil around a protruding cliff, grateful for the creature's aid in increasing their traveling speed.

"We are open targets in this barren land—and we are not alone," he said.

Fingering the arrows in her quiver, Gwyndel appeared calm—yet alert. "Then we must stay where we will not be seen," she replied. A grove of pines in the valley below offered potential cover. On one side of the grove, a hole in the treetops allowed a view of the sky above without revealing what hid in the shadows.

"We will rest for awhile there," Eyoés decided, pointing toward the small clearing. "We can keep an eye out for any threats from above." Cautiously, he steered the griffin toward the trees. Gwyndel nocked an arrow to her bowstring in case of a sudden attack. Sensing the tension between the riders, Gibusil hurried his pace, diving into the cover of the trees. As the creature entered the clearing, the shade of the pines wreathed them in shadow. Gibusil pulled up short of the forest floor and landed with care, wings cupped to slow their momentum. Eyoés released the reins, untying the rope from his belt and hopping off the griffin's back. Drawing his sword, he ventured into the dark wood. The wind droned through the dark branches above them. Weaving its way through the boughs, sunlight lit sections of the whitened forest floor. A creeping uneasiness gripped him. There was no assurance they were alone.

Gwyndel dismounted while keeping a watchful eye on her brother. Gibusil settled down to enjoy the meal he'd snatched in flight. Ducking under a low hanging branch, Eyoés stepped lightly through the brush. He glanced toward Gwyndel.

Bow drawn, she stalked across the terrain like a wraith in the forest. Taking one last look at the wood, she relaxed her hold on the bowstring. "No danger in sight," she announced, keeping her voice low.

Eyoés nodded and jogged to where Gibusil waited. "I'll keep an eye in the air. Make sure we are not attacked from behind," he commanded. Gwyndel turned away, scrambling up a nearby tree for a better vantage point. She fluidly ascended into the upper limbs as bark gathered under her fingernails.

With a wide yawn, Gibusil laid down upon the hard ground, tucking his head against his body and covering his back with folded wings. Sheathing his sword, Eyoés sat underneath the open sky, leaning against the griffin's massive frame for support. The minutes stretched as his vigilance waned.

As they waited, the sun began its descent into late afternoon. Fidgeting with a blade of grass, Eyoés hung his head, no longer attentive to the sky above him. His eyelids fell.

A rough shake on his shoulder roused him. Crouching in front of him, Gwyndel continued to shake her brother. Suddenly aware of his negligence, Eyoés leapt up. At the sudden unrest, the griffin abruptly stood, sensing the impending peril. Gwyndel seized her brother's arm.

"Get down! We must move before we are discovered," she hissed.

Eyoés gripped the pommel of his sword with white knuckles. He peeked around Gibusil and into the dark forest. "How did it get past your watch?" he inquired in a whisper.

Gwyndel flinched at the sound of a broken twig. "We must leave *now*!" she replied.

A blur of silver burst from the forest, emitting a piercing, metallic shriek.

31

Eyoés and Gwyndel clung desperately to Gibusil's furry hide. The griffin shot into the valley. Eyoés hurriedly looped the rope around one hand and looked back at their silver pursuer. An immense monster tore through the grove of trees, leaving a flattened path in its wake. Diamond scales covered its long body, linked together in a smooth chainmail. Ruffled by the mountain wind, a long, dark fur mane covered the creature's shoulders and back. The reptilian head glared at its fleeing prey. The beast's otherworldly dark green eyes were devoid of any pupil. The beast emitted another shriek, revealing hooked jaws ridged with rows of teeth. Gibusil darted upwards, dodging the clawed fingers at the apex of each wing.

Eyoés watched in horror as the unearthly creature sprang forward. "What sort of fiend is this?" he shouted, his racing pulse pounding in his skull.

"Kalakill," Gwyndel yelled over the sound of the rushing wind. She drew back her bowstring and fired. The arrow lodged into the Kalakill's eye, bringing a screech of pain. The beast fell back. More fearsome cries echoed across the valley in response. Several more Kalakill rose from behind the mountain peaks and took to the air.

Eyoés drew his sword, then stopped as the futility

of his position struck him.

I cannot even injure the monster with this weapon,
let alone kill it.

His father's sword, the weapon that had fought
countless battles, had suddenly found itself in a conflict
it could not fight in.

Gwyndel loosed another arrow, finding its mark in
the creature's eye a second time. The Kalakill fell from
the air, crashing to the rocks below. The pack of
monsters rushed into the fray, darting toward them.
Eyoés turned to seize Gibusil's reins.

They are going to hem us in.

Strange formations of rock columns protruded
from the valley below them, like trees in a stony forest.
Gibusil plunged toward the cover of the columns.
Eyoés squinted his eyes to shield them from the dry,
whipping wind as they dove. He gripped the rope
harness, overtaken by the terrifying sensation of an
uncontrolled fall. With a cry, he shielded his face from
the fast approaching mass of rock. The jolting impact
never came.

Gibusil weaved through the maze of columns to
shake the pursuing beasts off his trail. Awkwardly, one
of the Kalakill swayed to the side to avoid a stone
pillar. The monster slowed its momentum too late as it
smashed into one of the columns. The crashing of
stone behind them caused Eyoés to turn. The stone
collapsed upon its foundation and buried the creature in
a cloud of dust. Concentrating on their prey, the other
Kalakill ignored the death of one of their own.
Gwyndel loosed another arrow before the griffin

rounded a bend in the maze and hid the creatures from view.

Releasing a strained sigh, Eyoés lowered his sword.

That was too close.

A Kalakill burst through the pillars to their side, raining down rubble. Gibusil darted under the massive predator's body and away from the swiping claws. With a roar of fury, Eyoés sliced across the Kalakill's abdomen with his blade. The creature's scales sustained only a slight scratch.

Fóbehn will not fail me.

Sheathing his sword, Eyoés yanked the powerful weapon from the sack and slung the quiver over his shoulder. Quickly nocking one of the strong arrows onto the bowstring, Eyoés struggled to draw. A Kalakill soared above the maze, waiting to scoop up the griffin with its claws. Its haunting eyes locked upon them like a vise. Inhaling deeply, Eyoés relaxed the tension in his fingers and let the bowstring slip from his grasp.

Slicing the air like hot metal, the finely crafted arrow struck home. The shaft disappeared beneath the Kalakill's armored skin and plucked it from the sky. Embedded in the stone behind the creature, the arrow vanished from Eyoés' sight and reappeared inside the quiver. A bark of astonished laughter escaped him.

It is not by chance that this weapon has come into my possession.

Gwyndel watched the spectacle with awe and shouldered her bow. Nocking another arrow to the string, Eyoés searched for a second opportunity. Gibusil darted further into the maze. From between the pillars, fractured images of the hunting Kalakill sowed seeds of dread in the hearts of the riders. The deafening wingbeats ricocheted off the stone surfaces, competing with the blood pounding in their ears. The Kalakill awaited their chance. As soon as Gibusil entered a wider pathway, the beasts broke through the barrier and surrounded their quarry. Their wingbeats sent clouds of dust rising into the air. Gibusil screeched, brandishing his claws in preparation for a last stand. Shielding his eyes from the blinding dust, Eyoés searched for an escape route. His eyes darted to the empty sky above. He yanked the reins backward.

Violently tossing its head in response to the rough command, the griffin shot upwards through the ring of dust and leveled in flight. With a shout, Eyoés glanced behind, watching in triumph as the beasts lunged into empty air. He turned ahead, barely able to bring Gibusil to a halt before colliding with a large obstacle.

Wedged between the sides of the valley, an old dwarf bridge barred their path. The uneven surface of the stone boasted the dwarves' geometric style, remnants of past glory weathered down to near invisibility. More screeches erupted behind them. The hunt was not yet over.

With a thrust of his wings, Gibusil darted over the bridge. Eyoés wasted no time. Swallowing his fear, he urged the griffin onward as the shrieks from behind increased.

A blast of wind from the side tore Gwyndel from

her seat, sending her spinning toward the valley below as one of the Kalakill rushed past. Eyoés stiffened in horror. Her screams faded below him as she writhed in midair with stricken eyes. Time seemed to slow. Memories of her constant sacrifice on his behalf flooded his thoughts.

I cannot bear to think of being without you, Gwyndel.

Eyoés gave a desperate shout and pulled downwards on the reins, stirred to action by his father's last journal entry. Gibusil tucked his wings inward and dove. Eyoés forced himself to watch as the valley floor neared. In the blink of an eye, the griffin opened its wings and snatched Gwyndel from the air. Without guidance, Gibusil leveled his flight, swooping into a jagged crack in the side of the mountain. The speed and momentum sucked the breath from Eyoés' lungs.

Gathering Gwyndel close to its body, the griffin slipped into the hidden cavern. Eyoés pulled gently back on the reins and brought Gibusil to a stop. The shrieks of the Kalakill faded away, soon overtaken by the howling wind. Trembling, Eyoés bowed his head and let the reins slip from his grasp. He slumped in his seat, letting the stillness sink in.

Thank the King we're alive.

32

After a fitful night's sleep in the hidden cavern, they rose early. The bleak stone morphed into rolling hills as Eyoés and Gwyndel spent the day navigating through the Iostan mountains. As they departed the peaks, undulating fields of white, dusted grass were sparsely broken by small pine copses bent from exposure to the elements. They were thankful for an uneventful day of flying.

The sun above glowed a deep orange with the oncoming sunset. Eyoés guided Gibusil in the direction of a small thicket. Gliding close to the ground, the griffin pulled its wings upward, puffs of snow curling underneath. Untying their sack of supplies, Eyoés hopped off Gibusil's back and set them aside. He watched with glassy eyes as Gwyndel dismounted and patted the griffin on the neck. Her brush with death still unsettled him.

"We'd best camp here tonight," Eyoés reasoned, feigning normalcy to mask his stress as he watched the sun disappear below the horizon.

She almost died, and in my fear I nearly failed to act. Again.

He stared down at his empty palms, reliving the terrifying moment. Even though she goaded and challenged him constantly, he couldn't help but care for her.

I have done nothing to deserve her loyalty.

Gwyndel crouched by the supplies and untied the sack. Searching for some hidden item, she paused before pulling a small book from within. The light flap of turning pages drew Eyoés' attention as she thumbed through the book's contents. Gwyndel turned and extended the open book toward her brother.

"I'll get started with supper," she announced. "Think on this." With a probing gaze, Eyoés accepted the book. Once it left her hand, Gwyndel moved to prepare their meal.

Glancing toward her one last time, Eyoés retreated into the shelter of trees, eager to be alone. The tall grass brushed against his waist, slowing his steps. Streaks of red penetrated the boughs and shined upon the parchment pages. Eyoés kept her place with his finger and closed the cover to read its title.

The Proverbs.

His free hand clenched as anger flared within him. Her convictions about his quest were clear.

She is as stubborn as a mule.

Cursing under his breath, Eyoés opened to his saved place. It was not the first time he had seen its pages. Aványn had immersed him in its lore and wisdom. He never shunned its teaching, until finding his father's journal. Too stricken by her lies, he had discounted the book's words as a manipulative tool in the hands of a deceitful woman. However, his irrepressible concern over Gwyndel prompted him to comply.

What have I to lose?

Watching Gwyndel cook out of the corner of his eye, Eyoés leaned against a tree and read.

The Proverb of Rytsgard: It is his duty to avenge and judge—the doom of every wicked one will soon come to pass.

A pang of conviction struck him. Shaking his head to dispel the sensation, he pushed aside the statement. The words convicted him all the more. Eyoés closed the book with a thud.

How can one King bring every evildoer to their knees? How can he reach the evil in Zwaoi?

Eyoés started toward camp, biting the inside of his cheek. Still, his dismissal of the Proverb seemed inadequate to quiet the conviction.

If the King is powerful enough, why was Asdale destroyed? Does the King even know about the Ashen Specter?

Eyoés halted, forced to confront the saying that circulated in his thoughts. Tucking the book under his arm, he considered the Proverb's words.

Maybe the King chooses someone within his kingdom to avenge in his name. Or perhaps he has warriors planted in the right locations?

Troubled, he returned to their encampment, head tilted downward as he endeavored to reconcile his own beliefs with the King's words.

Gwyndel stirred the campfire with a stick, watching the sparks flare up and die down. At the sound of her brother's approach, she looked up, bringing a shaking hand to her forehead. The sight of him sent a wave of heat through her.

Without him, I would be dead.

Mumbling to himself, Eyoés sat by the flames, setting the Proverbs next to him. "All these questions," he mused. "What does it all mean?"

Gwyndel stirred the coals again, watching her brother through the sparks.

Looking into the fire, Eyoés mulled over the Proverb of Rytsgard in his head.

How could one proverb give rise to so many questions? Where are the answers?

He gazed off toward the distant mountains of Zwaoi. Taekohar seemed so far away. Overwhelmed, Eyoés met Gwyndel's gaze. "I feel so alone," he declared, despondent. "No matter who I am with, or where I am, I am alone."

Setting aside the stick, Gwyndel moved to his side and embraced him. "You are not alone," she replied.

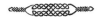

Confused by the darkness, Eyoés wiped the sleep from his eyes, snow coating his blanket as he sat up. A cool breeze coursed through the tall grass, nipping at his bare face. Crossing before the moon, misty clouds filtered the light shining upon the silent landscape. Trees transformed into black towers, gathering together in council among the fields. The hooting of a distant owl drifted along the wind. Eyoés covered himself with his blanket.

"Eyoés," a quiet whisper urged from nearby. Leaping up, he fumbled around, confused about the speaker's identity. Eyoés opened his mouth to speak. A hand briskly cupped over his mouth from behind. Seizing the man's arm, Eyoés made an effort to throw him to the ground. With uncanny speed, the stranger swiped the young man's ankles from underneath him and shoved him to the ground.

Eyoés sat up from his humble position. He recognized the white cloak. The stranger withdrew his hood. Straight hair ran to his shoulders, and a neat beard gave him a noble air. As Eyoés stared into the man's blue eyes, he edged backward.

"I've seen you before, but we've never met," he quavered. "Who are you?"

The cloaked man scanned the tall grass surrounding them to assure their safety. "I am the Guide," he whispered in reply. "I mean you no harm." Extending his hand, the Guide pulled the fallen youth to his feet. Eyoés gave a brief smile of thanks. The man retrieved a staff from where it had been laid aside, leaning his weight upon it.

Eyoés noticed the ornately carved crook formed at the top of the staff.

A shepherd's crook—why would he carry such a humble tool?

The Guide stared at the young man with piercing eyes. "Flee from this place," he implored, gesturing toward where Gibusil lay, asleep by the smoldering ruins of their campfire.

Eyoés swallowed. "Why?" he said. A low howl

broke the midnight silence, its deathly moan echoing across the empty field. The hair on his arms lifted as more wails followed.

Swiftly, the Guide tossed his white hood over his face. "I threw them off your trail several miles back," he spoke in a low tone. "Flee now, before they discover you," Without further notice, the Guide rushed into the grass, a white apparition in a moonlit sea. Fastened to the spot by a strange mixture of fear and admiration, Eyoés stared in the direction the stranger had run. Another ghastly choir roused him to action.

Seizing his blade from its place by the fire, he fastened it to his waist. He rushed to where Gwyndel lay, fast asleep. As he roughly shook her shoulder, Gwyndel woke, eyes open and alert for danger. Seeing no threat, she looked to her brother for an explanation. Deep, sinister howls from the netherworld answered her. She flinched, breaking out in a cold sweat. Eyoés held back a cry of fear, holding his breath in order to silence himself.

"They're onto our trail," he whispered.

Gwyndel sprang up, snatching up her bow and quiver and scattering the ashes of the fire with her boot. Gibusil's head perked up. The choir of death rose and fell like the song of a shade, louder by the second. Stuffing the remainder of their supplies into the sack, the two riders hastened toward the griffin. Eyoés leapt onto Gibusil's back, pulling Gwyndel up into her seat. With a flick of the reins, they launched into the crisp night air.

Eyoés gazed down at the field below, watching a

dark circle close in on their camp. Even from the sky, the identity of their attackers was clear. Each Hobgoblin held a leash in one hand, against which a Kélak strained, and a weapon in the other. Eyoés scanned the fields below. The Guide had vanished. "How did he know?" he whispered under his breath.

Robbed of both sleep and peace of mind, they fled.

33

A bead of ink dripped from the pen's white tip. Falling into the clay inkwell, the ebony tear of woe sent ripples across the black sea inside. As the quill touched the tan parchment, its message of foreboding streamed from its mouth like a snake's venom— inciting the death of a kingdom.

Skreon was ready. With a lavish flair, he signed his name at the message's end, the style elegant in design —yet sharp-edged like a tongue of steel. Enraptured by the moment, Skreon sat unnaturally still in his chair, eyes riveted upon the document as he returned his quill pen to its inkwell.

Far too long have I waited for this. Everything must be perfect.

Reading the message one last time, he assured himself there were no mistakes. Satisfied with his work, Skreon flipped the parchment over and smoothed it flat. A green candle burned upon his desk, the small flame casting light shadows along the length of the wood grains. He set a leather cord onto the back of the parchment and carefully removed the melting candle from its stand. With a quick breath, Skreon silenced the flame, the trail of smoke ascending to the ceiling like a soul set free.

He tipped the candle over the center of the leather

strip. Drops of hot wax puddled across the leather and onto the parchment. Skreon returned the candle to its proper place, slipping an iron ring from his finger and pinching the metal band between two fingertips. As he pressed the ring's face into the puddle, the wax spread under the pressure. After holding it in place for several seconds, he removed the ring, slipping it back onto his finger with satisfaction. Emblazoned in the drying wax was his personal insignia—a broadsword, flanked by two dragon wings.

Once the wax cooled, Skreon rolled the parchment and tied it with the leather strip. He stood, shoving his chair behind him with a screech as the wooden legs scraped against the stone floor. Rushing toward his chamber door, Skreon grasped the handle and paused.

Who will deliver this message? I must attend to the army. If this dispatch fell into the wrong hands...

As he considered the solution, a dark sneer built on his features.

Makulazai. He must deliver it.

Skreon grimaced at the thought of entrusting the message to his rival. If the Hobgoblin chief was to lose the message, his campaign against King Fohidras would fail—and the loss of surprise would result in the suffering of the Hobgoblin race on the battlefield.

We both have something to lose. I will keep Makulazai in fear—then he will not disobey me.

The iron doors of Nys-Felz slammed shut, the clang resounding across the drill field. At the sound, the Hobgoblins turned, tense at the expectation of their master's scarlet gaze. Stirred into action by the sudden noise, Makulazai faced the entryway, forcing himself to maintain a steady gaze. His eyes narrowed. Skreon was nowhere in sight. As a ripple of conversation spread throughout the ranks, the Hobgoblin chief briefly closed his eyes, releasing a controlled sigh. With a shout, he commanded the troops to return to their drills. Focusing on the task at hand, Makulazai clasped his hands behind his back. His breath caught in his chest as a compelling dread urged him to take one last glance. The Hobgoblin chief turned back toward the iron doors and stiffened.

Emerging from the shadows, the tall form of Skreon sent a wave of cold across the Hobgoblin's skin. Pinning Makulazai with a fixed stare, the albino gestured toward the far side of the drilling field. With a slight bow, the Hobgoblin chief silently departed from the ranks, following his master across the plateau. They halted at the side of the mountain. As Makulazai neared the spot, the overcast sun caught the mountainside from a new angle, revealing a lone causeway. Silent, Skreon led the way, pressing himself against the rock face as he traversed the precarious pathway. Following the albino's example, Makulazai stepped onto the narrow ledge.

The path came to an end, delivering them to the jaws of a dark cavern. The wide, jagged wound grew diagonally across the mountainside like an old scar. Stepping into the wide breadth of the cave, Skreon turned toward his second-in-command. Makulazai blankly stared into the black cavern, feeling the malevolent darkness seeping out like a disease. Although the Kóenar had repeatedly invoked roars from within, the cave had seemed too distant to fear from the drilling field.

"Why did you bring me here, Kóenar?" he questioned, his unease pleasing Skreon.

The albino seized the Hobgoblin chief's arm and pulled him into the cave entrance. "I want you to see the bane of your ancestors, Makulazai," he replied, laughing. Skreon shoved him further into the cave. A low, rumbling growl proceeded from the depths of the cavern, hailing their arrival. Flinching at the sound, Makulazai stepped back, grasping the sword underneath his cloak.

A ghostly pale apparition emerged from the depths of the cavern. Groping out of the darkness, massive claws pressed against the walls of the cave. Chains fastened to the creature's wrists and ankles clinked against the stone ground. Its giant wings were folded close to its body. The dragon's powerful upper jaw gave the appearance of a grim smile. Behind a crown of horns, a red frill lay against each side of the beast's head.

Skreon glanced toward Makulazai, watching with amusement as the Hobgoblin chief trembled as the dragon's red eyes locked upon him. "Behold—the Norzaid," Skreon hissed, locking eyes with the ghastly dragon. Noticing the presence of its master, the Norzaid released a low rumble from within and bowed its head. The albino glimpsed one of the whitened, uneven scars normally hidden by the frills. Over time, the creature's attitude toward him had made a favorable turn, allowing for the shards of iron to be removed without consequence.

He turned to Makulazai. Like lightning, Skreon seized the Hobgoblin's hidden sword and gruffly tossed it aside. The weapon clattered onto the stone, amplified by the cave walls. Makulazai bared his teeth and lunged to reclaim the stolen blade. The albino shoved the infuriated Hobgoblin back. Drawing a small dagger from his belt, he extended it to Makulazai blade first. The Hobgoblin chief glared at the small weapon, clenching his jaw before taking the knife. The idea of obeying Skreon's iron will made him feel weak.

Removing the message from his pocket, Skreon passed it toward the Hobgoblin, the parchment crinkling as it changed hands. "You are to take this to the Hobgoblin tribes in the southernmost region of Zwaoi," he commanded. "If you lose this, your people will reap the consequences."

Skreon was satisfied to read the hatred in the chief's eyes as a desire for revenge—not escape. Taking the message in hand, Makulazai turned to leave. Skreon's hand shot out and snatched the Hobgoblin by the shoulder. With a growl, the albino spun his subordinate back toward the pale dragon.

"You will ride the Norzaid on your errand," he insisted.

Makulazai gulped, stricken as he recalled the tales of his ancestors. A hollow silence filled the cavern, kindling the flame of anger within the dark lord. Roughly, Skreon shoved him toward the awaiting dragon. At the sight of the approaching Hobgoblin, the Norzaid hissed in expectancy of a meal. The beast's teeth gleamed in the dreary light. A growl from Skreon dashed the creature's hopes. Immediately the dragon drew back.

With vacant eyes, Makulazai swallowed, knowing he must bow to the Kóenar's wish. Rebellion was quickly quenched by Skreon's dark words. Silent, Makulazai approached the dragon, shoulders curled forward. In the darkness, the Hobgoblin chief noted a saddle upon the Norzaid's back. Lifting his foot into the stirrup, he paused. The dragon's eyes gleamed luminously as they watched his every move. Makulazai felt the urge to wipe away the cold sweat on his brow, yet held himself in check, feeling Skreon's dark gaze upon him. Mustering what courage he had, the Hobgoblin hoisted himself into the saddle and grabbed the reins.

Skreon held up his hand. "Should the Norzaid— begin to hunt among the ranks of the Southern Tribes —jab it behind the frill with the pommel of your dagger. It will back down," he added.

Perhaps the dragon will be provoked by the act and end his miserable life. Still, this message must get through.

Skreon approached the dragon. Removing a key from his belt, the albino unlocked the beast's shackles. As soon as the final chain hit the cavern floor, the Norzaid burst from the cave, its wings opening with a loud rush of wind. Released from its bondage, the dragon released a deep, ear-splitting roar of freedom.

From the scar in the mountain, Skreon watched as the messenger disappeared into the black mountains.

They will reach the tribes within the next few days. I must continue preparations.

34

A suffocating night gripped Zwaoi in its cruel
hand, the breath of winter frigid as it swept through the
black trees. Boughs of evergreens stretched into the
dark, like arms grasping for prey. Drifting through the
forest like a tormented wraith, long, mourning cries
rang in the ghostly hills, betiding dreadful things to
come. The land itself seemed to forbid its light as the
moon was smothered by thick clouds. Deep within the
snaring wood, an orange glow pierced the twisted
branches and fog. Within the relative safety of cleared
ground, two figures each leaned against a nearby tree.
A crackling fire burned at their feet. It had been four
full days since their departure from Nubaroz.

Gwyndel adjusted her blanket, trying to calm her
racing heartbeat. She flinched as another shrill screech
sent her blood cold. Glancing toward Eyoés, she
watched his chest rise and fall as he leaned against the
crooked stump of a maple for support. His father's bare
sword lay across his lap in case of attack. Gwyndel
gripped the handle of Fóbehn with white knuckles.

The fear of prying eyes forced her head down. She
refused to give into the impulse to flee. Flexing her
muscles to fight back the weakness in her limbs, the
young elf looked up into the darkness. Another wail
lifted the hairs on her neck. She set Fóbehn onto her

lap and moved closer to the fire. The heat of the flames fought back the icy breeze rustling the limbs above. Gwyndel sighed, wrapping her blanket tighter around her shoulders. The fog had been merciful enough to hide them from prying eyes on this first night in Zwaoi. As for its protection in the future, she remained uncertain.

We are in enemy territory now—we cannot take anything for granted.

Quietly uttering a prayer to the King, Gwyndel watched as shadows danced through the woods like phantoms swaying to the beat of a silent drum.

A rustling in the brush from the outskirts of the camp made her freeze. Listening intently, Gwyndel searched the dismal shadows. Silently removing her blanket, she withdrew an arrow from Fóbehn's quiver. At the click of her nocking the arrow to the bow, the rustling ceased. Slowly, she drew the bowstring to her cheek, waiting for sign of movement. Two yellow eyes pierced the fog. The orange glow of the fire revealed the dark, hunched shape of the beast's body. Staring into the eyes of the ghoulish creature, Gwyndel tried to aim with shaking hands.

She started as a shriek erupted above her head, sending the fiend fleeing into the dark forest. Gwyndel leapt up, searching the treetops. Scared awake by the cry, Eyoés sprang to his feet, throwing his blanket just shy of the campfire. Perched upon a thick, high branch, Gibusil looked down upon them, golden coat transformed into a dark grey by night. The griffin cocked its head with a warble.

Gwyndel released a tense breath, shaking her head as she organized her jumbled thoughts. "Gibusil scared off some prowling monster. It's alright," she assured her brother.

Drawing a deep breath, Eyoés relaxed his guard. He noticed dark patches underneath Gwyndel's weary eyes. "Get some sleep," he whispered, pointing to her former spot with the tip of his blade. "I'll take the next watch." Returning the arrow to Fóbehn's quiver, Gwyndel set the weapon aside and gathered up her blanket. As Eyoés knelt by their struggling fire, she leaned against the nearest pine, drawing her blanket up to her shoulders. Exhausted by the terror of the night, she fell into a fitful sleep.

The dreary arrival of morning did nothing to ease their spirits. Although the fog's grip on the wood had weakened, the mystery of what lie further into the gloom disturbed Eyoés. Sitting next to the dying fire, he loosely bounced a crooked stick in his palm. He stifled a yawn and rubbed at the dark shadows beneath his eyes. The night's watch had taken its toll. With a sigh, he prodded among the coals with the tip of his stick. Broken chunks of charred wood and ash were streaked with an orange glow that pulsed across the dying embers. Tossing the stick aside, Eyoés stared off into the forest. Images of the single, pale dragon among the flames of Asdale came to mind.

My enemy is within reach. If I find this Whiteblood, it will lead me to the Ashen Specter.

A grin of triumph slowly spread across his face as the realization sank in. Months of endless travel had delivered him into the dark land. He would not leave until vengeance had been realized. Standing, Eyoés grasped his father's blade, holding it close for inspection. The sight of the knotted designs etched into the metal crossbar evoked memories of his father, strengthening his resolve.

I will avenge the innocents' blood, Father, and make you proud.

Something stirred behind him, causing him to turn. With a yawn, Gwyndel wiped the sleep from her eyes, casting aside her blanket. Standing, she shivered as the cold wind bit through her clothing.

Eyoés sheathed his sword. "Good morning," he said, scattering the ashes of the campfire with his boot. Gwyndel gave a weak smile, rubbing her face to wake herself up. Unsettling dreams had tormented her sleep, haunted by horrid creatures and vivid memories of falling from the sky. Eyoés stepped around her, gathering her blanket into a bundle and stuffing it into their supply bag along with his own. Removing some jerky from within, he extended a handful toward his sister. They ate in silence, hurrying to get to flight before being discovered. As they packed their supplies, Gibusil woke in the treetop above them. The griffin stretched its wings and leapt to the ground.

With a loud snap, the branch Gibusil had perched upon crashed into the underbrush, rending the silence of the morning in two. Eyoés cringed. A sudden coldness seized his gut as he listened for sound of pursuit. Rooted to the spot, he took shallow breaths to stay quiet. For several minutes, they waited, painstakingly listening for the slightest indication of attack. Only the whisper of the breeze and the creak of the branches above met their watch.

Pulling a second cloak from the sack, Gwyndel fastened it around her neck to fight off the chill wind. Silent, the two sprinted toward Gibusil, quickly lashing the pack onto the griffin's back. Gwyndel started to mount. Eyoés seized her shoulder. Startled, she looked at him, examining his features for an answer. Jaw clenched, he listened intently with a furrowed brow. Closing her eyes, Gwyndel focused on the sounds around her. At first, she heard nothing. Then, carried on the wind, came the faint sound of guttural conversation. At the sound, Gibusil's ears perked. Her hands fell to the dagger on her belt, gripping the shaped oak handle.

"We should go—*now*," she whispered, looking back toward her brother.

Her breath caught in her throat as she watched Eyoés disappear into the forest, the deception of the shadows covering his advance.

35

Drawing her dagger, Gwyndel plunged into the dark timber. The boughs of the black pines choked the light above with their shadows. Needles covered the forest floor. Gwyndel scoured the darkness for sign of Eyoés, her neck stiff from straining to see. Ahead in the path, the scabbard of a sword disappeared around a corner.

"Wait!" Gwyndel whispered, her voice raspy as she attempted to remain undetected by an enemy. With elvish speed, she pressed further into the ebony forest, the thorny underbrush scraping against her boots. Dashing into the foggy wood, Gwyndel sheathed her weapon as she weaved through a maze of thick, overgrown roots. A bend in the path suddenly revealed the form of Eyoés hiding behind a fallen tree. Tripping over a root, she fell at his side. Looking toward the black roof of conifer boughs, she shook her head.

When will he learn to think before he acts?

With a huff, she reined in the words of rebuke coming to her tongue. To speak now would reveal their location.

Noticing her arrival out of the corner of his eye, Eyoés held his finger to his lips. The sound of guttural, savage conversation increased. Leaving the cover of the fallen pine, the two hastened down the forest trail, the words becoming clearer with each step. The debris beneath their feet changed to packed ground, leading further into the forest. Eyoés cautiously followed another bend in the path, hand resting on the pommel of his sword. Assuring the way ahead was free of danger, he glanced behind. Gibusil forced himself through a narrow opening in the brush. The cracking of the breaking branches seemed like thunderclaps.

Leaping over a large root, Gwyndel seized the griffin's reins and quickly tied the beast to a thick stump. Gibusil, sensing the riders' displeasure, remained still. They ducked into the cover of the fog and black wood, unsure if their presence had been detected. Eyoés' grip on his sword relaxed as the voices continued. He came out of the forest, followed by Gwyndel as he cautiously ventured further into the fog.

The light fog dissipated into a haze, revealing a complete picture of the surroundings. Ahead, Eyoés glimpsed the trail coming to an end at the border of a large clearing. Shadowy forms walked back and forth as the sound of voices increased in volume. Veering off the trail into the cover of brush, Eyoés crept toward the edge of the treeline. A thick oak championed the border of the forest, scarred with age and twisted into two individual trunks. Keeping a wary eye open, Eyoés ducked behind it. His heart raced. Crudely constructed tents of tattered animal hide were scattered over the expanse of the clearing, like fangs crowding the mouth of a nightmare. Hobgoblins went about their duties, conversing with their fellow tribesmen in their wretched language. Stationed along the forest's edge, several guards each clutched a weapon in hand, some stained with grisly marks of combat. Smoke from many campfires ascended into the overcast sky, carrying with them the stench of putrid meat. Repulsed, Eyoés spat into the nearby bushes, even recoiling at the sound of their gravelly speech. He heard the faint stirring of brush as Gwyndel crouched beside him.

She shuddered at the sheer number of the hideous creatures. "We must go—we will be spotted if we linger," Gwyndel whispered into his ear.

Pulling his gaze from the camp, Eyoés sharply shook his head. Although his reaction did not surprise her, she couldn't help her disbelief at his reply. "We might not get an opportunity like this again," he said in a whisper. "We will gather what information we can."

Gwyndel's mouth hung open. It was too much. With a glare and a wave of her hand she dismissed the idea. They jumped as a harsh shriek shook the ground. Circling over the camp, a long, dark shadow slowly descended. The Hobgoblins looked toward the sky. Again, the roar fell on them from above, spreading a panic among the creatures below. Shaken from their daze, the Hobgoblins fled, the chorus of their screams deafening as they shoved past each other to reach the safety of the forest. Eyoés pressed himself against the tree, clapping his hands over his ears. The stench of singed flesh returned to his nostrils as images of burning homes flashed through his memory. The distinct roar seemed strangely familiar. Prying his hands from his ears, Eyoés peered around the trunk of the oak.

With a rumbling growl, an immense, pale dragon landed amid the stricken camp with a thud, its wings billowing in the wind. The sight of the crimson eyes and icy blue underlid sent a wave of cold through Eyoés' body. With a growl, the beast revealed dagger-like teeth. The vile odor of old, rotting flesh emanated from the dragon's jaws. Dark blood-red frills rested behind a sinister crown of horns. Eyoés shuddered, then fumed with rage as he recognized the horrible beast. The Whiteblood dragon had not changed since the night of Asdale's burning.

A movement atop the dragon's back caught his eye. Dismounting, a single Hobgoblin leapt to the ground, falling into a crouch to absorb the impact. He carried himself with authority. Eyoés frowned, recalling the legend.

That's not the Ashen Specter.

Casting a wary glance back toward his steed, the Hobgoblin regarded the fleeing crowd with a haughty —and dismal—air. With a scoffing grunt, he whistled. At the piercing sound, the rushing crowd halted, trembling as they turned. The tension in their haunted eyes waned at the sight of their chief. Angered by their slowness to act, Makulazai barked orders in his native tongue. Glancing amongst each other, the Hobgoblins approached their former leader, trembling under the piercing eye of the Norzaid. Eyoés turned to Gwyndel with a raised eyebrow as words passed between the Hobgoblin chief and his people.

The conversation among the beasts ceased. Looking back, Eyoés held his breath as the Hobgoblins withdrew into their encampment. The dragon obediently followed. Eyoés stared at the ground as he remembered the dragon's devastating power.

Why does it not attack? Have these brutes tamed the beast?

He regarded their dwellings. These Hobgoblins were primitive. They were no match for such a wild creature. He caught sight of a tall flag near the outskirts of the camp.

The Commander's tent.

Eyoés gestured for Gwyndel to follow and left the cover of the oak. Circling the camp from the shadows of the forest, the two crept in the direction of the billowing flag. Eyoés grimaced as the toe of his boot caught an exposed root. They edged along the perimeter of the encampment, careful to conceal their movement from the guards on patrol.

Eyoés halted behind a large bush across from the commanding tent. A small band of officers escorted Makulazai toward the tent entrance. Noticing the tip of the dragon's wing above the tent roof, he swallowed the lump in his throat. Gwyndel set a firm hand upon his shoulder. Giving one last glance toward the large tent, he turned toward her.

She stared daggers at him. "What is your plan?" she hissed, her rushed speech venting her inner frustration. "We have no hope of escape if we are discovered!" The presence of the Whiteblood held them in terror. Suppressing the urge to glance in the dragon's direction, Gwyndel envisioned the beast crashing through the trees above their heads with its mouth open wide.

Eyoés noticed his sister's restlessness. He looked away, unwilling to look her in the eye lest his own fear be revealed. "We will *not* be discovered," he whispered with confidence. "Just trust me."

Gwyndel clenched her jaw. His past actions had fallen short of trustworthiness. Before she could rebuke him, Eyoés left the safety of the shadows and crept toward the back of the tent. With each step, the thought of the beast's eye trained on him grew stronger, as if to warn him before it was too late. Pausing, he looked toward the top of the tent. The dragon remained still, unaware of his presence from the opposite side of the tent. Eyoés closed his eyes and took a deep breath. He stepped out of the forest directly behind the Commander's tent.

As he squatted by the wall of animal skins, he looked behind to assure himself. Gwyndel waited in the cover of the forest, bow drawn to cover his escape. Closing his eyes, Eyoés leaned closer toward the tent wall. The flap of the tent announced the entry of the officers. Gravelly voices rose in conversation. Eyoés opened his eyes as the crackling of parchment met his ear.

This parchment must contain important information to deserve such an imposing arrival.

A movement near the tent caught his eye. Standing sentry, a lone Hobgoblin absentmindedly reclined against a nearby tent pole. Rising, Eyoés backed away from the tent and vanished into the forest.

As her brother returned to the cover of the trees, Gwyndel stood, struggling to return the arrow to her quiver with her shaking hands. Eyoés shook his head, leaning to her ear. He pointed toward the Hobgoblin sentry. "There is some valuable letter inside. Shoot that guard in the leg—we need a distraction," he whispered. Gwyndel gritted her teeth. She knew he would not relent. With a parting glare, she crept toward the forest line. Estimating the distance, she ducked behind a tree and nocked another arrow. Eyoés returned to the tent wall, his posture rigid as he awaited the shot. The wind slowed to a gentle breeze. She let the bowstring slip from her fingers.

The Hobgoblin dropped its weapon, giving a howl of pain while clutching its leg wound. Gwyndel froze. The ghastly head of the Whiteblood rose above the tents, nostrils flaring at the scent of Hobgoblin blood. With a rumbling shriek, the dragon leapt toward the stricken soldier, the frills behind its skull unfolding into a bloody halo. With a crunch, the beast clamped its jaws upon its prey. The screams of the victim melded with the cries of the others as they abandoned their posts. Followed by his subordinates, Makulazai burst from the tent, expression distorted in panic as he watched the dragon lock eyes with another victim. Chaos erupted. Eyoés looked away from the grisly scene. He had not meant to condemn the sentry to death. Drawing his sword, Eyoés sliced open the leather tent and slipped inside.

The pungent smell of burning oil nearly choked

him upon entry. He held back a cough, searching the interior of the tent for sign of the parchment. Several oil lamps cast dim shadows against the fur walls. Two poorly hewn chairs laid sideways on the dirt, thrown to the ground in the commotion. Eyoés darted toward a single large table placed in the center of the tent. Even in the dim light, the parchment was in plain sight. Eyoés seized the scroll, a shudder running up his spine as another thunderous roar shook the tent's frame. The parchment crackled in his grip as he formed a fist. Dashing back out of the slash in the tent wall, he fled into the forest, the silent form of Gwyndel on his heels.

Should the Norzaid—begin to hunt among the ranks of the Southern Tribes—jab it behind the frill with the pommel of your dagger. It will back down.

Terrified, Makulazai yanked the dagger from its sheath, recalling Skreon's words. Snatching two Hobgoblins in its teeth, the Whiteblood threw them into the black forest with a roar before whipping the ranks of its attackers with its jagged tail. The survivors fled from the bloody carnage, screaming in horror as the dragon shrieked in reply. Makulazai trembled as he eyed the red frills flaring behind the beast's skull, and then the massacre unfolding around him.

Skreon has reduced me to a slave. I am not a coward—I am a chief!

He was tired of the terror—the ever present fear of death at the dragon's teeth. Jaw set, he gripped the handle of his dagger. Watching its prey scatter, the dragon pounced after the fleeing Hobgoblins, maw gaping wide in preparation to spit flame. Makulazai made his move.

Intercepting the rampaging creature, he latched onto the dragon's folded wing and clambered up its neck, avoiding the sharp scales protruding from its spine. Surprised by the sudden weight on its back, the Whiteblood reared upon its hind legs with a roar. Makulazai seized the beast's horns to steady himself as the dragon thrashed its head in an effort to throw off its attacker. The creature scratched viciously at its neck, ripping scales off with each swipe. Ducking underneath the dragon's crown, Makulazai hammered the handle of his dagger behind the beast's frill with all the strength he could summon. With a scream of pain, the monster relented. The Hobgoblin chief leapt from the dragon's back. Shaking, he sheathed his weapon, turning back toward the subdued creature.

The return journey North to Nys-Felz would test his nerves.

36

Gibusil glided low above the black treetops as the riders left the Hobgoblin camp behind them. Clumsily gripping the reins with one hand, Eyoés clutched the letter in the other as the parchment was buffeted by the wind. He bowed his head, unable to believe he had escaped with his life.

Speechless, he looked at his prize with a weary smile. Eyoés looked up, blasts of wind nipping at his face as he searched for a place to land among the dark mountaintops. Gwyndel slumped against his back, weak with relief. Spying a small patch of flat rock below, Eyoés tucked the message inside his shirt, fearful of the wind claiming his trophy. A pained roar burst from the mountaintop behind, causing him to glance back to where they had come from. He guided Gibusil to the patch of open ground, eyes darting.

Sensing the urgency, the griffin dove, abruptly bringing its wings back to smooth its landing. As soon as Gibusil's feet hit the ground, Eyoés leapt off its back. He withdrew the message from inside his shirt. The sweat on his hands dampened the corners of the letter as he untied the leather bond. He paused. How had such a letter come within his reach?

Pondering his luck, Eyoés unraveled the parchment. Elegant, sharp words glistened upon the parchment surface, pointed like jagged teeth. He exhaled, brow furrowed. Although difficult to read, the harsh script was clearly written in the Common Tongue. Puzzled, Eyoés looked up from his musings. He had not expected the Hobgoblins to speak another language. The contradiction of brutish creatures being educated in the Common Tongue was astonishing. The appearance of this understandable language was fortunate. He returned to the script.

TRIBES OF THE SOUTHERN REGIONS –
The time has come. Muster your forces and return north as soon as Makulazai arrives with this letter. The ships await to escort us on our voyage to the river of Larimar. I can assure you that the fleet will not be detected – the fog will hide us, and the people of Toekohoar are too distracted over Castle Asdoie's destruction to guard the coast. Soon we will be victorious against Fohioroes and bring him to his knees. I await you at Nysfelz.
SKREON, KOENAR OF ZWaoi

His breath caught in his throat. From the depths of his memory, the discord of the legends of old returned to his thoughts. Eyoés regarded the signature with horror. The atrocities associated with that name caused him to shudder.

Skreon is the Ashen Specter.

Disturbed by her brother's expression of shock, Gwyndel dismounted. "Is there something about the letter?" she inquired. Shaken from his stupor, Eyoés passed the letter to her. He loosened the upper button of his shirt to allow the cold wind to dry the sweat on his chest. Sensing his unrest, Gibusil nudged him. Eyoés flashed a fake smile and patted the griffin on the neck. A dark rage burned behind his gaze as his smile of assurance faded. His fists shook as his mind rolled over the history of Alithell, the truth beginning to fall into place.

Skreon had personally directed the murder of hundreds of innocents—merely for their alliance with his enemy. More than one massacre had stained the fiend's hands. Eyoés recalled the tales told in the books of his childhood.

Centuries before, war had erupted between the King and his emissaries—the Gahrim. Created to serve him and do his bidding throughout the Kingdom, it was said the Gahrim possessed incredible abilities given to them in order to accomplish their duties. Among the strongest and most able of them all was Llumiael, Commander of the Gahrim. Prideful in his strength, Llumiael festered a secret jealousy for the King's power over the people—too blinded by his greed to see that his master's authority was based out of love, not dominance. Secretly gathering a faction of supporters, the Gahrim Commander plotted to poison the King at the annual banquet. For months he waited, assuring that every possible threat to his plan was eliminated. However, when offered the poison cup—the King was completely unharmed, and knowingly confronted Llumiael with a stern glare. Exiled for his rebellion, he fled, followed by the other fallen Gahrim.

Incensed by his failure, Llumiael ventured across the Kingdom, sowing seeds of discontentment, discord, and greed among all of its inhabitants—Men, Dwarves, and Elves. Once sure of the loyalties of the deceived, he declared open war against the King. For over four hundred years, battles of the bloody War of Adrógar swept the land of Alithell, including the fabled Draed. Countless lives were destroyed in the dire struggle as Gahrim fought Gahrim alongside those allied with their masters. King Fohidras, sorrowed by the death and destruction of his people, ambushed the Rebel's forces in a decisive siege at Edonsbreach. Unable to withstand the power of the King, Llumiael surrendered.

The King cursed Llumiael, transforming the Rebel into a black mist that revealed the darkness within his heart. Stripped of his name and form, Llumiael henceforth became the Black Presence. He fled into the depths of the world along with the deceived Gahrim who survived the war. Turiel, Llumiael's second in command during the war, refused to hide underground.

In retaliation for his master's defeat, the rogue Gahrim Turiel assembled a small contingent of Llumiael's defeated soldiers. Mounting upon the backs of Kélak, he led his troops in an attack against a village built upon the shores of Slóketal Lake. Ruthlessly, Turiel slaughtered them all for their devotion to their King. A week later, a party of the King's soldiers arrived at the village to recruit troops—only to discover the bloody streets littered with dead. Posted upon the wall of the local tavern, a large sheet of parchment boasted about the gory slaughter, signed in Turiel's hand. When news of his atrocities spread throughout the land, the people named him Skreon, meaning destroyer.

Eyoés bared his teeth, the whites of his eyes gleaming in the morning light. Looking northward with a dark fire in his eyes, he released a scream of rage against Skreon's heinous crimes.

Now there were two wrongs to be avenged.

37

Makulazai tried to appear natural. "The message has been delivered, Kóenar," he lied, standing deathly still. Turning to study his second in command, Skreon eyed the Hobgoblin chief with a probing gaze. Nervously, Makulazai met the gaze, measuring his breathing.

Skreon waved the Hobgoblin away. "Excellent," he remarked. "My army will soon be complete." With a hasty bow, Makulazai departed from the chamber.

Clasping his hands behind his back, Skreon stood before his chamber window. Above the ebony mountains of Zwaoi, tendrils of darkness strangled the dying light of day, transforming the sky into a dreary twilight. Skreon stepped back from the window, taking one last look at his domain before returning to his solitary desk. He pulled his chair back, shaking the candlelight shining upon his desk amid the dusk.

Skreon felt the presence first. He froze, his ruby eyes inspecting the shadowy recesses of the immense chamber with a haunted gaze.

No—not now. I am not ready!

Swallowing, he let his hand drop from the back of his chair, envisioning the arrival of his nightmare. The desire to vanish pressed upon him, yet he restrained himself and took several steps forward. He could not hide. Clearing his throat, Skreon spread his hands wide in greeting.

"Welcome, Llumiael," he stammered through his forced smile. "I was not expecting you." A long hiss severed the thick silence, like the last breath of the dying. A chill crept up Skreon's spine. The corners of his lips trembled as he struggled to maintain his facade. Seeping from the dark corner of the room, long tendrils of dark mist crept along the stone floor toward him. The albino flinched.

Suddenly the mist halted. Climbing upward, the streaks of black mist wove together, intertwining into the black, legless form of a man. Two, lidless, milky white eyes pinned Skreon to the spot.

"That name is dead to me," the apparition hissed, his voice stale. Skreon's smile faded as he kneeled before the Black Presence, his long white locks sweeping the floor. The figure's white eyes narrowed, "Arise."

Silent, Skreon obeyed. Many years had passed since his master's last visit. "Why have you come, my lord?" he inquired, voice cracking.

The Black Presence glided closer, extending an accusing arm of mist. Instinctively, Skreon stepped backward, repulsed. "I have seen you assembling this army without my instruction, Skreon," he declared in a biting tone as he swept his arm across the room.

Skreon's breath caught in his throat.

If I reveal my intention to conquer Fohidras, he will kill me for my treachery. By usurping the throne, I rob him of his only chance at vengeance.

Staring blankly at his master, he searched for an explanation to hide his true intent.

"I—I am mustering an army for your return, my lord," he quavered. "When you acquire a human form once again, I shall await your command." An uneasy silence hung between them as shadow finally ensnared the sunlight, forcing it to abandon its realm below to a deep, smothering night. Skreon clenched his jaw.

The Black Presence glided back a step. "Very well," he hissed. "I shall expect you to keep your promise."

Maintaining his composure, Skreon nodded. "So be it, my lord," he declared. As quick as he had come, the Black Presence vanished into thin air. The albino gasped, falling into his chair.

Has my master believed my lie?

38

Choking the skies, a thick mist hid the mountains below from their sight. Wisps of white fog entwined amid the clouds into a blanket of grey, tainted dark by the rain. Eyoés adjusted his hood, hands numb from the hours of rain and wind. The soaking cloth wrapped around him did nothing to warm him. Eyes straining, he shook his head, attempting in vain to guide Gibusil through the mist. He furrowed his brow, struggling to see even the tips of the griffin's wings. The reins slackened in his hand. He swallowed, turning in his seat. Clutching the compass in one hand, Gwyndel studied the map, looking up to squint into the mist for any landmark. His heart sank at her vacant gaze. For hours, they had flown through this fog, trying to grope their way northward.

As if to will their fortunes to change, Eyoés closed his eyes, gripping the reins with shaking fists. "Have you found where we are?" he inquired, holding his breath.

Gwyndel slumped in her seat, refusing to look him in the eye. "No," she replied in a toneless voice. "We are lost in this mist."

Eyoés swore under his breath, turning away. Violently, he shook his head.

We are not lost. This mist will lift.

Gwyndel looked up, sensing her brother's denial. Tears obscuring her vision, she punched his shoulder with a cry.

"Look around you! Can you make this veil lift? Can you search for an enemy whose trail you've lost?" she shouted, her voice cracking. "You are not a hero— you're a fool who cannot accept or realize his own failures!"

Dropping the reins in his lap, Eyoés turned and seized her shoulder, the wildfire of his hatred burning behind his flinty glare. The muscles on his neck tensed. "I was trying to make it right!" he roared. "My father gave up his life in service to the people. Avenging them was the only way to pay for my cowardice!" Gwyndel looked into his eyes, shaking her head. The fury burning inside him waned as a tear ran down her cheek and she averted her eyes. Clenching his jaw, he turned away again.

"You are not like Father—and never will be," she whispered, her voice weakened by grief.

Eyoés tried to swallow the painful tightness in his throat. He hung his head, watching the mist below race by as Gibusil flew deeper into the blinding clouds. "Yes," he muttered to himself. "I am doomed to die in these dark mountains." Eyes watering, he took the griffin's reins in hand, peering into the fog for a place to land. A black mountaintop pierced through the mist.

Contemplating his fate, Eyoés guided Gibusil toward the solace of its peak. No longer could he hide from his shortcomings.

Lying on the cold, wet ground, Eyoés stared up into the sky. Rain dripped on his face, trickling into his eyes and mouth. He sat up, heart dully beating in his chest. Gibusil slept with his head tucked, extending his wing over the sleeping form of Gwyndel to shelter her from the rain. Thrown aside, their supplies waited, water seeping through the canvas. Eyoés stood, viewing the bare patch of ground with a blank expression. Memories of the journey circulated through his mind, thrusting him deeper into despair.

I have failed. I am unfit to follow Father's footsteps.

Eyoés stumbled further into the open, his clothing splattered with mud. The screams of the dying innocents of Asdale echoed in his ears, begging for a vengeance he could not provide. Chin trembling, he unbuckled his sword belt, feeling the familiar weight of his father's sword lift. He gripped the scabbard, trembling as he looked upon the weapon for the last time.

I am unworthy to own this weapon.

With a cry, he threw it across the clearing, watching with reddened eyes as the sword landed in a large puddle of rainwater. A gust of wind surged through his hair. Swaying unsteadily, he turned away.

"This revenge has destroyed you. It was not your responsibility to claim it," declared a gentle voice from behind. Eyoés spun around, his expression darkening at the familiar face.

You're following me?

Leaning upon his staff, the Guide ignored the youth's accusation, instead gazing into his eyes to expose his thoughts. Eyoés held his head high.

"It was forced upon me," he replied coldly.

The Guide shook his head. "A painful event does not force one to take action against it—revenge is not inevitable. It is a choice," he replied, setting a hand on Eyoés' shoulder.

Gruffly, the young man swatted it aside. "Was I supposed to watch them die, and do nothing to defeat the evil responsible?" he spat, pointing an accusing finger. "Why did the King let the citizens of Asdale burn? If the King really cares about his people, then why did Asdale fall?" He stepped back, tears welling in the corners of his eyes. His arm fell to his side.

A tear glistened on the Guide's cheek. "Asdale's destruction grieves me as well," he replied.

Eyoés hesitated, then strode toward the Guide, thrusting himself into the man's face. "Why did my parents die?" he shouted, teeth bared in a snarl.

The compassion in the Guide's eyes pierced him like a sword. "A world of suffering was never the King's intent. He is not responsible for evil. It is the Black Presence who brought bloodshed and death to this land," the man declared, throwing back his hood. "When the Deceived surrendered themselves to the Black Presence's power, they spread lies about the King's character, wreaking havoc among his people. Despite their evil, the King let the people choose their allegiance. He desired a chosen love, not a forced one. Those who rejected him blinded themselves to the truth. The only way sincere love can exist is by choice."

Eyoés stepped back with a spiteful laugh. "I know nothing of love," he snapped. "*Aványn* I once loved as a mother—before her lies were exposed. She robbed me of a true family, and instead kept me blinded because of her own fear!"

The Guide stepped closer, his cloak flowing behind in the wind. "She hid the truth because she knew you were not *ready* to face the evil in the world," he remarked. "And she raised you upon the King's words."

Sneering, Eyoés waved aside the man's statement. "I barely know Gwyndel because of Aványn's—"

"You barely know her because of *your* foolish actions," the Guide interrupted. Silence hung between them, broken only by the breeze and the haunting cries within the forest. The wind howled across the mountaintop, and Eyoés struggled to stand against the force of the gale. Shivering, he wrapped his arms around his shoulders. The Guide tossed aside his staff, grasping the young man's shoulders to keep him from falling.

Eyoés looked up into the man's deep eyes, hair pasted to his forehead by the rain. "If it is the King who avenges, why should I not follow his example, and execute vengeance for the wrongs of wicked men?" Eyoés said, voice faltering as his teeth chattered.

The Guide removed his white cloak and secured it around the young man's neck. "Look around you—has your quest for revenge brought anything else but pain and failure? No one can ever pay evil back its full measure. You will only destroy yourself in the attempt. It is the King's responsibility because he can never be led astray by passion. If he were to allow you to take up the mantle of judgement, its consuming power would ruin you," he answered, pulling the white cowl over Eyoés' head. "A bitter rage against your enemy has fueled your vengeance. You cannot deny it."

Wrapping the Guide's cloak tight around himself, Eyoés closed his eyes, recalling the fire and terror that had eclipsed the noble desires within. In his thoughts, he returned to the outskirts of Asdale, watching his home turn to ashes before his eyes. Dark patches hung below his bloodshot eyes. The warmth in the Guide's tone soothed the turmoil within him. Even as Eyoés kept his eyes closed, he felt the man's captivating gaze.

It is true. All I have is hate—and it will not leave me.

Eyoés leaned against the Guide's chest, shoulders heaving as he sobbed.

The Guide embraced him, the broken youth's tears wetting his garment. "Your father had a unique purpose. His legacy does not define you," he proclaimed.

At the mention of his father, Eyoés stifled his grief and left the Guide's embrace. "He was a hero," he stammered. "Noble and kind. I only wish I could be half the man he was."

244

The Guide stared into his eyes, his steady, firm gaze demanding attention. "The King was proud of him," he assured. "Yet you idolize him because, in your mind, he embodies everything good. He made mistakes. As do you."

Eyoés gritted his teeth, face contorting in disbelief. Drops of rain flew from his hair as he vehemently shook his head. "My father's mistakes never cost lives! Surely he was no fool!" he insisted, struggling to keep the image of his father from shattering. Staring at his feet, the Guide shook his head. Eyoés seized the man's arm, his gaze pleading.

"In one battle, your father rashly decided to attack the enemy head on. Half of his forces fell because of his decision. Élorn was crushed by his failure. The blood of those men haunted him for the rest of his life," the Guide revealed, setting an arm around the young man's shoulders. "You rob yourself by looking to your father to know who you are. Your failures become an obsession, forcing you to strive harder to achieve the false image of your father's greatness." Gently escorted by the Guide's arm, Eyoés walked beside his comforter. Mud caked his boots and spattered the white cloak he wore as he trudged further into the clearing.

His hands dropped limply to his sides. The jagged pieces of his father's broken image pierced him.

My father—responsible for the deaths of his own men?

Observing the youth's fallen countenance, the Guide smiled. "And *still* the King calls him a noble man," he maintained. "Yes, the events of a man's life influence and change him—yet the King openly offers him a new identity instead."

Eyoés said nothing, his expression grave as he weighed the Guide's words. Despite the wrenching pain at the mention of his father's failure, a sense of similarity pointed to a shared struggle. The truth of his father's character seemed more attainable than the image he had struggled to maintain.

How could I have been so sure of his character when I had never known him?

Eyoés recalled the many nights spent longing to be like his father. The sting of his failures pricked him, fiercer than the bite of the cold.

Perhaps I can start anew. No longer will I let these failures and losses determine my course.

He looked into the Guide's patient eyes. "Aványn —I was indebted to her, yet I refused to admit it. Why did I not apologize? If I had known of the attack—" he confessed. His stomach surged with nausea at the thought of her death. The Guide's kind gaze convicted him. "I have only destroyed myself—and those around me," he admitted, voice broken. "What must I do to leave this behind?"

With a smile, the Guide stopped. He grasped Eyoés by the shoulders and turned him around to look him in the eye. "Leave the hatred and bitterness behind, and seek your identity in the King's good grace," he answered.

Releasing one of the young man's shoulders, the Guide flattened his palm and pressed it against Eyoés' heart. Eyoés cried out as a sudden jolt raced throughout

246

his body. Strength filled him as the tingling electricity coursed through his limbs like fire, raising the hairs on his arms and legs. A disarming warmth replaced the cold grip of despair holding him captive. A wide grin spread over his face, unable to be contained. The heaviness of his desire for vengeance vanished from his thoughts as a peace took its place. Then, as soon as it had begun, the strange sensation ceased, fading from his limbs as the Guide withdrew his hand.

Eyoés released a sigh, kneeling before the man who had cleansed him. "I owe you my life," he declared, unbuttoning the white cloak from around his neck. He reverently folded the garment and extended it to the Guide. Taking the cloak from the young man's hands, the Guide fastened it around his own neck. The mud that had splattered the white cloak faded to nothing.

With a chuckle, he grasped the youth's hands and pulled him to his feet. "Your journey is not yet finished," he chided kindly.

Eyoés frowned, furrowing his eyebrows as he tried to understand. "This quest was rooted in revenge," he pointed out. "If vengeance is dangerous, then why should I continue? I don't understand."

The Guide extended his hand, pointing to Élorn's sword, covered in mud and lying in a puddle of rain. "Sometimes, the King will work through a person to aid in the restoration of integrity to the land," he explained, letting his hand fall to his side. "However, you must remember that he chooses you because of *his* plan, not yours. He will give you victory in your time of need." The Guide strode to where his staff lay on muddy ground. Taking it in hand, he stood, leaning his weight upon the solid rod. He locked eyes with Eyoés.

"In later days, when evil swarms over the land, the King will sound the horn to summon his army. Await it," he called over the rushing wind. Eyoés bowed his head in submission. "I will," he answered, the conviction in his tone stirring the gratitude in his heart.

The Guide continued, "Tomorrow morning, at the second hour of sunrise, look for the light amid the mist. I will show you the way."

Eyoés looked up. The man was gone. Pursing his lips, Eyoés turned toward his fallen sword.

I no longer will carry this sword for myself.

He dashed toward the fallen weapon, mud spraying with each step. Halting short of his mark, he studied the familiar crosspiece with a new mind.

My father carried this for a noble purpose, and so will I.

Reaching down, he grasped the weapon with soiled hands and tears of gratitude. He buckled the sword to his waist.

"How does it feel to stand in freedom?" Gwyndel inquired from behind. Eyoés jumped, spinning on his heels to face her. Wrapped in her thick wool blanket, Gwyndel shivered, yet her eyes glowed with a brightness he had not seen before. Looking into the sky, Eyoés smiled to himself.

"It's frightening—as if I'm not sure I belong there," he replied, his voice choked with emotion. "Yet, I don't want to leave."

39

Gripping the reins, Eyoés peered into the mist, eyes bright with hope. The previous night's sleep had been unlike any before, full of peace and an assurance that the King watched over him. He recalled the Guide's words.

Tomorrow morning, at the second hour of sunrise, look for the light amid the mist. I will show you the way.

Eyoés steadied himself as Gibusil caught the wind underneath his wings. He leaned forward, holding his breath as he sought for the promised beacon. From her seat, Gwyndel searched the fog behind them for the Guide's sign. She marveled over the unexpected change in her brother.

Although welcome, the absence of his hate and foolishness had transformed him into a man she could hardly recognize. A smile built on her face.

Thank the King he has seen the truth.

Eyoés cried out, rising in his seat as he pointed into the deep fog to their right. An ethereal glow pierced through the mist. Sensing the riders' eagerness, the griffin surged toward it. Gliding through the thick fog, they trusted in the light they followed.

Suddenly, Gibusil burst out of the choking mist. Eyoés squinted at the sudden brightness of the overcast sky and gave a shout of triumph. Squeezing her brother's shoulders, Gwyndel smiled as they left the oppression of the fog behind them. Below, a wide, blackened valley gaped like the jaws of the underworld. From the top of a nearby mountain, the brilliant light guided them to a safe landing. Shielding his eyes with one hand, Eyoés guided the griffin toward the mountaintop. As they approached, the radiance grew, casting a stark shadow as in competition with the sun. Unable to see to steer Gibusil any further, he relinquished the reins and let the beast find its way.

Through the halo of light, he glimpsed the ground as the griffin came to an uneasy landing, wings spread wide to slow its descent. As soon as the beast had steadied itself, Eyoés untied the harness from his belt. Patting Gibusil's shoulder in appreciation, he dismounted along with Gwyndel. The glow quickly dimmed, revealing the cloaked form of the Guide awaiting their arrival. Eyoés leaned forward, watching with awe as the last remaining light faded from within the crook at the top of the Guide's staff.

The cloaked man struggled to contain a chuckle at their amazed expressions. His countenance grew serious. "Behold, Nys-Felz," he declared, sweeping his hand across the landscape behind him, "the Forgotten Place."

As Eyoés followed the man's hand, a sudden coldness seized his heart. Another hulking mountain loomed from across the broad valley, its jagged peak like a wolf's fang. From within a deep gash in the mountainside, an ebony fortress dared them to approach. Eyoés felt the hair rise on his arms as deep, rhythmic chants of drilling troops came from the mountain. A sensation of dominance emanated from the fortress as its haughty, dark gaze contemplated their arrival.

Eyoés turned to the Guide. "Why have you brought us here?" he inquired with a tremor in his voice.

The Guide stared into the young man's eyes. "Skreon plans to muster his forces and usurp the King's throne—and you are the one to bring about his downfall," he declared, striking the ground with the bottom of his staff.

Running his hand through his hair, Eyoés glanced toward the dark fortress and shook his head. "I cannot," he hastily replied. "I am alone! I will die if I set foot in that murderous place! There are too many of them."

The Guide stepped forward, his piercing gaze demanding attention. "You will not be alone!" he reassured him. Eyoés opened his mouth to object.

The hushed, steady procession of soldiers marching in time rose above the silence of the mountaintop. Eyoés and Gwyndel turned in wonder. Dark teal flags towered above a nearby ridge, rising higher by the second. Sucking in a quick breath, Eyoés set aside the thought of the imposing fortress. Emblazoned upon each flag—was the familiar diamond and pick emblem of Nubaroz.

How did they find us?

He spun on his heels to face the Guide. "I don't

understand," he remarked, eyebrows furrowed together. "Why are they here?"

The Guide glanced toward the approaching army of dwarves. "They have come to aid you in the coming battle," he answered.

The cadence of marching grew louder. "Why continue this quest of vengeance if it is not my responsibility?" he asked, shaking his head.

A smile spread across the Guide's face as the youth's inner change was evidenced in his words. He set a hand on Eyoés' shoulder and his expression turned serious. "More people will die in this war than in Asdale's destruction if Skreon carries out his plan," he urged. "The King will lead you to victory—but you must *face* this evil."

Licking his lips, Eyoés stared vacantly at his feet. As the haunting cries of the dying returned, a pang of grief struck him with the force of a knife.

I cannot run again. The time has come for me to stand.

Looking up, he tightened his fists. He held himself high. "I will fight Skreon," he avowed with a curt nod.

The Guide nodded in return and pulled him aside. Glancing toward the fortress, he leaned closer to the young man's face. "I must tell you another thing," he whispered. "Skreon's pride is his weakness. He assumes his enemies to be inept. He will not expect to be the target of a united attack."

Swallowing, Eyoés looked down at his sword with a frown. "Am I ready?" he questioned.

The Guide nodded. "Your father's journal taught

you what you need to know," he said, looking into the sky. "He smiles upon you from the Kingdom above the stars."

Looking skyward, Eyoés wiped a tear from his eye. The thought of his father's loving gaze looking upon him with approval stirred his confidence. He met the Guide's eyes and cleared his throat.

"Thank you," he said, relieved. The Guide smiled and removed his hand. As the dwarves' march came to an end, Eyoés hurried to Gibusil, eager to make amends to the Dwarf Lord.

As the dwarves went about their duties, they spoke with their comrades in hushed voices. Tents of thick, blue waxed wool were framed by sturdy wooden rods, each boasting the insignia of their assigned division. The monotonous clang of the blacksmith's hammer resounded deep within the camp. From the forge fires, wisps of smoke rose into the air like columns, accompanied by the grating shriek of sharpening weapons.

Dismounting from Gibusil's back, Eyoés helped Gwyndel down from her seat. Wrinkling his nose at the pungent odor of smoldering metal, Eyoés spotted the roof of Lord Ardul's pavilion. He hesitated, recalling the insults he had spoken against the Dwarf Lord.

I must apologize for my actions. It was wrong of me to disregard his concern for his people.

Noticing his hesitation, Gwyndel strode into the dwarves' midst. Eyoés tucked his head and followed. As the two pressed on toward Ardul's pavilion, they felt the stares of the dwarves on their backs. Rounding a bend in the central pathway, they stopped. Amid the haste of the camp, a quiet path led to the pavilion entrance. Gwyndel paused to collect herself. Sighing, she led the way with Eyoés in tow. Masterful artwork adorned the walls of the tent, and a large flag crowned its roof. At the tent entrance, they halted. Gwyndel knocked on the frame of the doorway.

"Enter," the strong voice from within beckoned. Lifting the flap with her forearm, Gwyndel entered, followed closely by her brother. Large animal pelts covered the ground within. Several chairs were scattered around the interior, awaiting the arrival of various officers and aides. Situated in the back of the tent, a large table was flanked by two pennants bearing the symbol of Nubaroz. Leaning on the corner of his desk, Lord Ardul turned. His tawny hair was braided behind his head for ease in battle. At the sight of Gwyndel, his countenance brightened.

"Welcome, my friend," he beamed, gesturing to one of the chairs. Bowing, Gwyndel grabbed the back of the nearest chair and moved it closer to the Dwarf Lord's desk. As she seated herself, Lord Ardul's gaze drifted to Eyoés. The grin on his face faded into a curt smile.

Eyoés bowed and stepped forward. "Lord Ardul," he sighed, clearing his throat. "I was a fool to disrespect you and mock your ways. I do not want to be an enemy. Please forgive me."

The disgust in Lord Ardul's eyes waned at the honesty in the young man's tone. Pausing, the Dwarf Lord lifted an eyebrow and nodded, releasing a sigh through his nose. "If we are to fight against Skreon, we must become like brothers. Trust is sometimes better than a blade," he declared, extending a hand toward the young warrior.

Eyoés took the dwarf's hand in a firm grip. "Then I will earn your trust," he agreed.

Gwyndel stood from her seat. "How did you find us? Why did you come to fight by our side?" she inquired.

Lord Ardul released Eyoés' hand. "The day you departed from my halls, the Guide came to me in a dream," he explained, looking away. "He told me of Skreon's fell plot and of the King's plan to use you both to bring the downfall of this wicked Gahrim. He beckoned me to come in haste." Stirring himself from his musings, Ardul strode to his desk. "My aides had the same dream. I could not disregard it," he concluded.

Eyoés glanced toward his sister.

This is no coincidence.

Meeting his glance, Gwyndel stepped toward the Dwarf Lord's desk, leaning against its sturdy hardwood frame. She locked eyes with Lord Ardul. "Are your people ready to die for this quest?" she asked.

The Dwarf Lord paused, then leaned in. "Yes," he replied with a furrowed brow. "The Guide himself has summoned us—we will not back down." His expression softened as he circled around the desk to where Gwyndel stood. "Your kindness gave us a glimpse of the King's love for us. We were wrong to estrange ourselves from his people," he confided, nodding toward Eyoés. "I have come to see that he can take even the worst of men and turn them into sons."

Exhaling, Gwyndel stepped back, face solemn. It was inevitable that dwarf blood would be spilled the next day. As she turned away, she muttered a fervent prayer to the King.

Let us have victory—do not let these lives be shed for nothing.

A moment of silence hung between them as they weighed the consequences. The swish of the tent entrance flap broke the stillness. Stepping into the pavilion, Ból opened his mouth to speak, then was silenced by the presence of the two warriors. He nodded toward Gwyndel in respect, then backed away from Eyoés. Eyes narrowed, he regarded the young man with a probing gaze.

Lord Ardul gestured for the dwarf to enter. "You may approach, Ból. Eyoés has expressed his regret at his actions and is to be treated as a friend and ally," he announced.

Ból bowed, giving one last glance toward the former troublemaker. "As you wish, Lord Ardul," he agreed, nearing the Dwarf Lord's desk.

Eyoés stepped forward. "What is our plan of attack?" he inquired, grabbing a nearby chair and setting it close to the desk.

Nodding in approval, Ardul reached under his desk and withdrew a large scroll. Smudges of dirt covered the creased parchment, and several insect holes pierced one corner. Untying the leather strip wrapped around its center, Ardul unrolled the parchment upon the desk. Although faded by age, the ink diagram sketched upon its surface could still be read. A small section of text was written in the top corner.

Eyoés raised an eyebrow.

A diagram of Nys-Felz?

"How did you get this?" he questioned, leaning in to closely examine the sketch.

Lord Ardul pointed to a dwarven emblem drawn below the diagram. "During the War of Adrógar, the dwarves of Qelezal ventured into Zwaoi, intending to found a colony for refugees. Nys-Felz was built as a military fortress to watch over the newfound settlement. However, near the end of the construction, a tribe of Hobgoblins forced my kin to abandon the outpost," he explained. "Two copies were made of these plans, and one of them fell into our possession at the War's end." The Dwarf Lord paused, inspecting the diagram as he strategized his next move.

Snaking through the peak of the mountain, several shafts were connected to central chambers deep below the fortress. Intrigued, he tapped one of the thin lines with his forefinger. "Air shafts—a necessary step to allow underground settlement. Too many, and you weaken the mountainside. If compromised, the tunnels could collapse upon themselves," he mused, stroking his chin.

With excitement, Bról nodded. "By dropping barrels of Duraval oil into these shafts, we might bring the mountain upon their heads," he speculated.

Lord Ardul nodded. "I will summon our best warriors for an assault from the air on dragonback. Our enemies will not be able to withstand such a bombardment," he declared, pointing toward a sketch of the drilling field. "Eyoés and Gwyndel will lead a squad of our troops to clear the front gate—most of the enemy's forces will be too occupied with our attack on their rear to notice. Bról, when Eyoés signals you, lead your battalion to the front gates. Break down the doors and fill the caverns with as many barrels of Duraval oil as you can, then torch the barrels and fall back. The remainder of our army will storm the lower gate at the mountain's base. We will rout these repulsive creatures from the mountain."

Bról bowed, hands clasped behind his back. "If it so pleases you, Lord Ardul. Your vassals await your command," he said, shoulders held back.

Stepping into the stable tent, Bról looked about the stalls. The racket of dragon chatter made his ears ring. Temporary pens separated the creatures from each other, lining either side of the long structure. At his entry, one of the dragons lifted its head and released a friendly yap. A stripe of dark red scales marked its forehead.

Striding over to the stall, Bról stroked the creature's cool, rough snout. "Good morning, Throggon," he replied with a smile. "Tomorrow we shall storm the gates of Nys-Felz together, as always." The dragon let out a low rumble, just as though he agreed. Giving the creature a pat, Bról moved on. A flash of golden feathers several enclosures away attracted his eye.

There you are.

He approached the pen with caution, putting some distance between him and the stall's gate. Settling himself in for a rest, Gibusil looked up. At the sight of the strange dwarf, the griffin came to its feet and snarled, its crowning feathers raised. Bról opened his palms wide to assure the beast of his good intentions.

"Throggon and I will fight by your side," he said, captivated by the griffin's graceful appearance. Gibusil studied the newcomer, then, sensing there was nothing to fear, lay down to rest once again. "I brought you something," Bról continued, letting his hand fall to the bag by his side. Opening the flap, he retrieved a small portion of meat from within and tossed it into the enclosure. The griffin paused, sniffing the food, then devoured it. With a chirp, Gibusil nuzzled the dwarf's hand through the gate.

Bról smiled, grateful for the calm before the coming storm.

40

Wiping sweat from his palms, Eyoés gripped Gibusil's reins as they drew ever closer to the black fortress of Nys-Felz. His heart raced as he looked furtively at the two dwarves beside him, Etherul and Fódral. Encased in thick plate armor, they looked grimly onward, steering their dragon mounts toward the enemy. As they rode the howling wind, the dragons chomped at their bits, stirred to aggression by hunger. Their dark grey scales seemed to be carved of stone, and short snouts gave their skulls a strong appearance. Large plates of armor were fastened over their heads and chests by chains.

Turning his gaze forward, Eyoés rehearsed the strategy to himself, riding behind Ardul's forces. The low rumble of Lord Ardul's war horn shook him from his thoughts. With a roar, the Dwarf Lord plunged toward the dark mountain, guiding his dragon around the back of the fortress. Screaming battle cries, the dwarf ranks followed their leader, each with a barrel clutched in their dragon's claws. Cries of panic rose from the fortress drilling field as the Hobgoblins ceased their training, rushing to form ranks against their attackers. Eyoés questioned his decision to leave Fóbehn behind.

It was the right choice. In the wrong hands, its

power would be used for evil.

Summoning his bravery, he furrowed his brow and pressed on. Deep, intermittent thumps added to the chaos of war. Flashes of brown tore through the air, whistling past Gibusil's wings. Screams burst from Ardul's ranks as thick darts plucked several dragons from the sky and threw their riders into the valley below. As Eyoés drew nearer, he recognized the familiar weapon.

Ballistas. Like in Father's journal.

Unfazed, Lord Ardul veered to the left, urging his dragon mount to a dizzying speed as he circled to the back of the mountain. The dwarf ranks followed on his heels, shielded by the mountainside. Clouds of smoke rose from the back of the mountain as the barrels of Duraval oil burst upon impact. The drilling Hobgoblins surged back into the gates to defend their stronghold. Eyoés loosened his sword in its scabbard. A small contingent of troops remained to man the ballistas. Gwyndel nocked an arrow, squeezing the griffin's sides with her knees to balance herself. Tensed for action, Eyoés spurred Gibusil onward, flanked by the two dwarves. The Hobgoblins failed to notice the three approaching attackers amid the chaos of battle.

Eyoés pulled up on the reins. With a screech, Gibusil landed. Hobgoblins whirled around to face them, screaming curses in their native tongue. Leaping from the griffin's back, Eyoés drew his sword alongside the two dwarves.

The nearest Hobgoblin fell victim to Gwyndel's readied arrow. Eyoés narrowly evaded a serrated spear point. Etherul smashed a massive war hammer into the creature's face in reply. His dragon raced toward the nearest ballista with a booming roar. With a thud, the Hobgoblins fired, lodging the bolt deep into the dragon's chest. The dragon released a stifled roar and plowed into the rock surface. Grieved by the death of his steed, Etherul hesitated. A Hobgoblin shouted in triumph, smashing its mace into the dwarf's side. Gwyndel leapt over one of the fallen brutes, her anger raging at the sight of the stricken dwarf. The hideous beast's triumph was cut short by her arrow.

Sickened by Etherul's sacrifice, Eyoés pressed on, determined to wipe out this loathsome enemy. Roaring, he lunged forward, viciously cutting down an enemy with his blade. At the twang of Gwyndel's bowstring, more of the repulsive savages felt the sting of her arrows. Two Hobgoblins dropped their weapons in pain as their fighting arms were strategically disabled. In a single stride, Fódral slew them with a swipe of his axe.

A surge of triumph swept through Eyoés as he approached the nearest ballista. Watching with dread, the two Hobgoblins struggled to wind the immense machine for the next shot. As they fumbled to lift the thick bolt into place, Gwyndel raced ahead of her companions. Shouldering her bow, she drew two throwing knives from her belt, and with a flick of her wrist, the first blade felled the closest enemy. Crying in agony, the creature tumbled back, its black, mottled face twisted in pain. The bolt clattered to the ground. Gwyndel's second knife cut the Hobgoblin's cries short.

Eyes wide with horror, the second beast struggled to draw his weapon. Gwyndel shrugged her bow from her shoulder and loosed an arrow in a single movement. The Hobgoblin fell with a shout and lay still. Eyoés sheathed his sword and beckoned for Fódral. He gritted his teeth as he lifted the fallen dart, struggling to place it correctly. The weight lifted as the dwarf added his strength. Hurriedly, they placed the bolt and fully cranked the rope trigger back. Gwyndel retrieved her dagger, a sheen of sweat covering her forehead and neck. She looked toward the ballista stationed opposite. The distant Hobgoblins shrugged the bolt off their shoulders and securely fastened the projectile with a click.

There was no time to lose. "Aim for the second ballista! Push away from you!" she commanded, pulling against the wooden frame. Setting their shoulders against the oak structure, Eyoés and his comrade strained against its weight. The ballista inched toward their target. Eyoés ignored the weakness in his thighs and planted his heels. The weapon gave way, scraping across the stone.

"Clear away!" Gwyndel shouted, yanking the rope trigger. With a shudder, the tension on the weapon's double bows was released. The bolt crashed into their target, throwing the Hobgoblins backwards amid a cloud of shrapnel. Gibusil and Fodrál's dragon bounded toward them.

Eyoés seized the war horn looped across his chest. The explosions from the mountain's rear echoed through the black mountain range.

Let the sacrifice not be in vain—and let this battle be decisive.

He pressed the horn to his lips and blew.

Like a swarm of insects, the dragons of Nubaroz dove as one upon the mountain's back once again, their grey hides morphing with the overcast sky. Tunnels peered out from the mountainside, rims blackened by the exploding barrels. Jagged craters were punched into the stone wall, stuffed with the debris and rubble of collapsed tunnels. Bellowing war cries, the dwarves swept across the mountainside, dropping several barrels of Duraval oil into the remaining shafts. Clouds of dust erupted from the openings as the stone crumbled.

Trapped within their stronghold, the Hobgoblins inside struggled to maintain their defense. Mustering their combined strength, they blocked the largest tunnels with great piles of rubble in hopes of withstanding the bombardment. Blowing a long blast on his war horn, Lord Ardul circled his troops about for another strike. The thud of the exploding barrels deafened those inside the fortress. Rubble exploded into the central chamber, burying a squad of the foul creatures. Escape was no option.

At the mountain's base, another battle raged entirely. Screaming cries of courage, the dwarf battalion readied themselves, lances bristling like a dragon's spines. Before them, an immense gateway jutted from the foot of the mountain, the steepled entry barred shut by a single metal door. Undaunted, the troops stepped neatly aside in two divisions to form a wide pathway between them. Their cries increased as a squad of their brethren ran through the path, carrying a thick log by the stubby ends of shorn branches. With a roar, they drove the ram into the door's center. The metal hinges shrieked in protest, twisting from the force of the impact.

Recoiling, the dwarves regained their hold upon their battering ram. Cheered on by their comrades, they struck again. The metal buckled under the pressure, its dented surface casting odd shadows. Muffled cries of anger erupted from behind the door. With a final roar of defiance, the dwarves thrust the ram forward with tremendous strength.

The door blew back upon its hinges amid a shower of splinters as the wooden plank holding it shut gave way. Carried by the momentum of the blow, the squad of dwarves burst through the shrapnel and into the entryway. With dark screams of rage, the Hobgoblins within swarmed over the invaders, slaying the small company of dwarves with their grim blades. The front line of dwarves marched forward to fill the void left by their comrades, kneeling before the oncoming foe and planting the bottom of their lances into the ground for support. As the Hobgoblins leapt forward, they found themselves pouncing on the bristling wall of pikes.

Ghastly howls issued from within the entry as a pack of Kélak pounced into battle. Many impaled themselves upon the dwarves' spears, clawing viciously at their enemies. Several narrowly avoided the iron tips and seeped through the dwarf ranks. Drawn by the clamor of battle, a second wave of Hobgoblins stopped short, then drew back into the darkness of the mountain. Absorbed with the rigors of battle, the dwarves saw nothing of their retreat.

Emerging from the darkness, a ballista rolled into view inside the entryway. A cracking snap pierced through the chaos of war as the bolt tore through the dwarf ranks, killing several of the skirmishing Hobgoblins alongside their foes. Raising their shields, the dwarves ran forward in unison, the ground quaking with their advance.

The Hobgoblins rushed to load another bolt, panic stricken.

41

A rush of adrenaline surged through Eyoés as the piercing blast of his horn rang across the valley. Glancing over his shoulder toward the fortress gate, he wiped the sweat from his upper lip. He could only hope the Hobgoblin army in the rear was too distracted by Lord Ardul's forces to hear them. From across the valley, another blast answered his call. He fingered the pommel of his sword. The weight of battle lifted as he caught sight of Bról's division of dragons racing toward them. Battered by the mountain wind, the dwarves struggled to control their flight path. Eyoés bit the inside of his cheek as they neared ever closer.

If they are caught out in the open...

A familiar, shrieking roar sent chills up his spine. Shaking his head in disbelief, Eyoés drew his sword, the heat draining from his limbs. A pale blur dove from the clouds above, ramming like lightning into the ranks of the oncoming dwarves. Several of the dwarves' dragons plummeted from the sky, crippled by the Whiteblood's strike. Blowing streams of fire as one, the survivors advanced upon the Norzaid. Their flames rolled harmlessly in spirals over the monster's pale skin. In retaliation, the ghastly wyrm lashed the dwarves with its sawtoothed tail, flinging a spray of mangled troops and dragons through the air. Eyoés screamed in anguish, unable to come to their defense. As if to increase his misery, the Whiteblood flared its blood-red frills and released a pillar of fire. Helpless against the beast's vicious attack, the dwarves fell back to their camp in haste.

Eyoés stepped back and gripped his sword with white knuckles, blanching at the carnage. With a roar, the Whiteblood Norzaid turned its fury upon the drilling field, its red eyes pinning the young warrior to his spot. Eyoés readied himself, encouraged by the presence of his comrades. He planted his stance wide.

I will not let this creature live.

The Norzaid raced toward them, its steady wingbeats thumping on the brisk air. As it approached, Eyoés could make out a bulky figure atop the beast's back, covered in lavish black armor. Though the man's face was hidden behind a massive helm, Eyoés knew his identity. Gliding to a stop, the Whiteblood landed at the drilling field's edge. Its curved, black claws gouged deep scratches into the rock. The armored figure cast aside the reins and dismounted.

Hiding his fear behind a dark frown, Eyoés pointed the tip of his sword toward his enemy. "Skreon. The Ashen Specter. I have been expecting you," he declared with a bite in his voice.

With a chuckle of derision, the figure removed his helm and cast it aside with a clang. Eyoés stood still at the sight of the fallen Gahrim's red gaze. A cold smirk spread over the albino's pasty features. "Have you?" he inquired with a harsh squint. "I would have expected a *man* to challenge me."

Eyoés swallowed hard, unconsciously letting the tip of his sword drop. He knew Skreon was right. The mistakes of his past returned to haunt him, and he looked away, pained. "Once, I was a boy who cared only for his own aspirations," Eyoés confessed, the burden of his foolishness pulling him downward.

Jutting his chin, Skreon smiled as his slander hit home.

A man's confidence is as weak as his skin. Break it, and he bleeds.

An inner glow grew behind the young warrior's eyes, wiping the smile from Skreon's face. Looking the albino in the eye, Eyoés stepped forward. "I've seen the King's grace, and I will never turn from him. I *am* a man," he proclaimed, holding his sword at the ready.

At the mention of the King's name, Skreon tensed and stared at Eyoés with a black anger. "Then prove yourself," he hissed, clapping his gauntlets together.

Shrieking in eagerness, the Whiteblood pounced. A blast of fire coursed from its mouth, consuming Fódral and engulfing the ballista behind them in a ball of fire. Eyoés fell back, heat sweeping across his face. Fódral's dragon rammed into the Whiteblood's side, scudding the pale beast across the drilling field. Its crimson gaze burning with hateful fire, Skreon's monster dug its claws into the stone.

Thrusting off the mountainside, the Whiteblood tackled Fódral's burly dragon and pinned it to the ground. Gwyndel fell back, waiting for an opening. Screeching, Gibusil sprang into the fray and latched onto the Norzaid's unprotected back. Shrieking, the dragon twisted violently backwards, releasing its victim and swiping at the griffin with its claws. The dwarven dragon pounced again, only to be knocked into the ravine below by a sweep of the Whiteblood's jagged tail.

Skreon gave a crisp nod, captivated by the unfolding chaos. Frenzied by the darting griffin, the Norzaid lashed out in anger. Eyoés wasted no time. Bursting into a sprint, he hacked at the dragon's tail, chipping a scale loose. Swatting Gibusil aside, the pale monster knocked Eyoés off his feet with its wicked whip. The young warrior bounced to his feet and sheathed his sword, wary of both ends of the creature. Infuriated, he scrubbed a hand over his face. This dragon was a distraction.

He shoved his fingers into his mouth and emitted a piercing whistle. The griffin bolted around the Norzaid's snapping jaws and swooped low. Eyoés leapt onto Gibusil, feeling a gust of wind surge against his back as the Whiteblood's claws swiped harmlessly behind. Turning to follow its escaping prey, the Norzaid shrieked in pain as Gwyndel's arrow suddenly sunk into its right eye. Flaring its neck frills, the beast fell back, clawing at the stinging thorn. Eyoés seized Gibusil's reins.

Approaching on its blind side will give us the advantage of surprise.

Wheeling the griffin around the dragon's blindspot, Eyoés jumped from his seat. He landed on the monster's neck, swaying unsteadily as he struggled to gain his balance. Sensing the unwanted rider, the dragon tossed its head with a roar. Eyoés flicked his head toward the valley.

"Get Bról!" he commanded. The griffin thrust its wings outward and wheeled away toward the valley. Eyoés laid against the smooth scales of the Norzaid, clinging for his life and grimacing as its short spines scraped his calf. Another of Gwyndel's arrows glanced off the Whiteblood's foreleg. Flaring its frills, the dragon answered with a blast of fire. Gwyndel fell to the ground as the dragon scorched the fortress wall behind her. She clenched her fists as her back blistered from the heat, and gagged at the putrid odor of her singed hair. The flames vanished into wisps of smoke above her.

As the dragon's frills retracted, Eyoés glimpsed the still form of his sister lying below a charred wall. Shaking, he willed her to rise. A sharp pain pierced him in the chest.

No. She cannot be dead.

A lingering uncertainty implored him to rush to her side. His throat lurched as the Norzaid reared with a roar. A soft patch of unarmored skin caught his eye, nestled in the crook behind the dragon's frills. Heaving himself further up the dragon's neck, Eyoés furrowed his brow and drew his sword. Time demanded action.

From the corner of his eye, he glimpsed Skreon seizing a fallen Hobgoblin spear. Instinctively, Eyoés whipped back. With a metallic hum, the flying spearpoint narrowly missed him, nicking his forearm as it flew past. Drawing his sword, Skreon vaulted over the Whiteblood's swinging tail and raced toward the fallen form of Gwyndel.

Eyoés looked on in horror, envisioning the black blade descending upon her neck. "Don't touch her!" he screamed.

The albino paid no heed. Startled by the sudden exclamation, Gwyndel slowly rose, emerging from the shock of her narrow escape. She caught sight of Skreon and backed away, nearly tripping over the fallen bodies of the Hobgoblins. Eyoés screamed in panicked fury, burying his blade into the dragon's soft skin.

The Norzaid's trembling shriek shook the mountainside. Eyoés clung to his sword, gripping with his legs as the creature thrashed its head. With a final cry of agony, the dragon fell into a shuddering heap—then lay still, its gaping maw revealing stained teeth within. Trembling, Eyoés set his foot against the creature's skull and pulled. His father's sword slid free of the wound. Memories of Asdale's bloody carnage flashed through his mind.

The Ashen Specter's steed has fallen.

Mouth agape, Skreon stared back at the slain carcass, frozen to the spot.

Leaping from the fallen dragon, Eyoés rushed to Gwyndel's side. Wild eyed, he stood between his sister and the shocked albino, extending his sword. "Do—not —touch—her, fiend," he commanded with a trembling voice. Gwyndel swallowed the knot in her throat.

Skreon turned, his unfocused stare riveted on the quavering hero. A bestial growl rose from within. "Say what you will," he snapped. "Luck never saved anyone for long." With a spiteful laugh, Skreon backhanded the youth with his gauntlet.

Clutching his cheekbone with his free hand, Eyoés stumbled backwards and lashed out with his sword. The tip of his blade etched a chalky white line into Skreon's ebony breastplate. Swatting the sword aside, the dark lord advanced, battering against Eyoés' meager defenses with his blade. Gwyndel retrieved her fallen bow and quiver and loosed an arrow. The arrowhead glanced off the albino's armor and disappeared among the fallen. Heart racing, Eyoés struggled to hold his own. A cold sweat broke out over his forehead.

I have seen the sun for the final time.

The thought of Skreon's blade piercing him made him cringe. His heart leapt into his throat as he tripped over a fallen spear shaft. Gwyndel's face turned ashen.

Eager to take his vengeance, the fallen Gahrim shoved the youth to the ground. "You are expendable —nothing more than a mere pawn," he laughed in mockery. The dark lord's contempt was eclipsed by a booming roar and the battle cries of a hundred dwarves.

Skreon spun on his heels. Directly above, a host of dragons bore down upon them, large barrels clasped in their claws. With shouts of victory, their dwarf riders followed Gibusil onward, brandishing their weapons with zeal and eagerness for battle. The albino's stomach clenched. Suspended by thick rope, a battering ram hung beneath two of the creatures. Skreon shook his head, running his hand through his hair. Even through the hatred of his heart, he could see the truth.

My forces are now spread between three fronts. I cannot defend this ground much longer.

Cheers from behind startled him. Thrusting his sword upward in triumph, Eyoés pulled Gwyndel close. "Bról! Gibusil!" he shouted with all the volume he could muster.

Skreon swiftly turned and kicked the young warrior backwards and renewed his attack with a growl. Shrieking in anger, Gibusil lunged toward the albino. Skreon fell to his knees, feeling the griffin's talons swipe over his head.

Pulling back on his dragon's reins, Bról turned to face them, his thick iron helm obscuring his features. Briskly, he gestured for his troops to press forward. The company of dwarves dove, pulling abruptly short of the landing point. At the blast of a horn, they severed the cords holding the battering ram in place. The dwarves dismounted at once and rolled the barrels into a large cluster, avoiding the body of the Norzaid. Spurring Throggon toward his desperate companions, Bról gripped the handle of his flanged mace. Again, the griffin dove, knocking Skreon to the ground with its wing. The dark lord sprang to his feet, slicing at empty air.

At the sight of the fallen Gahrim, Bról gritted his teeth.

I must catch him off guard.

He brought his dragon to a soft landing and threw himself from the saddle. Rushing toward Skreon from the rear, Bról slammed his mace into the albino's side. The dark lord reeled from the blow, gasping to regain the air knocked from his lungs. A booming thud on the fortress gate arrested his gaze. Again, the dwarves struck. Stricken by the sight of the growing dent, Skreon pulled his eyes away. Seeing the desperation in his black gaze, Gwyndel hastily shouldered her bow and seized a fallen Hobgoblin sword. Eyoés, blinded by the hope of victory, could not see her hesitancy. He dashed toward his fallen enemy.

Skreon vanished before their eyes like a wraith.

Gibusil pulled upwards, hovering in the air above. Breath catching in his throat, Eyoés skidded to a standstill. His wide eyes darted back and forth for sign of the hidden foe. "Where—" his remark was cut off as an invisible blow slammed into his midsection. Gwyndel fell back, swinging the Hobgoblin sword through the empty air.

Digging into a pouch on his belt, Bról scooped a pile of blue-green powder into his hands, careful not to expose it to light. "It takes deep concentration to disappear," he muttered. "He will not see this coming." The dwarf tossed the Gesadith powder into the air. Exposed to sunlight, the dust burst in a blinding flash. Skreon materialized with a cry and fell to his knees behind Eyoés, dropping his sword on the stone.

Gibusil bolted for Skreon. "No!" Eyoés commanded, holding out his hand. The griffin relented.

Bról chuckled in triumph. "Thought you'd torment us before running us through, did you?" he spat, the steady thud of the battering ram backing his words. "I've fought alongside your kin. I know their wiles."

The sudden, shrill creak of broken metal heralded

the dwarves' victory. With a final tumultuous shove, they drove the gates inward. Dropping the ram, the armored company cautiously tilted the barrels of Duraval oil on their sides and rolled them into the black cavern.

Skreon watched with a tormented gaze as his aspirations perished before his eyes.

Centuries of toil—for nothing. Nothing more than a meaningless ruin.

In a final act of desperate contempt, he turned to face his foes. "A coward conceals his flaws behind the veil of unity," he mocked, struggling to conceal his misery.

With a gleam in his eye, Eyoés tilted his head back and placed the tip of his sword against Skreon's breastplate. He smiled as the King's peace lightened his chest. "And a fool humiliates himself by his own insults," he replied.

Silent, Skreon gnashed his teeth in fury. "Who dares to ruin me?" he challenged.

Bról stepped forward. "Bról, son of Sûn, dwarf of Nubaroz," he answered, shouldering his mace.

Gwyndel threw the Hobgoblin sword aside. "Gwyndel, daughter of Élorn and Forester of Alithell," she declared firmly.

Eyoés locked eyes with the fallen Gahrim. His easy manner set Skreon's nerves on edge. "Eyoés. Son of Élorn," he proclaimed, pressing his sword against the albino's armor. At the mention of Élorn's name, Skreon's eyes lightened with the fire of spiteful victory. His strangely calm grin unsettled Eyoés to his core.

Eyes narrowed, Skreon swatted aside the youth's blade with his gauntlet. "I ordered your father's death," he said.

Gwyndel's bow clattered to the ground. Speechless, she looked away. A piercing cold seized Eyoés. He stepped back, the tip of his sword falling to the stone. Eyoés held his head in his hand, despondent. The black fingers of this demon had woven themselves throughout his entire life.

Nothing has been done to avenge these deeds or stop this beast.

The dark lord picked up his sword where it had fallen. "What a pity the Phantom League did not kill all his kin," he hissed, poising his blade for the final blow. Eyoés lifted his head, a flare of rage surging through his strained, bloodshot gaze.

A primal roar burst from within as he swatted away Skreon's sword. With a speed driven by hate, Eyoés kicked the albino backwards. Bról bolted forward to restrain the youth. Lured by the stricken cry, Gibusil screeched in anger and dove from the sky above. The dwarf commander leapt back as the griffin rammed into Skreon, knocking him to the ground. Sprawling, the dark lord raised his hands to ward off the attack. Gwyndel cried out as Gibusil circled back to deal another blow.

"Enough!" Eyoés commanded. Snarling, the griffin withdrew, its crown of feathers flattened against its neck. Heartbeat pounding in his ears, Eyoés advanced, driving the toe of his boot into Skreon's side.

Coughing, Skreon struggled to rise. Gwyndel trailed behind Eyoés, his rage causing her mind to swim.

Beneath their feet, the percussive rumble of the bombing ceased. Emerging from behind the fortress, a dark cloud of dwarves returned in haste to their camp across the valley. Placing the last barrels of Duraval into the fortress gateway, the remaining dwarves mounted their beasts and fled with their brethren.

Looming over his fallen foe, Eyoés shakily pressed the tip of his father's sword against the hollow of Skreon's throat. "My father and countless others have met their end at the tip of your blade," the youth growled with a faltering voice. "Now you will face mine."

Skreon chuckled with a triumphant smile. "You're just like me—a cold-blooded murderer. Your father would be ashamed," he taunted. The pressure against Skreon's chest ceased.

Eyoés hesitated.

A murderer. This is what vengeance would turn me into. A murderer with an excuse.

Swallowing, he looked up. His heart sank at the horror and pain in Gwyndel's eyes, and the doubt in Bról's. The full extent of his hatred was now exposed to scrutiny. The urge to return to vengeance beckoned him, yet he found himself unable to listen.

To give in would be to trade my rescue for refuse.

Withdrawing his weapon, he stepped back and sheathed his sword. "I am nothing like you," he declared, voice shaking.

The smug victory in the albino's eye faded.

Grimacing, Skreon stood.

We shall see.

Drawing his dagger, he dashed toward Gwyndel. Caught off guard, she tripped over the Whiteblood's limp tail.

Eyoés broke into a sprint, the heavy weight of nausea accompanying his lightheadedness. "Leave her!" he screamed.

Hurtling through the air, a blackened throwing knife stuck into Skreon's neck.

The albino staggered to the side, his iron dagger clattering to the stone. Gwyndel stepped away, dumbstruck. Slowing to a dead stop, Eyoés gripped his sword. A movement from the fortress entrance caught his eye. Previously concealed by the shadows, Makulazai stepped out from behind the cluster of Duraval barrels. Clutching a wound in his midsection, the Hobgoblin chief limped toward them.

Face twisted in a fevered stare, Makulazai eyed the stricken Kóenar. "It was only a matter of time," he hissed. As Skreon stared into the Hobgoblin chief's hateful eyes, his vision faded into an inky blackness.

Makulazai spat in Skreon's face and kicked his limp body to the ground.

The war horn's haunting cry echoed from across the valley. Eyoés spun toward the sound. His eyes widened. One solitary, riderless dragon darted toward the fortress like a bolt of lightning.

Sheathing his sword, he dashed toward Gwyndel and seized her shirt, causing her to wince. "Come! We must leave!" he said. With Eyoés gently assisting her,

Gwyndel limped to where Gibusil waited, gritting her teeth against the pain in her back. A sharp crack rang above their heads.

Weakened by the bombardment, several boulders tore free from the mountain and plummeted downwards. Screaming, Makulazai lifted his arms in vain to defend himself. With a mighty crash, the rocks silenced his cry.

Hastily beckoning Throggon with a whistle, Król mounted and took to the sky. Eyoés leapt onto the griffin's back and pulled his sister into her seat, her arms encircling his waist. Immediately, Gibusil burst into flight, his speed robbing the riders of their breath. With a roar, the riderless dragon flew over their heads and shot a ball of fire into the cluster of Duraval barrels before pulling away.

A deep rumble shook the ground. Spewing great clouds of dust from the gates, the mountain imploded in a mass of jagged, broken stone. Glancing backwards, Eyoés watched as dust spiraled upwards from the collapsing fortress, reminding him of Asdale's burning ruins.

The irony brought a slow smile to his face.

42

By the time they arrived at the dwarf encampment, the sun's choked rays had descended into twilight, masked by the overcast sky. Assembled before the entrance to Lord Ardul's pavilion, a large unit of dwarf officers hung their heads, their soiled faces consumed with grief. Out of reverence, none wished to break the gloomy silence.

Within the pavilion, several candles lit the interior, casting unsteady shadows on the sides of the tent. In the center, lay Ardul's desk, covered in lavish carpets and scented oils.

Upon this covering lay Lord Ardul.

A white cloth staunched the spear wound in his ribs, turned scarlet by his blood. Had he not joined the fight at the mountain's base, the Hobgoblin javelin would not have found its mark. Gathered around him, Eyoés, Gwyndel, and Iról stood silent. Eyoés regarded the dying dwarf with dull eyes. He wiped at his nose, chest aching. Hiding her face in her hands, Gwyndel wept openly. Hand clasped to his chest in salute, Iról looked on. Despite his attempts to hide his grief, his slack expression seemed dead and cold. A rattling cough racked Ardul's frame as he tried to sit up.

Exhausted, he fell back onto his pillow. "Iról," he called, his weak voice barely audible.

Bról rushed to his friend's side and held Ardul's hand. "Yes, my liege?" he asked, voice breaking.

Another cough. Lord Ardul winced, then smiled. "You—have been loyal to the end," he choked. "Our brothers need a leader such as you."

Bról shook his head in denial with a quivering smile. "Fight! You will survive this. The throne of Nubaroz waits for you!" he insisted with tears. Setting a comforting hand on Bról's shoulder, Eyoés bit his lip.

Lord Ardul grimaced and looked his friend in the eye. "Soon I will reside in the Kingdom above the stars. I cannot leave our people leaderless," he declared. Rolling onto his side, he removed the forged crown from his brow and placed it upon Bról's head. "I appoint you, Bról, son of Sûn, as Lord of Nubaroz and the mountains of Iostan. Unite our people and put the shame of the Draed to rest," he ordered. Shuddering, Ardul collapsed onto his back. A growing peace eclipsed the pain in his side like a soothing salve.

The last page of my tale has been written.

The Dwarf Lord looked to Eyoés and Gwyndel, his face softening. "The journey has changed you both. We shall meet again, children of Élorn," he sighed.

Pulling Gwyndel closer, Eyoés gave a firm nod. "So we shall," he declared.

Ardul gasped, his gaze suddenly pulled upward. "You have come to take me to my fathers," he whispered to one only he could see. A final sigh escaped his lips.

Eyoés closed his eyes, feeling hot tears run down his face. Eyes reddened with grief, Gwyndel turned away, at the mercy of her thoughts.

Liftng his shoulders shook with silent sobs as his head sank onto Ardul's still body. He recalled the comfort Ardul had given him in his darkest times. Lifting his head, the dwarf removed his crown and looked at it with an intent stare. The weight of his newfound leadership seemed too immense to understand.

Where will this crown lead me? Am I fit to take this responsibility?

Through the pain of his broken, troubled heart, a gentle thought came to his mind.

If you were unfit, this crown would never have come to you. Do not let fear decide your fate.

The thought struck him. Furrowing his brow, Bról pondered the words, struggling to think past his grief. He looked back to the still form of his dear friend.

I do not understand why I have been chosen.

Another thought broke through.

Must you understand?

Bról swallowed as the Crown of Nubaroz drew his gaze. The vision of his people wandering leaderless through the cold mountains tormented him. Wiping the tears from his eyes, he lifted the diadem over his head. He hesitated. Clenching his jaw, Bról set the crown upon his brow.

I will take what the King has given me.

The cries of the forest grew louder as the last light of dusk faded into darkness. Keeping the night at bay, the light from the Gesadith lanterns reflected off the dwarves' armor. With solemn expressions, they observed in silence. Stepping into the depths of the mass grave, two hooded dwarves placed the last body alongside the others. Weary from grief, Eyoés looked on, holding Gwyndel's hand.

Distraught, she let her shoulders sag under the weight of her sadness. She recalled the meeting in Ardul's garden, and the sincere words she had spoken. A strange relief comforted her in her mourning.

He resides in the Kingdom now—he does not share our grief any longer.

Eyoés swallowed. His sister's sorrow amplified his own. Sighing, he squeezed his eyes shut. The extent of the dwarves' sacrifice now made itself clearly known. A pang of regret swept over him.

I was the one to ask for their aid.

He hurriedly dismissed the sickening thought.

They chose to fight. I could not have forced them.

The low, mourning notes of a pipe roused him from his thoughts. Emerging from the surrounding darkness, a lone musician entered the funeral site, followed by several dwarves carrying a stretcher. All eyes turned toward them as the cold body of Lord Ardul was illuminated by the lantern light. Eyoés furtively glanced toward Aról. Struggling to maintain his composure, the new ruler of Nubaroz looked aside and blinked away his tears. Reverently, the party of dwarves stepped into the mass grave, carefully avoiding the bodies of their fellows. The dirge faded away as the dwarves gently placed Ardul's body among his warriors.

Taking a deep breath, Fról turned to face his troops. "Here lies Ardul the Steadfast, Lord of Nubaroz, and those who fought by his side against Skreon, the Murderer," he quavered. "From this day onward, let their sacrifice be remembered throughout the halls of Nubaroz, and in the hearts of our people. Ta Cahdûl Denbar—never forgotten!" Kneeling, Fról seized a handful of soil and tossed it into the grave.

The host of dwarves bowed in unison. "Ta Cahdûl Denbar!" they shouted. Each retrieved a shovel and marched to the heap of dirt at the grave's end. Releasing Gwyndel's hand, Eyoés strode to where Fról stood, mournful.

Pensive, Eyoés watched as dirt slowly covered the slain. "It feels strange, coming to the end of this journey," he pondered aloud.

Fról sighed. "My journey has just begun," he remarked, turning to look Eyoés in the eye. "Upon my return, I will commission a monument to be built in Ardul's honor. As for the future—I will seek the Guide's wisdom." Looking past Eyoés, Fról noticed Gwyndel standing alone. A look of concern crossed his features. "Will she be alright?" he inquired.

Eyoés looked over his shoulder and nodded. "In time this somber moment will be a distant memory," he replied. "She suffered a wound during the battle, but refuses any aid." Eyes widening, the dwarf took a step toward her. Eyoés grasped Fról's shoulder in restraint.

"She will not listen," he insisted, shaking his head.

Drawing back, Bról furrowed his brow. "Is it serious?" he questioned. His heart sank.

Eyoés hesitated, his gaze tormented and distant. "Her back is badly burnt," he admitted, looking Bról in the eye. "I am taking her to Gald-Behn." The name hung between them like a veil, like he had mentioned an unreachable dream.

Raising an eyebrow, Bról took a step back. For generations, the royal dominion had been thought of as forbidden ground, an unknown land. Many desired to see the King's palace, yet few dared to approach the territory. "The King's realm?" he asked incredulously.

Eyoés nodded, pressing his lips firmly together. "In the midst of my despair, the Guide healed my hate. Surely the King must know of his whereabouts. If I find him, he can heal Gwyndel," he maintained.

Bról frowned, turning his eyes to the stars above, imagining the majesty of the revered land.

The King will not turn them away, should they make it past the gates.

Meeting the youth's gaze, the dwarf sighed and extended his hand. "Then this is farewell," he admitted, leaning in. "Should we meet again, I shall welcome you into my halls."

Eyoés beamed and took Bról's hand. "Those who walk a common road never part ways for long," he declared. "We will meet again."

43

Eyoés spurred Gibusil onward at a frantic pace. Golden clouds raced by, bursting into puffs as the griffin's wings sliced them like a blade. Below, a sea of yellow clouds and mist obscured his view. Driven by desperation, Eyoés was blind to the beauty surrounding him. Unconscious from the pain, Gwyndel sat in his lap, her face leaning on his shoulder. Eyoés averted his gaze, broken at the sight of her stricken form. He wished with all his heart that he could take her pain. With renewed determination, he scanned the emptiness below for sign of open ground.

I must get her cured, even if I have to drag her through the gates and beg.

Doubt shoved the memories of his past misdeeds forward. Shaking the thoughts away, Eyoés tried to bring the Guide's forgiveness to mind—only to find his wrongs looming before him. He frowned, drooping his head. Remorse pricked at his heart.

If the King knows of my past, why should he welcome me? I have dishonored his goodness with hateful thoughts and vengeance.

The thought of being barred from the King's court with no hope of help for Gwyndel quickened his heartbeat. His eyes narrowed. "I will not be held back from him. She *will* be cured," he muttered under his breath. Gripping the griffin's reins, Eyoés brought the creature into a dive. The pounding wind made his eyes water, and he clenched his stomach to ward off the shivers. Like an arrow, they broke through the tawny veil of clouds below.

The wondrous sight stole his breath. Miles of plains stretched off into the horizon, rippling in the wind like liquid gold. Copses of willow stood guard about the plain, boasting leaves of amber and yellow. The sweet smell of honey hung in the air like a perfume. To his left, Eyoés glimpsed the shimmering blue of a cascading river. On the horizon, the faint chalky streak of a lofty watchtower drew his gaze. For a moment, he felt a sense of peace pulling at his anxiety.

Sitting upon a hilltop above the flaxen plains was the royal city of Gald-Behn. Mighty parapets stood guard over the milky white ramparts. Eyoés shielded his eyes against the sunlight reflecting off the bronze roofs. From the castle gates, a road of polished marble branched out into the horizon, its surface inset with gold designs. Eyoés drove Gibusil toward the gates. His breath caught as he spied the two massive sentries standing watch.

Please let me through! She could be dying!

Gibusil pulled up short of the gates and landed softly onto the marble road. The guards tensed, tightening the grip on their weapons. Eyoés felt their piercing stares from underneath their helms. Dismounting, he carefully leaned Gwyndel back. As the griffin bent low, Eyoés slipped his arms underneath her neck and knees with great care and lifted with a grunt. Gwyndel groaned in pain, the light of consciousness drifting in and out of her eyes. His heart leapt into his throat at the sound of rattling armor and heavy footsteps.

"Don't drive us away, please!" he cried in despair, spinning on his heels to face them.

The two sentries removed their helmets and cast them aside. Eyoés hesitated, confused by the concern on their faces. "Let us help," one of them declared, gently taking Gwyndel from him. For a moment, the youth hesitated, glancing uneasily at the two guards. Then, wetting his lips, Eyoés swallowed and stepped back.

"We must see the King," he insisted.

While the second sentry lead Gibusil to the nearest stable, the remaining Gahrim led Eyoés through the city square, carrying Gwyndel with ease. Buildings of speckled marble stood on either side, adorned with intricate, chiseled carvings. Clothed in bright robes, Gahrim went about their duties in a refined manner, making quiet conversation with their fellows. Colorful mosaics covered the streets, chronicling tales of courage and honor. In the midst of such splendor, Eyoés blushed, painfully aware of his tattered clothes. Sensing the bewildered looks of the inhabitants, he forced himself to look ahead, and halted at what he saw.

The King's palace towered above him, its powerful structure hinting at the majesty within. Polished slate tiles covered the walls in a smooth, elaborate armor. Pillars inlaid with gold and jade guarded the entryway. Three deep platforms stepped up to the palace doors, flanked on either side by a turquoise fountain.

"We must hurry!" the Gahrim urged, waiting at the palace gate with Gwyndel in his arms. With a nod, Eyoés darted up the steps to the gate to catch up. At the sight of Gwyndel's limp form, the guards beat upon the thick wooden door. Silently, the door swung open to allow entry. They hastily stepped into the lengthy hall. As the gate closed behind them, a tranquil silence pervaded the chamber. Finely embroidered pennants hung from the walls, adorned with various illustrations. At the far end of the hall was a solitary door.

Eyoés wiped the sweat from his hands. The air about him seemed alive.

I am standing in the King's own palace, about to boldly confront him.

The hair on his neck rose at the realization. Trembling, Eyoés drug his feet.

Am I worthy?

Heat surged into his face at the thought of his rage and hatred. Slowing his pace, he looked down to his feet in shame.

I am not a good man. I cannot face him.

Eyoés turned back toward the palace gate.

The Guide has restored you, has he not?

He exhaled, feeling the Guide's hand against his

chest once again. Lifting his head, he glimpsed Gwyndel's curly, charred locks. The thought of the Guide laying his hand upon her gave him courage. He clenched his fists.

The King may accept her and punish me for entering his presence. Nevertheless.

Eyoés quickly strode toward the door. Silent, the Gahrim stood before the entrance. He cast a furtive glance toward Eyoés.

The door suddenly swung open on its own. A magnificent hall stretched before them, illuminated with beams of sunlight from the many windows lining the walls. Emanating from within, a peace pulled them inward, yet carried a terrible awe with it. Standing at the far end of the royal hall, a magnificent throne expected them, the sparkling myriad of colors reminding Eyoés of the reflection of sunlight on water. Rubies, sapphires, and emeralds embellished its armrests.

At the sight of King Fohidras, Eyoés broke into a sweat, pale and trembling. Even from a distance, he felt the man's eyes pierce him, leaving no thought or deed unseen. Head throbbing with dizziness, Eyoés tried to step back, only to find himself glued to the spot. The terror of the King's glory nearly made him scream.

"Come here, my son," the King beckoned with outstretched arm. His quiet voice instantly penetrated the youth's fear, bringing the color to his face. Overcome with relief, Eyoés wept and advanced with the Gahrim behind. The tap of his boots on the golden floor clicked against the ceiling high above him.

Face wrinkled with grief, he stretched out his hands in supplication. "My sister will die without help! Please—where is the Guide?" he begged. Silent, King Fohidras stood, descending from his throne to stand before Eyoés. Compassion emanated from his blue eyes, penetrating deep within to remove his fears. Eyoés narrowed his eyes. The longer he looked into the man's face, the more familiar it seemed.

A smile crossed the King's face as he set a kind hand upon the youth's shoulder. "I am the Guide," he declared. "Do not mourn, for now is a time of rejoicing." Releasing Eyoés' shoulder, King Fohidras looked toward the Gahrim sentry, who cradled Gwyndel in his arms. "Lay her on the ground before me," he commanded. With a hasty nod, the sentry strode toward them. Crouching, he set the limp body of Gwyndel upon the golden floor. The King regarded the Gahrim softly. "Thank you, Chasan," he acknowledged with a smile. Smiling in thanks, Chasan bowed and vanished.

The King's smile faded. Forehead wrinkled with pain, he stared at Gwyndel, stricken. The passion in his eyes shocked Eyoés. Holding his breath, he watched as the King knelt beside her and set his hand against her side.

"Be whole," he ordered, the deep rumble of his voice shaking the ground. Eyoés stepped back, gaze riveted on Gwyndel. For several moments, she lay still. Then, like the dawn of morning, her eyes opened. Gwyndel leapt to her feet at the sight of the King, studying her surroundings with a confused look.

Before she could speak, Eyoés embraced her with tears of joy. The sight of her brother brought tears to Gwyndel's eyes.

Releasing her, Eyoés turned toward the King and fell to his knees. "Why would you help a guilty man like me?" he cried, awestruck. " I have done nothing to deserve it."

Smiling, King Fohidras grasped the youth's forearm and lifted him to his feet. "You can do nothing to win my grace. Only I can give it, and I give it freely to whoever will accept," he declared. "Because of it, you *are* a noble man, Eyoés."

A surge of heat radiated through Eyoés' chest at the words. The outrageousness of the statement puzzled him. For months, the hope of becoming honorable had seemed empty, a goal too distant to grasp. A peace assured him the truth of the King's words.

If the King himself has declared me noble, then I am.

Teary eyed, Eyoés drew his sword and extended it in allegiance. "I am your willing vassal," he proclaimed.

With a chuckle, King Fohidras pushed the weapon away. "My only wish is that you will heed the proverbs I have written," he instructed.

Sheathing his sword, Eyoés nodded. The King stepped toward Gwyndel, his gaze softening. Her eyes widened as she recognized the man's face.

Fingering her singed hair, she moved away from him, shaking her head. "I am not presentable," she muttered, her ears turning red. "But it will be much easier to hide myself in the treetops without this red banner giving me away." King Fohidras gently grasped her shoulders and shook his head.

"Appearance does not matter to me, it is the heart that is significant," he said. Gwyndel looked aside, struggling to accept his words. The King tenderly turned her face toward his own. "Your perseverance in the face of despair and darkness has pleased me," he maintained. "Your mother and father are pleased as well. You shall see them again in due time." Gwyndel's eyes shone with encouragement.

Leaning her head on his shoulder, she closed her eyes and smiled. "I am grateful," she said, sniffling to keep her composure.

The King caressed her hair. "There will still be scars to remind you of what you've been healed from," he added.

Joyous, Gwyndel didn't care. Stepping away from the King's embrace, she bowed low. "You are the true King," she declared.

With a smile, King Fohidras withdrew to the base of his throne, his pure white robe reflecting on the stone surface. Eyoés wet his lips as the King's gaze lingered on him. By the look in the man's eyes, something of importance was to be said. King Fohidras' smile faded behind a serious expression.

"For your courage and action against Skreon, the Murderer, I bestow upon you, Eyoés, son of Élorn, the Baronship of Taekohar. Rebuild what has been destroyed and restore the people," he commanded, shifting his gaze to Gwyndel. "You shall be temporary Baroness until the time arises when Eyoés shall bear the full responsibility of his position." Gwyndel gasped, touching her parted lips with her fingertips.

Heart racing, Eyoés studied his lord with an incredulous stare. "Me? The Baron of Taekohar?" he stammered, dumbfounded. "Am I ready for such a responsibility?"

At the youth's shocked expression, a grin broke through the King's serious demeanor. "There is more in store for you than you realize," he continued. "This is only the beginning." Leaving the throne, King Fohidras gestured to a nearby door. "Come, let us feast together," he invited.

With a click, two double doors swung open to reveal a beautiful table covered in red velvet. Lavish plates of food crowded the table's center, arranged with elegance. Seated around the table, four robed men ceased their conversation and rose at the King's entry. Following close behind, Eyoés studied the other guests with a curious eye. Gwyndel forced herself to appear calm and tried to ignore her disheveled appearance. Stepping to the side, the King swept a hand toward two empty chairs. Eyoés nodded in thanks, assisting Gwyndel with her seat before seating himself. Striding to where a grand chair resided at the far end of the table, King Fohidras took his seat. The guests eagerly followed his example. Eying the food before him with yearning, Eyoés moved to take some.

"Before we begin our meal, Eyoés, I must introduce our guests," the King declared with a smile.

"Your father, Élorn, was not only the Protector of Taekohar. He was the fifth warrior to bear the title of one of the Heroes of Alithell."

Eyoés stilled, transfixed. Recollections of his father's journal surfaced again.

The Five Heroes of Alithell—the few chosen as the King's own. I am both honored and troubled by this privilege.

At a loss for words, Eyoés leaned forward and let his gaze wander among the guests. The King signaled for two of the heroes to stand. Pushing their chairs backwards, they rose. The first dwarfed his comrade with his tall, burly frame. A crimson robe was fastened about his shoulders, emblazoned with the image of a white, clenched fist. The second, although small, carried an look of wisdom and intellect. He wore a purple robe, trimmed with fur and boasting the image of a quill pen.

"Sir Gwair and Sir Neifon," King Fohidras announced. "One renowned for his strength and courage, the other wielding his power in both wisdom and words."

Eyoés stood from his seat to bow. Neifon quickly held up a hand to stay him. "Do not bow before us, Eyoés, son of Élorn. It is an honor to know you," he spoke.

With a firm nod, Gwair looked to Eyoés. "Indeed. Your father was a great man," he said. Smiling, they returned to their seats. The King turned toward the final two and gestured for them to rise. The warriors stood. Shrugging his ice blue robe over one shoulder, the nearest examined Eyoés curiously. Embroidered upon his robe was a white crystal. His sharp features and raven hair seemed at odds with his warm eyes. He clapped both of his fists to his right shoulder in salute. The remaining hero smiled, stepping around his seat to approach Eyoés. His light brown robe swayed behind him as he walked, giving the youth glimpses of the mountain insignia sewn onto it. The man's swarthy features glistened. The two men shook hands.

"Sir Arthek and Sir Sabaah," King Fohidras continued. "Even in the harsh cold of Norgalok, Arthek has been steadfast in speaking of me among his lost people. The humility and adventurous nature of Sabaah has given hope when hope seemed far away."

Sabaah flashed a pearly smile. "Please don't speak to me of my humility. I only exalt the one who deserves it," he chuckled. "I look forward to many years of friendship, Eyoés."

As Sabaah returned to his chair, Arthek let his hand fall to his side. "So do I. One day, maybe the mountains of ice will separate us no longer," he mused. Grinning, Eyoés mimicked the man's salute. With a twinkle in his eye, Arthek returned the gesture and sat.

Once all were seated, the King clapped his hands. "And now, we may feast," he declared. With a hearty shout, the warriors gathered the food of their choice and ate. Between bites, Eyoés recounted his journey to them all, speaking openly of his struggles and the change within him.

All stood still, watching in expectation. Sunlight streamed in through the windows lining the King's throne room, bathing the assembly in gold. Gwyndel stood among their number, eyes sparkling with tears and heart swelling with pride. Eyoés kneeled before the King, eyes watering. His former dreams of heroism and honor seemed only a trifle in the shadow of this unfolding reality.

How far I have come.

A surge raced through him as he felt the light tap of the King's sword upon his shoulder.

"Rise, Sir Eyoés, Baron and Protector of Taekohar and member of the Five Heroes of Alithell!"

"Andíamas Radem—for Sword and Crown!" they shouted with conviction, lifting their swords aloft.

44

With the sun warming his back, Eyoés strolled through the ruins of Asdale. The rubble of the keep lay strewn across the scorched ruins of the town, blanketed by moss. All around him, hired laborers from across Taekohar cleared away the debris, their bodies shining with sweat in the noonday sun.

Eyoés sighed, stepping over a charred piece of wood. Replacing his old, tattered clothing, richly crafted attire spoke of his newfound status. Emblazoned with a golden flame, a dark green robe hung over his shoulders. Unaccustomed to the feel of his new boots, he stooped to adjust them. His soft, pensive features bore no mark of tension or strife. Inhaling, he relished the quiet whisper of the wind.

Even five days after the ceremony, the realization of his journey seemed strange, almost too baffling to comprehend. He shook his head as he recalled how desperately he had searched for his identity.

How lost one feels when his own character remains a mystery to him. To think of what I could have become…

Standing, he adjusted his robe, pondering the honor he now bore. He thought back to the days when he had sought for honor in retribution, and the acceptance of the father he had never met.

When I turned from my revenge, the King gave me

the warrior spirit I wanted all along.

He continued his walk, observing the workers going about their tasks. Stepping around a pile of scrap, he stopped. Only feet away from him, a thick wooden pell lay amid a pile of scorched wood.

It can't be.

As Eyoés moved closer, he noticed several laborers clearing away the remains. He raised his hand. "Please move on," he instructed. Wiping the sweat from their brows, the workers cast a puzzled glance toward the newly established Baron, then withdrew to aid their fellows. Heart pounding, Eyoés stepped amid the debris, carried back to the time before the attack. Tears welled in his eyes.

My home.

As he walked through the remains, his boot knocked a large stone from its place. A glint of light upon the ground caught his eye. Blackened by fire, a golden locket lay by his feet. Shaking his head, Eyoés stooped to pick it up.

Aványn's locket!

Affectionately lying it in the palm of his hand, he unfastened the clasp on its side and opened it.

Inside, carefully drawn by hand—was a picture of himself.

EPILOGUE

A thick, stale darkness permeated the very depths of the underground chamber. The cold air was imbued with the pungent stench of rotting flesh, hinting at hidden nightmares in the cavern's depths. Long, twisted stalactites hung precariously from the roof. Screams and howls echoed from deeper within. A small circle of orange light illuminated the ghastly grimace of a skull impaled by a fallen stalactite. A roughly hewn nook in the cavern wall was illuminated by a single candle. Drops of wax collected in a growing pile beneath it. Such an ordinary sight would have given hope in the somber depths—had the figure of ebony mist been absent.

Setting his unearthly hand upon the desk, the Black Presence closed his eyes, envisioning the past. He recalled the afternoons spent walking with King Fohidras in his personal gardens. To think he had walked alongside his enemy aroused a growl of rage from within.

That was before I resisted his tyranny.

He relished the acts of violent vengeance surging into his thoughts. A black smile spread across his dark, murky features. "Soon, the day will arrive when I will string his innards around the throne of Gald-Behn," he muttered to himself, picturing the King's flawless face.

Opening his pale, white eyes, he viewed his ghostly substance with distaste. If the assassination had gone through as planned, he would never have been cursed.

He had to move while he had the chance.

Bringing his fist down on the table with a slam, the Black Presence turned with a hiss. In response to his beckoning, a single apparition stepped into the light of the candle, cowering before the hideous presence of its master. The phantom's yellowed skin was covered in grievous wounds.

Two round, inky eyes briefly looked upwards, before turning away in fear. "What would you have, my liege?" the creature moaned.

The Black Presence gave a low laugh at the sight of his withered vassal. "Now that Skreon no longer can prove a hindrance, it is time to weaken the territories of Alithell. We start with Rehillon," he declared. "The Phantom League's greed has eaten away at them like a disease. They will prove useful." The specter gazed upwards at its master once again. This time, a twisted grin adorned the mutilated face.

With a piercing shriek of triumph, the ghoul dashed into the darkness.

To access exciting Sword and Scion freebies, please visit the Exclusive Content page on my website:

www.jacksonegraham.wix.com/jackson-e-graham

Password: AndiamasRademSS

Made in the USA
Middletown, DE
23 September 2018